BAD TEETH

DUSTIN LONG

BAD TEETH

NEW HARVEST
Houghton Mifflin Harcourt
Boston New York
2014

This edition published by special arrangement with Amazon Publishing

www.hmhco.com

Library of Congress Cataloging-in-Publication Data
Long, Dustin, date.
Bad teeth : a novel / Dustin Long.
pages cm
ISBN 978-0-544-26200-3 (hardback)
1. Authorship—Fiction. 2. Plagiarism—Fiction.
3. Paranormal fiction. 4. Satire. I. Title.
PS3612.O493B34 2014
813'.6—dc23
2013044252

Book design by Greta Sibley

Printed in the United States of America
DOC 10 9 8 7 6 5 4 3 2 1

FOR JEANNINE,

AND FOR QUENTIN

PART ONE

BROOKLYN

I turn now to a tale
so wrong no tongue can tell
it all, no pen record
it to its final word;
throats fail
and letters will not spell.

—Magnus Valison,
The Oneiriad, Canto 168

She was a cool black woman in a long dress and boxy spectacles, and she eventually taught Judas to score and unfold a mango so that it would yield bite-size cubes of flesh. "You look lost," she said.

They were standing in a dim, converted office space from which all of the cubicles had been recently ripped: outlines remained indented in a carpet the color of television snow. In one corner a longhaired DJ in a purple-and-blue vertical-striped blazer did his best to mix the danceable with the passably hip, though the floor was too crowded to permit much actual dancing. A bar at a table in the corner opposite was where the crowd was at its thickest, a young man and younger woman providing red plastic cups filled with either of two varieties of cheap wine or one variety of cheap beer; a tip jar reminded partygoers that this was a fund-raiser.

"What?" said Judas stupidly, a bit bewildered by the volume of the music.

The party was being held to celebrate the release of the fourth issue of a literary magazine called *E*. The title was supposed to be something like a joke, as the full cover text read, "*E: modern cultural criticism*," and they were trying to bring new *energy* to the literary scene. But those who got the joke tended to say, "That's kind of funny," instead of laughing, whereas those who had it explained to them just said, "Oh." The price of admission to the party was a ten-dollar donation (which also bought a copy of the magazine) or to help unload the issues from the truck at the *E* office a few blocks away. Judas had paid.

"Do you have a cigarette?" the woman asked.

Patting his pockets though he hadn't carried cigarettes in over ten years, since the end of college, worried as he'd been that they would stain his teeth: "No, sorry."

"It's okay. I'm trying to quit. Do you just want to step outside with me and get some air, then?"

"Gabriel asked me to save you," she explained once they were out beneath a lamp on the wet reflective street, half a block down from a hacking of smokers; she almost had to yell to be heard above the Q train shrieking overhead. It must have rained since the party's start, but it had since cleared up. The lamp shone orange—tingeing her tight-curled hair, catching the corners of her glasses—and her face looked golden beneath it.

Judas shivered; it wasn't cold, but he wished he'd worn his hoodie if only as one further item of familiarity, protection against the alien all around him. His stuff (books, clothes, dishes, and a few small pieces of furniture) had not yet arrived from California—and he'd only brought three changes of outfit in his backpack on the plane—so he'd shown up at this party short-haired and baby-faced, wearing baggy jeans, off-brand tennis shoes, and a grey T-shirt emblazoned in blue with the single word BERKELEY. Most everyone else was dolled up to some extent, including this woman, but he told himself he didn't feel embarrassed; rather, he felt a vague sense of Californian pride.

Attending this party was nearly the first thing he had done since arriving in Brooklyn. He'd dropped off some things at his new apartment, and he'd taken a long stroll around the neighborhood: great pizza parlor, though most of the other restaurants would be out of his price range if he stayed jobless for very long; convenient access to three major subway lines; and only a few blocks' walk from the Brooklyn Heights Promenade, from which he could take in the entire panorama of Manhattan. "All of those people," he'd said aloud upon sight of it. "And all of them have lives, and most of them have genitals." He slept alone that night, but the next night he attended this party.

"My name's Caissa," the woman said (*kah-EE-suh*).

He told her his name, and she immediately smiled as if she understood some hidden profundity in his statement. "Are you an *E*-tard, too?"

He gaped for a moment. "I'm not sure how to answer that. I'm not one of the editors of *E*, if that's what you mean."

"Oh, do you have a piece in the new issue or something?"

He shook his head. "I'm not really a writer."

"Not really?"

"I'm a translator, not a writer."

"A lover, not a fighter." She nodded. "That's a relief."

She spoke these words only out of some associational echolalia, but there was as much truth in her statement as in his. Judas had never had the discipline to follow through on any writing of his own, but he had an innate love of translation, decoding the text of another and recoding it for himself; he'd even made a little money the previous year from the translation of a Chinese detective novel that he'd done for the University of California Press. And while he usually went out of his way to avoid direct conflict, favoring the path of passive-aggression, loving—which is to say being in love—had always come naturally to him. He'd tried to explain it once to Hannah, the girl he'd left behind in Berkeley; it's unknown exactly what he said to her, but she interpreted it as something like this: "I occasionally find other women alluring, for one reason or another. In some cases it's physical attraction; in other cases it has purely to do with personality—usually some combination of the two. And every woman I find alluring, even as a friend, is a woman I'd like to sleep with, at least once. The thought invariably crosses my mind. However, my love for you is so powerful that it not only eliminates this desire but inverts it. I actively wish not to sleep with these women, as I realize that such an action would hurt you." Whatever he'd said had been meant as a compliment, but it hadn't been taken that way.

"Frankly, I'm not a big fan," Caissa said. It took Judas a moment to realize that she was still talking about *E*, but then she went on at length to explain the basis of her aversion. "Martin actually told me once that the reason there aren't any good 'ethnic' writers is because they all write about ethnicity," she said at one point. "I don't even know where to begin with that, but then he also said it was a waste of time to write about atrocities in Sierra Leone when the real revolutionary ideas that are going to advance the world are being conceived in New York. Which is completely ignoring SOFA, seemingly on no other basis than the fact that it started on the West Coast. And as if we really need more media devoted to the ideas of New York intellectuals. And when the big, new idea for the new issue is 'the environment.' Seriously? How revolutionary."*

"Martin Pope?" Judas asked. "That's Gabriel's roommate, right? I think I just met him and his girlfriend. Jasmine?"

Caissa snorted. "'Girlfriend' is a strong word. On again, off again—mostly 'off again'—but yes. He's Gabriel's roommate. As close as he comes to dating anyone, I suppose: that girl, not Gabriel."

"You sound as if you've dated him yourself."

She stared at Judas in silence for a second. "Shall we head back to the party?"

Back inside, Judas took a good look at Martin, who was wearing a black crushed-velvet coat. Though he'd seemed affable enough, ready with a smirk, Judas—who was more than capable of being capriciously judgmental—decided on second glance that he didn't like him. Still, he elected to ignore such negative thoughts for the moment, and after grabbing a pre-poured cup of merlot, he placed a dollar in the tip jar and pushed his way back out through the drinkless plebes. New acquaintances excepted, he didn't know anyone here apart from Gabriel Stilzkin, and their friendship had really only lasted about a year, long ago, before Gabriel had transferred to Yale. Judas had already started conversations with him twice this night, only to be gently redirected, but he made his way over once again.

Gabriel was talking to a young woman of Russian birth,

---

* This was, of course, still in the days when most perceived SOFA as a novel but ultimately harmless organization.

attractive—though platinum blonde, and thus not to Judas's tastes—who had a piece in the new issue.

"So why don't you tell me a little more about the guy I'm here for," Judas said by way of interruption.

"What?" Gabriel asked between gulps of beer. "Who?"

"Jigme Drolma, right?"

Gabriel regarded Judas with what might on another face have passed for a thoughtful expression. "Oh, right. I don't know much more about him, apart from what I already told you. You should talk to Walter."

"Good luck with that," Martin Pope said, arriving at Judas's side, persona projecting from his black coat and ironic bolo tie, eyes on the woman. "He's busy holding court at the moment."

Walter was another founding editor of *E:* Walter Benjamin, pronounced *Wal-ter Ben-ja-min*, Brooklynite author/critic (not to be confused with *Val-tair Ben-ya-meen*, German philosopher/critic). He was the one who'd had the money to found the magazine, having been in on the ground floor of an essay cheat sheet website that had been briefly profitable before its ultimate demise. The previous Sunday, the *Times* had published a piece in the Style section about his weekly Ultimate Frisbee game in Prospect Park, and it had given him a front-page slot in the Sunday Book Review for his first novel—the absurdly titled *Challah-caust*—the week before that. At the moment he was surrounded by interns and fact-checkers of both sexes and from a wide array of magazines.

Challah-caust was the story of a pretentious literary type named Ben Wallenstein, whose compulsive behavior one drunken night leads him on a series of comic misadventures through modern Manhattan culminating in the accidental conflagration of a kosher bakery. Wallenstein, who is Jewish (though only by heritage), almost immediately and coincidentally strikes up a relationship with the Sephardic arson investigator (female), who suspects him of the crime though she never uncovers definitive proof. Over the course of the book, Wallenstein finds himself strangely moved by the way the diverse urban neighborhood pulls together to help the septuagenarian bakery owner, and he comes to embrace his own Jewish roots, making for a self-consciously "meaningful" climax. The book then ends with a jarring, quasi-metafictional scene depicting Walter Benjamin himself typing out the last few pages of *Challah-caust* with one hand while he holds his tumescent dick in the other. For whatever reason, the book was a critical hit, and according to the *Times* Frisbee article, Walter was already working on a memoir follow-up about the youthful excess that had led to his only slightly less youthful success.

As Gabriel resumed his chat with the young Russian woman —his turn away from Judas and Martin was slight, but the few seconds of arc were definitive—Judas guzzled his merlot. But then upon reaching the bottom of the cup, he felt a sudden sense of unbalance, as if his soul were heaving up on a swell. It was probably just the alcohol hitting his empty stomach.

At this point in his life, Judas was one of those vague young men on the verge of no longer being young, now in his midthirties, whose sense of purpose in life had been too long dependent on early promise, and who was only just beginning to realize that this promise had been rescinded; he was still defining himself in terms of what he might become rather than in terms of what he was, but he was beginning to learn. For instance, he'd moved to Brooklyn in flight from a failed relationship, yes, but he at least had the pretext of other reasons. Gabriel had emailed him a month earlier asking if he could really read Chinese; it seemed that everyone was excited about a newly discovered author, but no one had actually seen his stuff.

"He's about to explode," Gabriel explained in the email. "He's supposed to be the next Sebald or Bolaño—the Tibetan David Foster Wallace. That's where you come in."

Despite this explanation Judas still hadn't been sure what they wanted of him. But later that night Gabriel sent a long, rambling follow-up email, and Judas managed to piece together a bit more of the story. The guy had been born in Tibet, but he wrote all of his books in Chinese, co-opting the language of the oppressor; Gabriel had seen an article in the Cal alumni magazine about the Chinese translation Judas had done the previous year, so he thought this might be up his alley. Judas thought so too.

"Maybe I should come out to New York for a week or two," he wrote back. "Or maybe I'll just move there indefinitely. I've been thinking I need a change of scene anyway, and it would be easier than working long distance, right?"

Gabriel hadn't replied right away, but when he did his response wasn't overly dissuasive, so Judas chose to ignore the obvious lack of enthusiasm, gave two weeks' notice for his job at the County of Alameda, cashed out his 401(k), found a trustworthy subletter (better safe than sorry), paid movers to ship a few necessities, and bought a ticket to LaGuardia. Gabriel said he could sleep on the couch at his brownstone in Park Slope until he found a place of his own, but that hadn't been necessary as Judas had lucked into a rent-stabilized railroad apartment on Craigslist before his two weeks' notice was even up.

Judas managed to corner Walter as the party was winding down and found out that *E* didn't have a firm deal set up with this Tibetan guy—Jigme Drolma—but Walter had heard that he'd just published his magnum opus in Hong Kong, and word had it he was looking for a small press to put it out in English: some ideological opposition to the big houses. Walter was drunk at that point and seemed a bit put out that Judas was even bothering him about any of this, but Judas figured a little enthusiasm on his part couldn't hurt. And so the morning following the party, after the remainder of a restless, alcoholic night spent alone on an air mattress in his otherwise empty bedroom, he went to the local branch of the Brooklyn Public Library to see what he could learn. He was standing in the lobby trying to decide whether or not he needed to apply for a card when he spotted someone he thought he knew behind the counter and beneath a bushy beard, and so he got in line.

"Jarrod?" he asked once he'd made it to the front.

The voice that answered him was both Australian and awestruck: "Judas? Shit, it's been a long time, man."

Jarrod had been a casual acquaintance of Judas's in his Berkeley days: not a fellow student at the university, but a traveling rugby player who had found a place to stay at Delta Kappa Epsilon, that being the fraternity most favored by Cal's rugby players; a friend of Judas's from high school had happened to number among those, which was how he'd made Jarrod's acquaintance.

"What are you doing here? Are you in New York now?" Jarrod asked.

"Yeah. Just doing a little research for this new magazine. Maybe you could help me out? My skills are kind of rusty."

Jarrod nodded. "Sure. We can catch up. Let me just see if I can find someone to switch me for the desk."

If he'd been left to his own devices, Judas's research might not have progressed far beyond a Google search (which didn't turn up much information: no pictures, no date of birth, though he found brief mention of a son who had been arrested at the Battle in Seattle WTO thing, and his first publication had been in the late seventies, so he couldn't be that young). But with Jarrod as a guide, Judas turned up some useful information in the microfiche. A few articles in small Chinese-language newspapers mentioned Drolma's work being condemned by the Chinese government, and how popular he was among former Chinese nationals living abroad. Then there was a 1995 article in *Time*'s online archives about the Dalai Lama's brother—a professor of Uralic and Altaic studies at Indiana University Bloomington—in which he mentioned Jigme Drolma as "a quintessentially Tibetan novelist who writes in the voice of the world." That one was interesting if only because it suggested that Drolma might be moving to the United States—more particularly, "back to the United States"—and Bloomington in particular; he wanted to get out of Hong Kong before the British turnover. Chinese-language reviews of new books appeared every three or four years, but it seemed that none of his stuff had ever been translated into English.

"Not quite," Gabriel countered via cell phone later that day. "Hal Auerbach's supposed to be publishing an early short story in the next issue of *Brother*. He was raving about dude in some online video interview. Kind of what set off the whole speculation about the impending boom. Surprised you missed that with your Google-fu."

Though, as of yet, he wasn't himself a part of it, Judas was aware that Gabriel and the other *E* editors felt a rivalry between the East Coast and West Coast literary scenes. Hal Auerbach and his *Brother* and *Sister* publications were West Coast, so he realized that it would sting extra sharply if they got the deal for Drolma's new book.

"Maybe I should head back to Berkeley—see what leads they have. Or maybe they need a translator."

Gabriel waited a beat. "*Chesko, Sebulba.*"

"What?"

"Huttese. It means you're walking on thin ice. Did you get an email from your ex or something?"

"I was kidding. But if they've contacted him about a short story, shouldn't we be worried about the book?"

"If they get it, they get it, nothing we can do. I just don't want to see you getting mixed up with those guys. They're bad influences. But, you know, do what you want. I'm kind of surprised you moved out here in the first place."

"Do we at least know who Drolma's agent is?"

"I don't know, man. I'll talk to Walter and get back to you, okay? Or, you know, I guess he's supposed to be handling this, but he's been a little busy with the book and everything . . . so maybe you should just keep digging and see if you can find some contact info on the guy yourself."

Judas paused, pursed his lips. "All right, will do."

He ran into Caissa again two days later, as he was standing outside his building watching the movers unload his stuff. They were three Chinese men from San Francisco, in their forties, and rather than welcoming Judas into their circle when he spoke to them in Mandarin, they switched to Shanghainese. Four narrow flights of stairs led up to his apartment, and Judas felt sympathy for the three men having to maneuver his big bookshelf and bed frame, but they wouldn't let him help. He was beginning to feel a sense of uselessness that transcended the realm of physical labor when Caissa walked up from behind and said, "Hey!" It was a Sunday, bright, a few clouds that smiled instead of frowned, and she told him that she was meeting a friend for brunch on Montague Street. She lived in Vinegar Hill, and while Judas's apartment wasn't directly between the one and the other, it was along one of the more scenic routes. Judas repeated all of these place-names in his head, trying to get them down.

"So you're just moving in?" Then, half biting her bottom lip to restrain a smile and adjusting her glasses with one hand: "That explains the way you were dressed."

He nodded and looked down at himself. He was wearing the same outfit he'd had on at the party. "I'm afraid most of my clothes are in boxes."

"I confess, I kind of just thought you were a jackass."

"Oh?"

"Yeah, like we were all out enjoying looking nice, and there you were trying to show off how above society's strictures you are. When really you were just ruining the atmosphere. Gabriel told me you were from California, so I thought it might be some weird West Coast pride thing." She shrugged. "Sorry."

"No, no problem. Natural assumption that I was a jackass, if that's what you were basing it on. But—" He struggled to find words to prolong the conversation. "I mean, so are you a native New Yorker yourself?"

She shook her head. "I was born in Guyana. But I've lived here most of my life." A short-breathed silence, followed by another of her expansive shrugs. "Anyway, I should get going or I'm gonna be late. Good running into you."

"Enjoy your brunch." Then, before she could take two steps, "But hey, could I get your phone number? Since you seem familiar with the neighborhood, maybe you could show me around a little?"

She turned back to look at him, dislodged tongue from cheek, and smiled. She added him as a friend on Facebook later that night.

Judas tried for a while to get in touch with the Dalai Lama's brother, but after a few telephone calls he discovered that said brother had died in Bloomington in 2008. Still, in the attempt, he did learn a few things worth noting: the Indiana town was something like a Tibet in exile, for one, with a whole department thus devoted at the local university and a cultural center on the outskirts. And the Dalai Lama's nephew still lived and owned a restaurant there. Though he proved a hard man to contact.

"Why don't you just go?" Gabriel suggested later that week when they were out at a darkened Park Slope bar for Balderdash-Trivia Night, at which points would be awarded for answers that were correct as well as for answers that were plausible and funny. Martin Pope and his girlfriend, Jasmine Green, were there too—apparently "on again"—but Judas and Gabriel had carried most of the answers in the first round. The competition wasn't exactly stiff, though. A few teams had turned up dressed like investment bankers, and rather than actually trying to answer any of the questions, they were just filling their answer sheets with complaints about poor people, boasts about their bonuses, etc.; Martin was annoyed that the MC was actually humoring them by reading it all out.

"Fucking SOFA kids."

Judas at this point was aware enough to know that SOFA was some sort of protest group, but he hadn't gleaned much else in the few months since its first appearance. It was his philosophy that the most important news—the stuff that would still be worth knowing ten years down the line—would eventually reach him by word of mouth, so he didn't ever bother trying to keep up with current events by himself, rationalizing that his time was better spent looking more deeply into the news that really interested him. That sort of apathy where the larger happenings of the world around him were concerned was one of his greatest character flaws.

"Shut the fuck up," Jasmine said, punching Martin halfheartedly in the arm. "I'm a fucking SOFA kid, for what it's worth."

"Oh yeah?" Judas asked.

"Well, I've been to most of their major happenings."

Jasmine was cute in an elfin way—her nose curving up unexpectedly just when you thought it would end, and with dimples that suggested a perpetual grin—brunette, which was to Judas's taste, though she had a shoulder-length cut pushed forward, so he couldn't judge the pointiness of her ears. Martin had been excluding her from the conversation all night, so Judas felt a little bad when Gabriel brought up the translation thing —another subject that she'd have little to contribute to—but it was rare for Gabe to actually want to talk about it, and Judas didn't want to miss the opportunity.

"So you think I should just fly out there?"

"Why not? I mean, if Drolma did move to the U.S. in '95 or '96, that's probably where he went, based on that article, right? And you don't seem to have much compunction about flying off to strange places on the flimsiest of pretexts."

"Yeah, maybe? It sounded kind of tentative, though. I mean, he really could have gone anywhere." Judas took a sip of his beer: a San Francisco microbrew. "But that would be cool, I guess: just turn up there and ambush him if he's actually there, show him we're the publisher he needs."

"Or maybe he'll just think you're a stalker," Martin said, standing and pulling a pack of cigarettes from his pocket. "I'm going out for a smoke." He headed for the door. Jasmine bit her lip.

"Anyway," Judas continued to Gabriel, ignoring Martin's comment. "I might at least find some people there who could put me in contact with him. You know, it might be easier to get some useful information in person than it would be over the phone. And it would be interesting to visit the Tibetan Cultural Center, since I don't really know all that much about Tibet. Right?"

Gabriel arched an eyebrow. "Wait, wasn't that like your major in college? I thought you were going to be my pan-Asian ringer, dude. I mean, what are you even here for?"

Judas shrugged, thinking of Caissa. "Comp lit. I focused on British and Chinese, but somehow I managed to avoid learning anything about Tibet."

"Didn't you have like a Tibetan roommate or something, though? That Thomas dude?"

"Chinese."

"Shit." Gabriel ran his hand over his head, revealing the base of his hairline to be a flattened capital M. "But I guess a lot of people don't know much about Tibet besides the Beastie Boys, Richard Gere, and gerbils." He smiled. "If we do get dude's book, I might have to write up a synopsis of the whole situation for *E*. Comparing the Chinese occupation to the hipster occupation of Williamsburg. Or maybe gentrification in general: tearing down beauty salons instead of Buddhas."

Judas only nodded.

"Anyway, what's this new magazine you're playing us against?"

"What?"

"I ran into that dude from Berkeley. Jarrod whatever from Australia. He told me you were looking into this Tibetan shit for some new magazine."

"I was talking about *E*."

"Four issues, man. Not exactly new."

"I guess he misunderstood."

Then Jasmine slid a *New Yorker* business card to Judas from across the beer-lacquered, wood-slatted table. She'd scrawled her cell number in red ink across the back. "If you need any help fact-checking this Drolma stuff, you should give me a call. I do some freelance work to make ends meet. Or if you ever want to check out some SOFA literature, learn what we're all about. You know?"

"Thanks." Judas took the card, considered, and only then noticed that Martin was already back, standing at the bar, chatting with the young woman who stood behind it—ironic mullet—and who was pouring him another Irish whiskey.

Around this time Judas decided to rent *Kundun* from his local video store since he thought it would at least be a good place to start the expansion of his knowledge. When he got home and opened the case, though, he found that the disc was unmarked—a burned copy—which he supposed wasn't too strange in itself considering the video store. But when he put the disc into his player it turned out not even to be the right movie. Still, it was drizzling, and he didn't feel much like going out again, so he decided to give whatever it was a chance.

The picture quality was poor, as if it had been transferred from an old VHS—pan and scan, with bad tracking—and it jumped right in without any menu or credits. The first few minutes were void of dialogue, but it seemed to be set in Paris in the days leading up to May '68, and visually it reminded him a bit of Alain Resnais's *Je t'aime, je t'aime,* except in black and white. But then people started speaking, and he thought it sounded maybe more Polish than French, though he spoke neither. Maybe it was Wojciech Has.

The subtitles were mostly lost beneath the edge of the screen, but from what Judas could piece together the plot centered on a young couple in love. The man was narrating—very matter-of-factly—and at first it seemed that nothing much of interest was going to happen: just a couple's mundane doings, going to an outdoor market to buy the makings for a romantic dinner back at their well-appointed apartment, taking the *métro* to museums and parks, etc.

"I knead my fingers into your shoulder blades and try to wipe away the knots and pains of Judo," the subtitles read at one point as the camera focused on masculine hands spreading out over the expanse of a feminine back. "My fingers move up your nape and into the soft, gentle scrape of your scalp. Thick tendrils resist as I try to pull out and away. Yet it's okay. I cease my attempts to escape and settle back into the squeezing again of your warm-skinned skull."

But as things went on, the narrator's voice grew increasingly desperate, and—from the flickers of subtitle—Judas thought he picked up a thread of paranoia that some of the shop clerks, *métro* riders, and other passersby were actually tourists from the future who had come to this moment in Parisian history in order to steal furtive glances of the narrator before he achieved some enigmatic fame (or infamy). Juxtaposed with all of the stirrings of the student uprisings that were going on in the background, it seemed that on one level at least the subject of the film was this young man's narcissism and how it contrasted with the social consciousness of the revolutionaries: his obliviousness as the world was changing all around him. But Judas wasn't watching this for film school; he just wanted to be entertained.

So, the guy's paranoia wound up resulting in a bit of erratic behavior that eventually led to tension in the relationship, until a scene about forty minutes in, at which point the narrator began to suspect that the temporal tourists were actually there to see the woman rather than him. His subsequent jealousy at this revelation eventually caused the woman to leave him, since she just thought he was crazy, and the movie's narrative proper ended with a shot of the man in an apartment now fallen into disarray, building a strange machine adorned with wire and clockworks: a machine designed perhaps to stop time, or turn it back, or to visit his now-former girlfriend at a moment when she still loved him. Judas wasn't sure about this last part, but he speculated that the machine was possibly going to be the cause of some chronotopic disaster, and that this had been the real item of interest for the time-tourists: it was the event that would result in the narrator's infamy. Upon reflection, he decided that the silent first few minutes of the film were probably supposed to represent a collection of the narrator's cherished memories, since they were played again at the film's conclusion.

Anyway, Judas didn't wind up learning anything at all about Tibet, but he was left with the feeling that he had learnt something about Jigme Drolma. Of course, this feeling was entirely irrational. He returned the movie the next day and asked the clerk about it, halfway hoping the conversation would lead to a DVD experience equivalent to Italo Calvino's *If on a Winter's Night a Traveler,* one mistaken or interrupted story leading him to another in a long, diverse chain of entertainments, but even though the clerk offered Judas a free rental of his choice (sadly, they had no other copies of *Kundun*), his best guess about the cause of the mix-up was that some renter must have switched the discs with a movie procured in Greenpoint (which had lots of video stores that carried nothing but Polish-language titles), but he didn't have any idea what the movie might be, nor did he have a best guess about which store Judas should investigate, and he couldn't even offer any help on who the renter might be, since there were plenty of Polish customers who frequented the store, and the last time anyone had rented *Kundun* had been before they got their new computer system so he couldn't check to see who it was, and though the clerk said nothing about it (and in fact could not have known), Judas felt something in the man's glance that suggested admonishment—a reminder that such an investigation wouldn't actually lead Judas any closer to this Tibetan novelist he'd never heard of—so Judas only sighed, nodded, and rented a talky romantic dramedy starring Ethan Hawke.

Judas didn't call Caissa until the following Monday. He was sitting on his bed, taking a break from arranging his bookshelves, staring out the window at the large apartment complex across the street. His own building was relatively small, six units, with a bar on the ground floor, but the building he was looking at from his window must have housed hundreds. And from what he had seen of them, the tenants were all old or businessmen, neither of which he wanted to be. After more than a minute of thoughtless staring, he took a deep breath, rose, and grabbed the scrap of paper that she'd written her number on from where it sat atop his desk.

He didn't think much about why he was calling her. It was action without premeditation. If he had been more perceptively introspective in this moment, he would have realized that he'd actually been intentionally avoiding thinking about it, as such thought would have set him on an obsessive path of planning in detail everything that he was going to say. And that sort of thing never worked out well.

It took four rings for her to answer, and he'd already begun to compose his voicemail message in his head.

"Hey," she said, and he thought he heard a smile. "How's it going?"

They only talked for a few minutes, as Judas paced the narrow stretch of floor between bed and window. He told her he was fine, and that he was eager to learn more about the neighborhood from her. She told him this was a busy week—she worked as an assistant editor at *Byner's*, a sort of third-tier magazine on the *New Yorker/Harper's/Atlantic* model, and they were just about to close that month's issue, and—in what little spare time she did have—she was working on a book that she was contractually obliged to finish. She said she could maybe hang out for a bit at some point on Saturday, though.

He paused as he reached the window again, pressed the fingers of his free hand against it, and nodded, forgetting for the moment that she couldn't see him. "Yeah, that'd be great," he added quickly. They didn't settle on a time or place, but she said that she would email him that night. He nodded again.

She didn't get in touch that night, or the next two days. Judas distracted himself by reading up on SOFA, since the topic had come up quite a bit of late. It turned out to be a harder task than he anticipated. The first difficulty he encountered was that he didn't know what SOFA stood for, either acronymically or ideologically, and neither, it seemed, did anyone else.* Ideas varied and rarely made any straightforward sense: Situationist Occupation Force Army, Social Opposition Forward Alliance; some held that it was actually S of A, for Soldiers of Apocalypse, or Socialists of America, while others said it wasn't an acronym at all and was merely a symbol of the endemic complacency that prevents people from effecting any real social change. The movement had apparently started in Berkeley, though it had never stood out to Judas among all of the other protest groups. But further difficulties arose from the fact that it didn't have an official website, so he couldn't be sure that any of the contradictory accounts he read were more accurate than any of the others. The best he could find was a quasi-affiliated social-change website designed like something halfway between Digg and Kickstarter, at which anyone could suggest activities or objectives, offering incentives in exchange for support; the most popular suggestions rose to the top, and the fringier stuff got buried. The goals and grievances of the organization itself were pretty vague, though. Which didn't seem to hamper its popularity.

The founder was a guy who called himself Viv LaRevolution. In the beginning he'd had a blog, but now it was long inactive and redacted. The posts that Judas was able to find via Google cache and Wayback Machine were inconsistent at best, more

* In fact, Viv's stroke of genius in planning the whole thing was precisely to place no limits on the imagination of others (e.g., never defining exactly what the Apocalypse Towers were there for). And as we have seen, it's amazing what you can get people spontaneously to do, especially when they've already projected their own meaning onto the situation. This is similar in principle, I think, to why he never provided a definitive interpretation of the acronym.

often than not contradictory. For instance, one of the first posts he'd made in the name of SOFA was a rant about how "effort" correlated directly with "meaning," and that, for example, having to search for a rare book in every used-book store you visited made it seem so much more special when you finally found it than when you could just search for it on eBay and have it at your house the next day, and he parlayed this into a larger point about how the increasing ease of modern life thus necessarily meant an increasing meaninglessness of modern life. Which, fine. But Judas found it odd that he used the acquisition of a commodity (rare book) as his main example, when so many of his other posts bordered on anticapitalist. And he found it even odder that LaRevolution was railing against the ease of modern life, and—more specifically—the internet, when his popularity seemed halfway founded on how well he had adapted to these very things. He had 38,128 followers on Twitter, for instance. As one follower put it, "Each Tweet is a 140-character manifesto." SOFA-related hashtags had been trending highly, steadily, for months, and SOFA "happenings" were apparently always a good time: as much entertainment as protest. There was a big concert/rally/meet-up thing in Brooklyn next month, planned to coincide with other similar events across the country; Judas wasn't clear on the details, but he decided that he would make a point of checking it out. On the day that Caissa finally emailed—a Thursday—he had pretty much exhausted his curiosity on the subject; yet he was having trouble focusing his attention on anything else, either. So after doing little more than opening and closing a few frivolous browser tabs until late in the afternoon, he decided on a whim to take a break and head deeper into Brooklyn to explore Prospect Park.

"Maybe I should walk," he said aloud to himself as he rose from his chair. "Making frequent stops along the way."

The day was sunny, but the breeze brought a slight chill; Judas couldn't decide whether to keep his hoodie off or on. In the park, women were pushing bulky strollers, dogs were romping in a half-moon pool, young people played all manner of ball sports, and, seated on a browning patch of grass, a serious young man read *Ulysses.* Judas felt that this tableau presented him with an array of choices about where to find fulfillment in life—family, pets, physical recreation, literature—and on the surface, literature seemed the least rewarding: the furrow in the young man's brow contrasted with the bemusement on the young mother's face as she regarded her pouting child or the joyful grimace of the hard-hit football player, not to mention the lolling canine tongues. Judas walked behind the reader to peer over his shoulder and see where he was in the novel, but before he could get a clear look he noticed that the young man had turned to look back at him. "Don't I know you?" the young man said.

Judas took a moment to think and found the man entirely unfamiliar. "No," he said. "I think you don't." Quickly, he walked on. Farther down the field, though, he saw someone whom he did recognize.

"Walter!" Judas called.

Walter Benjamin, in a popped-collar goldenrod polo, was standing with a group of six or so other guys, watched a short distance off by a slightly smaller group of girls seated on blankets. One of the girls was holding a baby dressed in a pink onesie, and a black Lab lounged in the grass a small distance off.

This scene complicated Judas's previous interpretation of the park's tableau. Walter looked up when Judas called his name.

"Hey, guy," he said. "You up for a little ultimate?" He waved a Frisbee in front of Judas's face like a taunt. "We're odd at the moment and could use an extra. Or if you just want to hang, you could sit out with the girls."

Judas was in jeans and uncomfortable boots, but he shrugged and trotted over. There didn't seem to be enough room to play, as a good deal of the field was overrun by people with smartphones, all clad in top hats, wandering around on some sort of scavenger hunt, checking in at various hotspots to earn new badges and unlock social-change strategies. Or this was roughly the explanation that he received from Walter.

"Is this another SOFA thing?" Judas asked. It seemed he couldn't get away from it.

"I think it's a spin-off. I tried interviewing a few people earlier, and none of them seem to know much of anything about anything." He paused. "I'm working on a piece for *Byner's* about Viv LaRevolution, you know. But let's get down to dividing up the teams."

Judas wound up with three of Walter's friends from Harvard, none of whom he knew, and when they found out he could only throw backhand they didn't seem eager to get to know him. From almost the beginning, then, he was sorry that he hadn't made some excuse to not join in the game. Luckily Walter gave him an out after about fifteen minutes, running into him so hard as he went to intercept a slow glider that Judas was sent flying face-forward to land at the feet of one of the top-hatted scavengers, jamming his right ring finger as he reached out to soften the impact. He yelped when he tried to support himself with the hand in his attempt to rise, winced, and then felt dog saliva being painted on his face before he opened his eyes to see the black Lab wagging its tail concernedly while the smartphone-clutching scavenger just shambled off.

"Sorry about that, guy," Walter said, offering him a hand. "You okay?"

"I'm fine." Judas stood without Walter's help, grasping right hand with left as the dog danced around him.

"Hey, Chester likes you."

Judas was in serious pain, more than he would have expected, but he managed to make a comment about Chester's attractiveness.

"Yeah, you should watch him for me some time."

"I should?"

"Yeah, that would be cool. You're not busy, are you?"

"Well, you know, I've just been looking into that translation stuff."

"Oh, right. Anyway, did Gabe tell you we're playing poker at my place next weekend? You should come."

"Sure," Judas said. "I'll see if I can make it." A sharp pain shot through his finger's middle joint as he reached to wipe mud from his forehead, and no one objected when he said he didn't think he could play anymore.

He went away feeling sorry for himself: seeing himself as Candide and wondering why he had even bothered moving here. But the reader shouldn't feel too sorry for him, as he was ignoring all of the times in his life when he had been the one who had acted like a total dick to someone else. He tended to express his aggression more passively than Walter and his friends, of course, but at least they were open about who they were. Judas, on the other hand, pretended even to himself that he was sweet, romantic, and innocent when in fact he was just as competitive, lustful, and petty as any of them. Which is to say that he kind of deserved to have his finger broken.

He felt slightly better that night after he checked his email and read what Caissa had sent him. She suggested that they start the next Saturday off by getting lunch and that they could maybe walk around the neighborhood afterwards. She'd done some research online and read about a Tibetan restaurant in Prospect Park South that was supposed to be pretty good—Gabriel had told her about Jigme Drolma—and she thought it might be fun to try it.

"Sounds great," Judas had replied. "When and where should we meet?"

She wrote back almost immediately, figured it would take maybe an hour to get there, and so they decided to meet in front of Judas's place at noon. He was waiting outside his building's security door by 11:55, though he tried to act casual and claim that he'd just come down when she showed up at 12:10.

"Good to see you," he said, raising his right hand in a half wave, displaying his grossly swollen finger.

"Ow, God, what happened?" Her face scrunched up either in sympathy for the pain or in horror at the purple deformity.

"I fell."

"Have you been to a doctor? Is it broken?"

"I thought it was just a sprain. I'll probably have it checked out on Monday."

They walked a block in silence.

It took an hour to get to the place. Plenty of time for small talk: what do you read? how do you like the city? etc. And it was a warm, sunny day, so the walk through the park itself was nice; some of the leaves were already beginning to turn. Judas had skipped breakfast, though—a tendency for which Caissa would later proclaim him a "manorexic"—and by the time they made it to the restaurant his head ached for food as much as his stomach.

"Any idea what's good?" he asked her once they'd been seated and had their menus in front of them.

She didn't look up. "The reviews I read said good things about the *ping* and the *momo*."

He tried in vain to find these items, quickly flipping plastic-covered pages, before saying, "Sounds good to me. Want to get an assortment and we can share? And maybe some of this butter tea? I read about it once in this Chinese swordplay novel. I'm thinking of translating it, actually. Maybe more up my alley than the Tibetan thing, you know?"

"That sounds horrid. The tea, not the novel. But I suppose we have to try it."

Over the course of that meal and subsequent others—always and almost only while eating—Caissa told Judas the story of her life. Though it took a fair amount of time for her to even reach her birth.

"Context is everything," she explained.

That afternoon she began by talking about her father. In the early sixties, it seemed, Myron Holly had been something like a Guyanese James Bond. That is: Oxbridge educated, taking a first in Oriental languages; spending a good deal of time in Jamaica; cultivating an interest in ornithology. And, Caissa suspected, being a secret agent.

"That's my mom's theory, anyway." She adjusted her glasses. "Officially, he was a journalist. But you know, she says she's pretty sure he helped CIA in their efforts to keep the PPP out of power. And I've actually got a pretty good angle on the whole thing, I think, about how the racial and political situation has played out in modern times; I managed to sell it as a book proposal, at least, though I'm kind of having trouble making any progress on the actual book. Despite looming deadlines."

"Wow, that's all really cool." Judas shoved a *momo* (steamed dumpling) into his mouth. He decided that he would wiki Guyanese history when he got home.

"Well, it's sort of cool." She shrugged. "Except it means I never got to know him. I mean, I was only five when he died."

"Wait, so he was still a spy like twenty years later?"

The waitress arrived with the *ping* at this point (bean thread noodles on rice, with chicken, vegetables, and a spicy sauce), and Caissa heaped some onto her plate before answering.

She made eye contact. "I don't think he was 'spying,' whatever that might have meant for a Guyanese American in the early eighties, but his journalism work took him to D.C. a lot. He was always going off to research stories that never seemed to get published. My mom said she wouldn't let him tell her he was a spy even if he wanted to. But then in 1981 he fell through a plate glass window and broke his neck." She looked down at her food. "The official verdict or whatever was suicide."

"God, that sucks." Judas was trying to serve himself some *ping*, though it was awkward to handle noodles with only one hand fully functional.

"Yeah. I know."

"I'm sorry." He tried to say it with emphasis but it came out sounding flat. He put down his fork.

"No, it's okay. I don't know why I even brought it up. I have a bad habit of dwelling on sad stories about myself. My old boyfriend Mike used to call me 'Niggarella.'"

"That's funny," Judas said without laughing. He picked his fork back up.

They didn't explore Brooklyn Heights as they'd originally planned—at least not that afternoon—but Judas rode the train back with her and then walked her to her apartment in Vinegar Hill. At the security door, she gave him a hug good-bye.

Judas was in high spirits as he headed home. He fell in love easily, but he had the sense that his feelings for Caissa were of a variety that he had rarely felt since high school and his first serious crush: a girl named April "the Magnificent" Amberson. He found Caissa attractive and he wanted to sleep with her, but his infatuation was somehow separate from this desire. He simply *liked her* a great deal, and their time together had elevated him. Part of him would have preferred to have slept with her, of course, but another part couldn't have been happier. And later that night as he lay sleepless—unable to distract himself with books or internet—this happiness gave him cause for worry.

In the past, he had always kept two loves in tension: one actual and one ideal. The actual loves, like Hannah back in Berkeley, had been women he dated long-term, whom he treated well, whose company comforted him, and with whom he was honest and open, sharing himself in all of his considerable imperfection; he'd been known to fart in front of them with only the slightest self-consciousness. The ideal loves he tended not to date at all. They were women he would spend time with in situations that were not explicitly romantic, and his gallant gestures towards them derived their meaning precisely from the fact that he wasn't attached to them. He didn't have to play games, hide his enthusiasm, or try to act cool, because he wasn't concerned with seduction; he could present his honest emotions right from the beginning. Or that's what he told himself, though in practice the presence of these women never comforted him but rather made him giddy with nerves: acutely self-conscious of every action and all its possible interpretations; whether he realized it or not, he was always striving to project an ideal version of himself in order to be worthy of the feelings that he harvested from his interactions with them.

Again, such feelings were entirely dependent upon his not dating these women. A high five or a hug from a love he'd never kissed was in some sense a greater thrill than an orgasm from a one-night stand. Yet any further intimacy or investment might ruin everything. In the ideal state, he never *had to* walk around with them as they shopped for clothes, and so he could take pleasure in doing so. And he never had to fight with them over the choices he made in his own life, or the choices that he wished they'd make in theirs. Because—unbound to them—their weal and woe had no direct bearing on him, and vice versa. With actual loves he had a personal stake in their lives, but with the ideal ones he could listen to the same problems and give the same unheeded advice, over and over, without ever feeling the slightest frustration. In short, with ideal loves, he could avoid any sense of responsibility.

The key to amorous equilibrium for Judas was that the ideal loves weren't meant to be competition for the actual ones; he was self-aware enough to realize that dating the ideal loves could possibly destroy, or at least alter, the feelings he had for them. But the system wasn't perfect. Part of the problem with Hannah had been that Judas's ideal love of the moment—Natalie, a coworker at the County who moonlighted in both modern dance and comic book illustration, and with whom Judas spent almost every lunch hour—had threatened to eclipse her, and he wasn't advanced enough a man to get beyond his immature inability to commit his mind to any singular avenue, romantic or not. But what worried Judas about Caissa was the fact that she felt too ideal, while he didn't have an actual love to hold her in tension against. Worst of all, he thought that he might want her to be his actual love and his ideal love together, though he knew this could never work out. The situation was untenable. As he'd always told his former roommate back in Berkeley, a cow won't give out the milk if she can get the hay for free, but with ideal loves Judas tended to dole out hay by the bale.

"So," he said aloud to himself. "I'll just have to sleep with her soon."

Caissa, meanwhile, was busy trying without much success to work on her book. And though she thought that Judas was nice and vaguely interesting, she wasn't yet smitten. She did, however, call him up the following Tuesday morning—just as he was leaving the office of a doctor who had given him a splint for his slightly broken finger—and ask if he was free for lunch. He occupied her consciousness enough that when certain subjects arose in conversation, he was the first person who came to mind. Which is vague, but so were her feelings, and so was what she said to Judas when she spoke to him on the phone. Her exact words were "I have a little surprise for you."

They decided to meet at a little café near the *Byner's* office at one o'clock. He got there first. It was a brightly lit place with big open windows on two sides, and he snagged a table in the corner where those two sides met.

"What's the surprise?" he asked as soon as she sat down across from him. She was wearing her widest grin.

"I'll show you."

It was a book by Jigme Drolma. Not the new one, she apologized, but she'd mentioned Drolma to a friend at Oxford University Press, and he happened to have a spare copy of this one lying around.

"Wow, thanks," Judas said. But he was thinking, *All right, she clearly likes me, now I just need to be careful not to blow it. Move quickly but not sleazily.*

The book was called *Xiangxin Qitan*, which meant something like "believe a crazy story," but which Judas figured was also maybe supposed to be playing on *xiangqi*, or "elephant chess," since that game was one of the novel's—novella's—central motifs; Judas actually used to play a bit with his old roommate Thomas, though he'd almost always lose.* The book wasn't much more than a short story, really, and even with the occasional need for his Chinese dictionary, Judas made it through the whole thing between lunch and dinner. The plot

* I tried multiple times to explain to him that material advantage matters far less in *xiangqi* than it does in Western chess; position is everything.

sort of reminded him of another book he'd read recently, *Tourneé du Chat Orange* by Magnus Valison. That one—basically about a chess match in 1950s Algeria between an Arab and a Frenchman, set against the backdrop of impending revolution—was a little weird, even for Valison, but Judas had enjoyed it, and the plot was this:

The day before the match is scheduled to begin, the Arab spends the afternoon walking around Algiers, which is the city he grew up in, though he's since relocated to Switzerland. He's walking and he's thinking back on his life, memories evoked by the street scenes around him, and he starts reflecting on all that he's given up and passed by (family, friends, love, etc.) in order to pursue a life completely devoted to chess. There are a few poignant memories dilated into scenes, but he eventually ends up at a café where he runs into his French opponent, and—feeling lonely after his walk—he shares a drink with him. After a frivolous but strangely pleasant conversation in which neither man mentions anything about chess, they both decide to head back to their respective hotel rooms, which is when the story picks up: the Arab has just made it to his door and is thinking to himself that his opponent seems like a decent fellow when someone grabs him from behind and chloroforms him.

He wakes that night in a plush chair in a lavishly decorated drawing room, where he's confronted by three men in tuxedos and paper animal masks (a rooster, an orange cat or tiger, and—most interesting to Judas now, in light of the Drolma book—an elephant). Their dialogue is very polite; they offer him food, drink, a cigarette, all of which he refuses, demanding instead to know who they are and where he is and by what right they've brought him here. The rooster is angered a bit by the Arab's perfectly reasonable indignity, but the elephant suggests that everyone just relax. The tiger thus far has not spoken. The elephant then explains to the Arab that masks will not be removed, that names will not be given, and that they've only brought him here by right of force.

"However," he says, his accent decidedly French upper crust, "we have no wish to inconvenience you any longer than necessary, and the sooner you agree to assist us, the sooner we can arrange to have you taken back to your hotel room."

After considering his options, the Arab decides that the best thing to do is just to ask what they want from him, but the elephant is anything but direct in his response. He starts off by apologizing for the necessity of all this theater, but then he explains that, as the Arab is an extraordinary man, extraordinary measures were called for.

"I'm anything but extraordinary," the Arab answers. "Except when it comes to chess, perhaps, but even then—"

"*Au contraire*," the elephant says. The novella had been written in French, but Judas had read it in English translation, and this was one of the few remnants of the original language. "If you were any less extraordinary you wouldn't be here. We would have kidnapped your wife or your daughter, sent someone to hold a knife to your mother's throat or cut the tail from your cat. But you have none of these things. Family dead, you are close to no one, and you seem to have no interests at all . . . aside, as you say, from chess. You seem to be almost suicidally apathetic. How is one supposed to threaten a man such as you? And if not threaten, then bribe, yes? But despite all of your success you live in a small apartment with no luxuries, and you regularly turn down generous offers to play exhibition games, even in your own city. Extraordinary."

The Arab then repeats himself. "What is it that you want of me?"

"Well, that," the elephant says, raising one shoulder in a half shrug. "That is nothing extraordinary at all. We would like you to play your game tomorrow to a draw. Give it the appearance of a hard-fought contest in which you never seem able to gain the advantage. Then, spirit crushed, we would like you to forfeit the rest of the match."

The Arab takes a moment to consider all that's been said, but then he refuses, pointing out that the elephant himself has just finished explaining that there are no compelling reasons for him to accept. Besides, the fact that the three men are wearing masks suggests that they are people the Arab would recognize if he were to see their true faces, and since there can't be many people who would gamble on a chess match, and even fewer who would have taken the long odds of a draw, he doubts he'll have much trouble uncovering their identities whether they reveal their faces or not; he plans to go to the police as soon as they release him. The rooster gets a bit apoplectic at this, but the elephant again calms him.

"You have no idea how many people are invested in this match," the elephant says to the Arab. "But I don't expect to garner your sympathy. I can only ask you to keep our request in mind as you play tomorrow. And keep in mind that your actions will have consequences."

"You'll kill me, then, if I don't go through with it? Is that what you're saying?"

"No." The elephant shakes his head, paper trunk pendulous. "We will kill your opponent."

For the first time the Arab is actually shaken, as he thinks back to the pleasant Frenchman whom he shared a drink with that afternoon.

"It takes two to draw," he finally says to the elephant. "Are the three of you going to have a conversation with him, as well?"

"No, but you are heavily favored to win, are you not? If he had been the favorite, this all would have been a much simpler matter."

The Arab can't handle the absurdity any longer, and he tries explaining how ridiculous their logic is, and how there's no way he could be sure of pulling off what they're asking even if he wanted to. "I'm favored to win the match, but I still might lose a game," he says. But the men in masks aren't interested in his protests, simply telling him that it's his responsibility to comply and that he knows what the consequences will be.

After this, not much happens in the drawing room. Some indecipherable bickering between the rooster and the elephant and then a murmured apology in Arabic from the tiger before a goon, who's not wearing a gorilla mask but might as well be, comes in to put a bag over the Arab's head and escort him back to his hotel room.

Unsurprisingly, the Arab has a hard time falling asleep. He thinks briefly about drinking until, considering the chloroform, he thinks better of it. Then in a scene revealing a slight mistake in the elephant's estimation of his character, he pulls a book by Maupassant out of his luggage and holds it on his lap before opening to a story in the middle and reading the inscription scrawled there by a secondary school sweetheart. Judas couldn't recall exactly what the inscription read, though he had the feeling that the words might have been one of the secret keys to the story. In any case, the Arab cries a little or something and after a sleepless night heads out to meet his opponent without having come to any decision about what he's going to do: whether his respect—if that's the word—for this man across the board from him would outweigh his vague ideal about the purity of play. Which seems like it would be an easy decision—human life versus a vague ideal—but the story makes it clear that the real dilemma is in whether or not the Arab can face the fact that his whole justification for continuing his own existence is based precisely in this vague ideal.

The story—which to this point has been focusing very closely on the Arab's psychological interiority—then shifts into a detached, technical mode, describing the moves of the game and the notes made by each player. Which isn't to say that this section is completely dry; it's actually one of the more interesting sections, as the Arab's notes quickly devolve into unhinged musings that have little to do with the game itself ("The English call the fool a 'bishop,' the Germans a 'runner.' They sense that he is a holy fool, running happily off a ledge despite the barking of his dog. In India, he was an elephant."). The game develops quickly and it seems like it's really close, just as the men in masks wanted it—dramatic sacrifices, complex threats and counterthreats—and the rising action here culminates in the Arab's decision to split the game in two. That is, at some point he decides that he can't decide whether he should try to preserve the Frenchman or his own ideals, and so he tries to do both, making one move with his hand while verbally announcing an entirely dissimilar move. It takes his opponent a few minutes to figure out what's going on, and there's some absurd humor involved in consulting the judges, but ultimately the Frenchman seems to intuitively understand the Arab's turmoil, and he responds in kind, making one response to the physical move while announcing a separate response to the verbal, and in the text the two parallel games continue to progress alongside each other in algebraic notation.

The Arab's notes are largely concerned here with pseudo-philosophical/poetic musings on the idea of parallel realities and divergent time lines, a particular emphasis given to imagining what sort of life he might have lived had he not devoted himself so single-mindedly to chess: how a sense of meaning in life can come from such devotion, but how he fears that there might be something more fundamentally meaningful that he missed out on. The climax of the story comes with the simultaneous ending of the two games: the actual game a stalemate to satisfy the men in masks, and the verbal game a dramatically unexpected loss on the Arab's part, the implication being that his best game led him to a defeat even greater than compromise. The story ends with the Arab in his hotel room receiving a letter of condolence signed with the cartoon image of a tiger's face.

The Jigme Drolma book was basically identical to this, plot-wise, except that it took place in Tibet and was about a relatively casual game of elephant chess between a Tibetan and a Chinese who'd never met but had a history of sparring with each other long distance through newspaper columns. Otherwise it was the same.

Judas preferred the Valison book. It not only had the virtue of coming first (both in terms of when it had been published and when he had read it), but also was subtler. Both books had a postcolonial subtext, for instance, but at least the Ghana-born Valison's direct concerns were transposed onto the French-Algerian conflict, making it seem somehow more universal than Drolma's very specific take on the subject. But maybe it was meant as slight: a fairy tale. If Judas were trying to preserve the poetry of it, he probably would have translated the dedication as something like, "To my son as he lives and learns, a revolution as it turns." So maybe it was an attempt to make political ideas digestible for young people. But in any case, the overall effect of Caissa's gift was to make Judas wonder how much he would actually enjoy translating a full-length novel by the guy.

On the subway over to Walter's place for poker, Judas reflected that he needed to start making friends outside of the circle of Gabriel Stilzkin's acquaintances. His growing doubts about the prospect of the translation he'd supposedly come here to do were making him feel generally ill at ease, and it was simpler for him to place the blame with Gabriel rather than to accept it as his own. This was unfair to Gabe, of course, but sometimes it was hard for Judas to think of his erstwhile friend as a human being, either physically or mentally. There was something almost parodic about Gabe's appearance—his stooped shoulders, patchy hair, bad teeth—like an ineptly made golem. And although it hadn't seemed to hold him back too much professionally or personally, Gabriel's sense of social propriety was rudimentary at best. To all appearances, he operated on the principle that any attention was good attention, so he chose to offend when he couldn't dazzle. He wasn't the best at joining a conversation already in progress, for example, but instead would try to derail it, waiting for the slightest pause between sentences in order to insert a non sequitur on whatever subject he would feel more at ease talking about.

But what bothered Judas most about Gabriel was how sleazy he was when it came to women. Judas was, of course, ignoring his own sleaze on the basis of the subtler form that it took. But Gabe was almost ridiculously straightforward, his smoothest pickup line being something like "You should come home with me tonight," which was only smooth in relation to the more common and direct "We should totally fuck" that he usually used. Judas had heard that Gabe was repeatedly warned about sexual harassment at his job before *E*.

And yet Judas liked him. He liked him, in fact, as a direct consequence of all these supposed deficiencies of character. Gabe was ridiculous, but he was unapologetically the person that he was, and Judas admired that; apparently there were women who felt the same way, since he was rarely at a loss for a date. He at least seemed to be a happier person now than he had been freshman year, back in Berkeley. When Judas had first known him he'd been pretty fragile, crying weekly on the phone to a girl whom he'd had a crush on throughout high school, converting to Catholicism to be more like Auden, and drinking far too much almost every night. The last bit, at least, hadn't really changed, and Judas had mentioned to Caissa that he was actually a bit relieved at the familiarity he felt whenever glimmers of Gabe's old nerdiness managed to shine their way through the crust of his current persona. Having occasionally observed Gabe's nerdiness herself, she laughed at the idea of him attending a poker night.

"You sure it's 'poker night' and not just 'game night' or

something? I've known Gabriel Stilzkin for a while, and I think *Dungeons & Dragons* is definitely more his speed. Just wait, he's going to be wearing a cloak. And I bet he slips up and calls the dealer a dungeon master."

He didn't do anything so extreme, but during the course of the game he did reference the movie *Conan the Barbarian* with regard to his sexual exploits and "the lamentations of the women." Recalling Caissa's comment, Judas laughed aloud, but Gabriel just took the laugh as a compliment to his wit.

In general, the conversation that Saturday was less focused on the subject of fantasy than on the subject of women. *E* interns, mostly, and how great it was to watch them bend over to change the ink cartridges in the office printers, or how fixing the air conditioners hadn't been a huge priority over the summer since it kept the girls scantily clad. These supposed intellectuals were turning out to be a bit more corporeal in their concerns than Judas had anticipated, and he was mildly disappointed to learn that these guys were just like other men, no better or worse, though he still irrationally preferred to think of himself as an exception. There was also talk of women whom players were, to various degrees, dating: Jasmine Green, for instance.

"So, what's up with her?" one of Walter's Frisbee buddies asked Martin Pope. "The skinny one from the party, right? You hitting that?"

Martin, again in his black crushed-velvet coat and bolo tie, shrugged. "Sometimes. She's a little too into me. Doesn't know how to keep it casual and cool."

"Or you don't know how to just nod and play along," Walter said. "You have to admit she's hotter than your usual fare."

Martin shrugged again. "What about you and that Dorothy Horowitz chick?"

"That's different. She had an entire blog devoted to the experience of dating me. And people were actually reading it. It was messing with my game."

"Speaking of messing with my game, can you deal, please?" This was Jon, another of Walter's friends from college—this one a novelist whose books were all based around the theme of searching for lost loved ones in the aftermath of tragedies, like World War II or 9/11 (the American one in his first novel, the 1973 Chilean one in his third).

"I mean, it was good on one level," Walter continued, passing cards around the table. "Girls would read the blog and think maybe they could reform me, or that they could get some secondhand fame as a guest slut in one of Dorothy's posts. So it kind of gave me license to be an asshole. But it just got to be too much to think about."

"Yeah, sounds horrible," Martin said.

Walter smirked, and Judas took advantage of the pause to insert some innocent comment about Drolma, asking Walter if he'd found anything out.

"I'm not sure if I should tell you. I mean, how can I be sure you're not just trying to get our angle for this new magazine I hear you're playing us against?"

"What?"

"Yeah, Gabe told me about your Aussie friend."

"That's— There's no other magazine, I just— I mean, Gabe's email made it sound like you guys were pretty enthusiastic about this guy, you know, and you just haven't really told me much about what I'm supposed to be doing."

"Dude, I was coked out of my mind when I sent you that email," Gabe interjected. "Besides, I thought you'd be the one telling us shit. When are you headed to Bloomington, anyway?"

"What? Since when am I going to Bloomington?"

"I thought you said you were going there to track down the Tibetan dude."

"I said that maybe I should."

"Right. So maybe you should. I already emailed a guy there who wrote a piece for the first issue of *E*, and he said he'd probably be able to put you up while you're there. You're not doing much else, are you?"

Judas nodded. "I'll think about it."

"Just don't forget that you're watching my dog this weekend, though," Walter said.

"What?"

"When we were playing ultimate. You said you were going to watch Chester. He liked you, remember?"

"Whoa, yeah, I didn't know you meant any time soon."

"I mean, what else do you have going on?" Gabe asked. "Why not head to Bloomington? Anything happening with you and Caissa?"

"Dude, deal already."

"I'm off to Berkeley in two days for this *Byner's* story," Walter said. "I told you that. I'm kind of counting on you, guy. Don't let me down here."

"Yeah, don't let the rest of us down either. Are you going to see or fold?"

The game was Texas Hold'em, six-man table, fifty-dollar buy-in. Judas had played a decent amount of poker during college, but that had been before Hold'em had threatened the death of all other forms, and in the past he'd always stuck to basic varieties of draw and stud. The first warning sign that he might be in over his head had come when Walter had laid a green velvet surface over the table. And then his broken ring finger made it hard for him to deal—especially with the unfamiliar practice of remembering to kill cards before the river and the turn, especially since he hadn't known beforehand what the river and turn were—which only increased his already considerable self-consciousness. So tonight he was just trying to get his bearings with these strange players and odds. He kept getting off-suited ace-nines in the pocket, which was just on the border of tempting, but folded most hands before the flop. Judas nursed his beer and decided to play it safe.

"So what's going on with you and Caissa?" Gabe asked on a hand that both he and Judas had folded. "Did you guys hook up?"

"Not really," Judas answered.

"Not really?" Jon echoed. "What's that supposed to mean? You give her the head and dodge or something?"

"'Head and dodge'?"

"Yeah, she gives you head, then you get the fuck out of Dodge."

Judas tried to smile. "No."

"Heh. Did she give you the head and dodge, then?" Gabriel asked.

Judas looked him in the eyes. "No."

"So what'd you guys do?" Jon asked. Then, to Walter, "I'll raise you ten."

"Do you even know the girl we're talking about?" Judas asked.

"No," Jon said. "But I do know that 'not really' is a bullshit answer to 'Did you guys hook up?' So what did you do?"

"Nothing," Judas said. "We hugged."

"They hugged." Walter smiled. "I'm all in."

"I fold," Jon said, and Walter pulled in the chips. Then, Jon to Judas, "Was it at least like you tried to go up to her place with her and she turned it into a hug? Because you know that if you didn't at least try for that you've already blown it, right? You've got to establish the possibility right away."

Judas sighed and shook his head. "Look, I don't need dating advice. Why are we even talking about this? It was just a hug."

"That's kind of sweet," Gabriel said.

"Or gay," said one of the players whose name Judas had forgotten. "Puerile, infantile . . . emotionally stunted, at best."

"What the fuck, I never claimed we hooked up." Judas was allowing his annoyance to raise the pitch of his voice. "We hugged. And all I'm saying is that that's the extent of what we did. I'm not saying I want to hook up with her, or that a hug is the same as hooking up, or that it meant anything at all."

"Not really," Martin said to the general amusement of the table.

Judas went home fifty dollars poorer.

The following weekend, he found himself starting a five-day stint of watching Walter's dog. More to the point, he found himself in Walter's brownstone while Walter himself was off in Berkeley to research his *Byner's* story about Viv LaRevolution and the founding of SOFA. Judas was the first of a few separate dog-watchers whom Walter had arranged to have come over. Judas understood from Gabriel that the others who would be coming after him were various young *E* hangers-on, editorial assistants and literary aspirants who wanted to ingratiate themselves to Walter so that he might remember them and maybe even publish them. Which made him wonder what he was doing here himself. He didn't feel as if he'd been bullied into it, exactly, but he just wasn't sure how it had happened that he'd come to agree.

The place was pretty nice, two stories, well lit, with lots of white furniture and mirrors. Judas didn't know design, but he would have guessed that it was maybe Danish in aesthetic. In any case, a welcome change from his little railroad. He spent his first few minutes in the place rummaging through drawers and medicine cabinets, but he didn't come across anything particularly worth noting.

Despite Chester's initial enthusiasm when they'd met in the park, he now seemed to be giving Judas a wide berth. Which Judas was fine with, though he had a hard time getting him on a leash to take him to the park, which he was supposed to do three times a day. The weather had warmed a bit since the previous weekend (Indian summer), so come one o'clock, while he was out for the day's second walk, Judas decided to text Caissa to see if she was maybe up for a picnic.

"With my mom right now in Manhattan," she texted back. "Already ate. Maybe call you later this afternoon."

"Sounds good," he replied. He took Chester home, and then for the next two hours before she called he was unable to think of anything else.

• • •

They wound up meeting the following Tuesday at a fashionable restaurant in Brooklyn Heights renowned for its cocktails, and they each ordered strange drinks with silly names ("O Captain, My Comfort," "The Ginger-Headed Sailor") just for the novelty. Judas was at his most amusing, or at least he thought so. As the night drew on, his remarks became ribald without crossing into lewdness, and somehow—after the main course—he managed to grasp her hand from across the table; the waiter came by and asked if they'd like to see the dessert menu, and without looking up or letting go Judas told him they'd have another round of cocktails. Then with hardly a segue, she said something that he couldn't have anticipated:

"So, I hear you're in love with me."

"What?"

"That's what Martin says."

"What? Martin Pope? When did you talk to him?"

"I had brunch with him this weekend. So, are you? In love with me?"

Judas exhaled through his nose and cleared his throat. "No." He paused. "I mean, especially at this point, that's just a silly question. I don't even really know you well enough to say I love you and have it mean anything."

She nodded. "I know, that's why I thought it was kind of psycho. But Martin said you were acting all dreamy about having hugged me the other day, so I just figured I should ask."

"He said that?"

"Was he lying?"

"Yes. I mean, I may have mentioned that I hugged you when he and his friends wouldn't shut up asking if we'd had sex, but I wouldn't say I got all dreamy about it."

"You think the fact that we hugged is a step on the path to sex?"

Judas sighed. "No, it was more like, 'We didn't have sex, we just hugged; stop bugging me about it.' Are the two of you dating or something?"

"Me and Martin? We're just brunch buddies."

"I mean, I do think I kind of like you."

She nodded and lanced him with her eyes. "Well, I like you too." He could hear a qualifying tone in her voice. "I'm glad I met you. Fair warning, though. I just want to say up front that my last relationship was kind of tough . . . and I think after that, I kind of formed this idea that the next time I got into something, I hoped it would be something obvious and clear from the get-go."

A sort of panic came over him and he withdrew his hand. "That's cool. I mean, I like you, but I'm not saying we have to be in a relationship or whatever. I mean, apparently I'm headed to Bloomington soon, and who knows where I'm going from there, or when I'll be back. I just like hanging out with you, though."

She shook her head and waved her right hand in the air, simultaneously making a sound that could only be described as a vibrato "blah."

"I guess your ex must have screwed you up a lot."

Caissa nodded and wound up telling him more than she'd meant to.

Michael Harmon first achieved notoriety for his short-story cycle *Sand Niggas.* The book was predominantly about African American soldiers in Iraq, though the two most praised stories —the two that had been anthologized—were those that deviated most sharply from the mode: one was about gangbangers who had returned home from war and were trying to bring their military experience and knowledge to use in Compton, fighting for turf. The other—the title story—had focused on a group of young Iraqis who dreamt of becoming hip-hop stars, and their fateful encounter with two black Muslim American soldiers. Sales for the book had started off slow, but they'd picked up after Mike had managed to convince a *Los Angeles Times* reporter that he'd received a death threat from Osama bin Laden over the book's depiction of Islam. Though Caissa didn't know it, it was this stunt rather than the quality of his fiction that had eventually granted Mike access to Viv LaRevolution's inner circle, once he'd moved to the West Coast to become an acolyte of Hal Auerbach.

But Mike had met Caissa a few years before all of this, while he was a graduate student in creative writing, and Caissa, an undergrad, had enrolled in the fiction workshop he was teaching. Over the course of the semester, he'd wooed her with the multipronged attack of praising her work for its amazing potential and then ripping every sentence apart and pointing out all the flaws in her fundamental premises—though always implying some sort of assurance that she could become the successful writer she'd always dreamed of being if only she would submit herself to his guidance. They began sleeping together shortly before the semester's end. The relationship lasted three years, so Judas assumed it must have had its good points, but as Caissa described it for him now, it consisted of anecdotes ranging haphazardly back and forth in time and linked only by the fact that they all portrayed Mike as an asshole.

"During our second year dating I got an ovarian cyst,"

she said. "I didn't have health insurance or money, but Mike thought I was just using it as an excuse not to have sex with him. He paid for my surgery. But then when we broke up he made me pay him back."

And on it went, tales of Mike subsuming Caissa into his world of sexual deviancy, ex-lax and porn, careerist self-obsession, all punctuated with episodes of cheating, emotional abuse, petty competition—

"Wait a second," Judas interrupted. "Is this another one of your Niggarella stories?"

"Excuse me?" She removed her glasses and squinted at him.

"I asked if this—"

"I heard what you asked—I just can't believe you asked it. Don't ever call me that again."

Judas paused and took a sip of his Ginger-Headed Sailor. He glanced around the restaurant to make sure they weren't being too loud. "I didn't call you that," he said. "I just asked if this *story* was—"

"Don't give me semantics, just apologize."

"So I can't say 'Niggarella' just because I'm white?"

"Oh my God." She laughed and put her glasses back on. "I can't believe you. The answer to your question is no. You can't say 'Niggarella' because I find it offensive."

"All right." He sipped his drink. "But did you find it offensive when Mike said it?" A pause. "I mean, at the time?"

"Yeah, a little," she said, with no hesitation. "And looking back now, a lot. Besides, you're not Mike, and after what I've just been telling you about him, I wouldn't think you'd even want to remind me of him."

Judas saw the wisdom in this line of argument and relented.

"I'm sorry," he said. "You're right. Should we get another drink?"

She downed the remainder of her second O Captain, My Comfort. "Yeah," she said. "I think I could sit here and wind down for a little while longer."

And so, the subject changed, Caissa didn't get to hear the story of Hannah—at least not that night. Though such a story, if properly told, wouldn't have been very flattering to Judas in any case.

Thus far we've hewn fairly closely to Judas's point of view, and so it's understandable if the reader has developed a less than favorable opinion of, say, Martin Pope. Caissa at least—based on a few casual comments that Judas made over dinner—had gotten the impression that Judas didn't look on Martin very kindly. Yet it's important to realize that Martin was a human too, with all of the complexity that this implies. If he seemed somewhat more cavalier than Judas in his relations with the opposite sex, it didn't necessarily mean he was any worse of a person. It simply pointed to different formative experiences, a different personality—a different way of insulating himself from the hardships of the world. Caissa had occasionally seen another side of Martin—she'd seen him open up—and she thought a few of Judas's remarks about him unduly harsh; in some ways, his seemingly unprovoked malice bothered her more than the Niggarella comment.

None of this stopped her from being at least minorly infatuated. Or perhaps "intrigued" was a better word. It had been drizzling as Judas walked her home, and despite her slight pique, she found herself inviting him up out of it.

"Good job," she said.

"For what?"

"For getting through all of this, whatever it is. I feel like you deserve a prize."

As soon as she spoke the words she worried that they made her seem too easy—which she wasn't, having slept with maybe ten guys in her life, depending on how you counted—but then Judas spoke.

"This rain's just going to get heavier; I should head home."

Sometimes a woman wants a man to be gallant, and sometimes she wants him to lift her off the ground and take her to bed. Caissa had thought it apparent that asking Judas up should have been a clear signal that she was leaning towards the latter, so his refusal only added to the pique she'd been feeling. Until, in the next moment, he gave her a kiss that she felt all the way up to her nucleus accumbens—a term that occurred to her she knew not whence and which caused her immediately to acknowledge her own tendency to analyze and aestheticize the events of her life coincident with the moment of experience—even despite the direct assault of his garlic breath.

"Or not," he said.

And so she opened her door and took him up.

The next day, after he'd headed home, Caissa found herself wondering why Judas liked her, not out of any sense of self-doubt so much as out of simple curiosity. He seemed to like her a lot from the way he doted in the morning, but she just couldn't see any objective correlative for his emotions. She worried that he just wanted to like someone. But then, she wasn't sure how she felt about him, so perhaps that didn't matter yet. Still it was something to think about.

She saw a therapist every Wednesday during her long lunch hour. She'd mentioned Judas once or twice in passing but had dismissed his importance when the therapist had asked to know more about him. So on the day after dinner, she didn't feel as if she could just launch unexpected into a full run-through of her conflicted feelings about having slept with this guy she'd hardly mentioned before—she didn't want her therapist to feel as if she were keeping things from him—so instead, because she felt she had to say *something,* she told him about a dream she'd had.

"I had a couple dreams, actually, but one was just about my iPhone falling apart, and that's pretty obvious, right—like my life is falling apart, or I'm worried that it's about to? But anyway, the other one was more complex. My mom, my sister, and I were going to a day spa. Which is weird in itself, since my mom wouldn't do anything so frivolous, and Marfa, of course, is way too butch. But otherwise, at first, it was fairly normal. We were sitting in a sauna talking about the towels we were wearing. I knew that mine was a hand-me-down from Marfa, from when she was in high school, and my mom was saying it looked much better on Marfa, while Marfa was saying she hated it and she'd only ever worn it because my mom had made her. Pretty normal.

"But then after that the people who ran the spa came in and said we had to go to separate rooms for our massages. I said I wanted to get the same massage that Marfa got, but they told me that mine was special, just for me, so I went along with them to this room made all out of stone. Granite or something. Possibly limestone. Anyway, I took off my towel and lay facedown on a giant stone table, which was freezing after the sauna. But when the massage started, it was like a pleasant buzz that made me forget the cold of the table. Not too drunk, not too high, just nice and comfortable all over.

"I noticed something odd, though. All around the edges of the table I was lying on, there were these jars. Not really formaldehyde jars or pickle jars, but kind of both at once. They'd been empty when I climbed up onto the table, but I noticed now that they had body parts in them. My body parts. While the person was massaging me—I think it was a woman—she'd been reaching into me and pulling out all of my internal organs and putting them into brine without my being aware of it. I was bothered by this, but I thought it would be rude to say anything, so I just watched as she placed my lungs, and heart, and liver, and ovaries in jars in a circle around me. After almost all of the jars were full, I noticed that they were labeled with the names of different vegetables that you might pickle. And I think on some level I knew I was dreaming then, because I recall thinking that if I could just remember, after I woke up, which organs went into which jars, then it would reveal some great metaphorical truth about me. Like my heart is pickled okra. But when I woke up I couldn't remember any of the details at all." She paused. "That's the end. Why can't I dream about horses?"

"So how did this dream make you feel?" the therapist asked. "What was your emotional state upon waking?"

"Aren't you supposed to tell me how I'm feeling? Isn't that what I pay you for?"

He smiled. "You're the only one who can feel what you're feeling. Nothing I say can express it as well as you can."

She shook her head. "No, I know—but I just expressed it. I

mean, my dream is the expression. It's the objective correlative. But then you're supposed to tell me the feeling that the dream correlates to."

"Excuse me?"

"The objective correlative. Like how things and events in a story evoke a particular emotion. T. S. Eliot had this essay on *Hamlet* where—"

"Allow me to stop you there. Can you see what you're doing? You're launching off on a tangent in order to avoid engaging directly with the situation in front of you."

"So you're saying I'm not even good at therapy?"

He paused. "Do you amuse yourself?" he asked.

"What?"

"Viewed externally, do you find yourself amusing?"

Caissa didn't say anything.

"I think you do. I think you're trying to make this session into something that you can tell your friends about later as an amusing anecdote. Acting aloof so that you can later mock yourself for 'not being good at therapy.'"

Caissa thought for a moment and then nodded. "Yes, but see, that's the point I was trying to make," she said. "When I tell my friends this story later, they'll know the emotion it's supposed to evoke: amusement."

"Caz, how many times have I told you that the only thing I care less about than your therapy sessions is your dream life?"

"I'm just—"

"No. There are two types of people you can go to with your problems. One to tell you that you're perfectly justified in feeling bad about whatever you're feeling bad about, and the other one to kick your ass and tell you to stop whining and feeling sorry for yourself. Now, have I ever been anything to you but the latter?"

"No, but—"

"Then why are you even sticking that 'but' in there?"

Caissa had no answer. She and Marfa were facing each other from either end of an orange, vinyl-covered couch in Marfa's Park Slope brownstone, both resting bare feet beside empty teacups on a circular mirror-faced coffee table. Marfa's newborn son, Flynn, was sleeping in a bassinet on the table's other side.

"How's the book about Father coming?"

"It's not. I mean, it's about Guyana, not Dad, and it's not coming. But I'd rather not talk about it."

"Hmm." It was both a musing and an affirmation. "For the writer in the family you don't seem to write much."

"I email people constantly."

"I always liked those fiction stories you wrote. Like the one with the cat and her clumsy girl owner, and the cat just keeps trying not to get hurt when the girl plays with her."

"I was ten when I wrote that."

"It was good." Marfa looked at the ceiling and smiled as if she'd just remembered something. "I think you do need to get around to writing something new, though. It doesn't matter what it is. Just clear away the brain clutter. It's all up there making you feel crazy because you haven't cleaned it out by putting it onto the page. And then you'll have plenty of energy for the book. But don't waste your energy complaining to me."

"I'm not complaining. You're the one who brought it up."

Marfa clucked again. "You're going to make Flynn cry with all your whining."

Caissa looked over at Flynn still sleeping soundly, and she sighed. "When you stare at a computer screen all day, it's not that easy to come home and stare at another one."

"So write in a journal."

"I don't have a journal."

"Then buy one."

"What color?"

Marfa frowned and Caissa placed her palmheels to her temples to stave off an impending headache. "Marf," she said. "I don't really know what I'm doing right now."

"Anyone can see that."

"I think maybe I just want to get out of publishing and become a woodworker. I was the star student in woodshop. I built a birdhouse while everyone else was making picture frames."

Marfa for once had nothing to say.

"Sanding was my favorite part," Caissa said. "And planing. The repetitive smoothing of surfaces."

It is the job of the eldest child to be dutiful. Parents deserve one dutiful child in exchange for bestowing life. The eldest child is self-sufficient. The eldest child may defend younger siblings against threats from outside the family, but part of him will always resent having had his singularity stolen from him, especially considering how dutiful he was. He isn't stingy, yet neither is he overly generous to those outside his family. The eldest child is the wisest of siblings. The others may come to him for advice. The eldest child shall inherit his father's shadow. Or her mother's, in the case of a daughter. Jupiter is the planet of eldest children.

It is the job of the middle child to be rebellious. Parents deserve one rebellious child in exchange for inflicting life. The middle child is mercurial. His rebellion is a cry for attention, but it also produces an agile mind, rejecting dogma in favor of original thought. The middle child admires the eldest, feels protective of the youngest, and is jealous of both. The middle child is overly trusting of flatterers. He yearns to find those against whom he will not rebel, but this is only his attempt to rebel against his own nature. The middle child is the most independent of siblings. Mercury is the planet of middle children.

It is the job of the youngest child to be adored. By the time this child arrives, parents will have received all that they deserve and the child's turn will have come. The youngest child is needy. He is used to getting his way and feels personally affronted when chance conspires against him. And yet the youngest child can be too giving, taking on the burdens of others in order to foster a sense of goodwill and thus satisfy his own neediness. The youngest child is the most compassionate of siblings. He is also the most easily hurt in love. Venus is the planet of youngest children.

Judas was an only child. Caissa was the youngest. Viv, of course, was a middle.

Judas rebounded from his carnal encounter with Caissa in a manner quite different from hers. It was what he'd wanted, but in the aftermath, he wasn't sure what it meant. And in the day that followed, he was confronted with a situation that only complicated it.

He was in Walter's kitchen, scooping a can of shredded

meat into Chester's bowl, when there came a ring of the doorbell. Despite knowing that the bell could not conceivably have been tolled for him, he went down to see who it was, and found that he knew the person whose finger had done the tolling: Jasmine Green, sometime girlfriend of Martin Pope, who was next on the list of those scheduled to watch Chester.

"I just thought I'd come by early to get the keys," she explained.

"There's only one pair." A pause. "I mean, I thought I had him tonight."

"Yeah, but I work tomorrow, and I wasn't sure how I'd get them from you otherwise."

Without any premeditation, Judas suggested that the two of them have dinner together before he headed home, as he'd already been preparing pasta. To his surprise, she agreed.

The conversation was awkward at first. They asked about mutual acquaintances that neither was interested in discussing; Judas was only mildly surprised to learn that she and Martin were currently having "difficulties." He didn't dwell on the subject. Instead they moved on to topics more mundane. They asked about each other's work, and neither had anything exciting to report. He told her about his upcoming trip to Bloomington; he'd just bought the ticket, and it was to be his first time in the Midwest. Jasmine was from Chicago but she didn't have any insights into the region that she thought would be particularly helpful.

"But anyway," she said, "I heard you're starting your own magazine to compete with *E*. I think that's great."

He just shook his head and told her that she hadn't checked her facts well enough. Which he worried might offend her;

instead, she laughed, and she told him that she liked the sauce he had made for the pasta. After a few glasses of wine, they found themselves on Walter's couch together, alternating videos on YouTube that each thought the other should see. Jasmine favored videos that served as propaganda for SOFA, like one in which a Fox News anchor reads from a teleprompter that has been programmed by an intern who also happened to be a SOFA activist, or a series of Wall Street–themed fat-cat videos. Viv LaRevolution was conspicuously absent from these. It seemed that he preferred to be the spirit but not the face of the movement that he had started.

"So what separates SOFA from Occupy Wall Street?"

"Completely different. I mean, any similarities are purely coincidental. OWS is about changing a corrupt social and financial system. SOFA is about changing the entire fabric of ideaspace."

"What does that even mean?"

"You should really check out some of our literature."

And then, with little in the way of preamble, either on her part or in the way of his own conscious emotions, Judas found himself leaning aslant to the screen in a way that brought his lips to hers, thus beginning an unconsidered and theoretically meaningless encounter that was to last through to the next morning. And it was with a blank mind rather than with any sense of guilt that he woke before her, dressed, and headed back to his own apartment.

Judas spoke to Caissa only two more times before he left for Bloomington. The first time was via cell phone. The conversation was awkward. They both had things to say to the other, but they had trouble with the diction. Caissa was halfway annoyed that she even had to deal with her own uncertain emotions when she would have preferred to put all of this energy into her book. Judas, meanwhile, was focused on wondering whether he would be able to engineer some other opportunity to sleep with her and thus cement what he hoped might become a real and meaningful relationship, though he couldn't think of anything that wouldn't come off as desperate. So, instead, they spoke mostly of other people: Gabriel, Marfa, Jigme Drolma, Walter Benjamin, Hal Auerbach, people at *Byner's*, etc.

This phone call happened on Thursday night, but then she didn't hear from him for the rest of the week. On the Friday following, though, she did receive a text message from Martin Pope. "911," it read. She called, and after listening to him, she agreed to meet up at a Park Slope bar as soon as she got off work. He was already halfway through a pitcher of something locally brewed by the time she arrived; he had broken up with Jasmine again.

"I think it's for real this time," he said. "I've never felt sad about it before."

She nodded. "At least that's a step in the right direction. I mean, in the direction of humanity."

He went through an exhaustive catalog of things that were great about Jasmine while Caissa listened: how she was hot, and she was always up for going out drinking or whatever, but also that she was smart and well-read, and that even though she was pretty quiet she could be funny when they were alone together. And she seemed to be genuinely enthusiastic about this SOFA shit, which he found kind of admirable, even if he couldn't quite see the point of it himself. Then he lamented his own inability to treat her well and expressed concern that he might be a sociopath.

Caissa, recalling her sister's assertion that there are two types of people that one can go to with problems, opted to try to be one of the ass-kicking variety. She started off by telling Martin that he was cheapening the word "sociopath." She was on her second glass of wine.

"I don't know," he said. "I've been talking to my therapist. I think it all comes down to my childhood. I think I decided early on that I couldn't open myself up emotionally, and I've never quite gotten over that decision."

Caissa's laugh was joyous. "Oh, please. You've told me about your childhood before. What was so bad about it? Sure, your mom and dad foisted you onto nannies and tutors, but that probably left you better off than most kids who actually have to deal with their parents."

Martin shook his head. "For the most part, maybe. But that's also the problem, right? Forming my strongest early emotional attachments to people who were paid to care for me." He looked at her in a way that he obviously thought was soulful, though it was actually more of a leer. "Besides, I had experience enough with my parents too."

She laughed again, knowing him too well to buy this act. "What, did they make you take riding lessons with your sister?"

He poured the last suds of the pitcher into his glass. "You know, my dad may not have been physically abusive, and he might have ignored me for the most part, but that doesn't mean it was easy growing up with him." He took a gulp. "I need more beer." Caissa's smile was his permission slip.

He got up and walked over to the bar to order another

pitcher while she sipped her zinfandel. He was still standing behind a group of expensively suited bankers, trying to catch the bartender's attention, when Judas texted Caissa to ask if she was free. She considered replying with "Sorry, out at a bar with friends," but then halfway through decided to go with the full disclosure of "Sorry, out at a bar with Martin." Though in retrospect she questioned whether her motivation had been honesty or cruelty. When Martin returned with his pitcher, her mind was halfway wondering whether Judas would respond, when, and saying what. The other half was thinking, *Fuck Judas. If he hasn't even tried to make another move after all of this, I shouldn't waste any more emotional energy on him.*

"I remember Christmas Eve 1982," Martin said as he settled back into his seat. "I was six years old. It was after dinner, and my dad had been drinking the eggnog. When I picture it now, I remember a discrete layer of rum floating on top. But I might have made that up. In any case, the old man was reeling by the time he got to the bottom of the bowl, and he pulled me and my sister over to the Christmas tree for a drunken ramble. My mom was out doing some last-minute shopping or something, so I had no one to shield me except my sister; she was seven years older than me and pretty desensitized to the whole routine by this point."

Caissa sipped her wine.

"He went off for a while on some drunken gibber that I can't quite recall. Probably something to do with one of his patients. But then, just when we thought he'd reached the end, he grabbed hold of each of us by a shoulder, and he started to list all the bad things we'd done that year. I had the habit of being too loud while pouring myself cereal in the morning and waking him up when he had a hangover; I think my sister had just had her ears pierced and looked like a slut.

"But anyway, I don't recall exactly what wound up pushing him over the edge; I think it might have been something I said in my sister's defense. I'm not sure. But the next thing I remember is him ripping the paper from one of my gifts, and how I had this moment of excitement mingled with uncomprehending horror. I remember the faces more than anything else: myself in the mirror, red, with mouth open, wailing; my sister, golden hair haloed in the firelight, and expressionless like I always remember her; my dad, his eyes striped like candy canes; and Castle Grayskull, which I'd been lusting after all year long, sitting where he'd shoved it in the middle of the fireplace, tears of melted plastic trickling down out of its empty eye sockets. I still have the little sword that you would stick in to unlock the door . . ."

His head was tilted forward, and he was looking at her from the top of his eyes, angle calculated for maximum sympathy. Caissa wondered how many times he'd practiced this affected little routine. She'd been considering talking to him about the Guyana book, but he was obviously too drunk to give her any useful feedback. She wondered, then, what Judas was up to.

Judas's night is a bit harder to reconstruct. There was drinking involved, begun at home alone, before proceeding to the bar downstairs: alone there as well. But the bar where he ended the night was many F train stops away, and there he'd had company. At some point he'd dug Jasmine Green's business card out of his wallet and given her a call. She was embarrassed about what had happened between the two of them, and she'd already been a little drunk—about to shoot an angry email off to Martin—but Judas had convinced her to come out and talk about it all with him instead. He told himself that he'd just wanted to find out what she knew about Caissa and Martin's relationship, and this justification was somewhat supported by Gabriel, who called him the next day to ask what the rambling voicemail had been about: "Caissa" and "Martin" had been among the few fully articulated words.

From what Judas could recollect, Jasmine had done much of the talking, complaining, with Judas nodding along supportively. He had vague memories of not knowing what to say. Part of the conversation went something like this:

"He doesn't even care what's happening in the world around him. Like, I don't care if he's not into SOFA in particular, though it would be nice if he showed a little interest in what matters to me. But I don't think he even cares who the next president is. It's like the universe doesn't exist beyond what he sees. But then when I try to show interest in his life, I'm apparently smothering him or something. He acts all offended if I even ask him about another girl. And like we haven't even been broken up for six hours and you're telling me he's already out with her? It's not fair."

"I know. But maybe they're just talking about your breakup, right? Just like we are. Maybe she's just being a friend, trying to help him get over it."

Jasmine did something with her brow that couldn't quite be called furrowing, and yet came closer than not. "I don't want another girl trying to help him get over me . . . Besides, it's different. He's totally going to go for sympathy sex. Or revenge sex. Using her sympathy to get revenge on me. Or just to hurt me, I guess, since I didn't really do anything he'd need to get revenge for." She gave Judas a look. "Well, nothing he knows about. But it's not fair. She has an unfair advantage."

"How so?"

Her eyes went wide. "Oh my God, what's wrong with your finger? Why's it all purple?"

Judas wasn't wearing his splint. "I broke it. You've seen it before."

"I didn't notice."

"But what do you mean about an unfair advantage?"

She inhaled and shook her head. "Well, I mean, I bet I could take you in darts right now. Or thumb wrestling. Maybe even arm wrestling, because I could just squeeze your finger to distract you and then throw your arm to the table. I'm stronger than I look. Are you right-handed?"

"Yeah." He nodded. "But no. I mean what were you saying about Caissa and Martin. What's her unfair advantage with him?"

"Oh. Oh yeah. She went to college with him. They were in the same dorm freshman year." She took a gulp of her gin and tonic, through the little black straw. "That's like an intimate bond."

"Which is to say," said Martin, elsewhere, audibly pixilated, "that I think, after all this time, and having come all this way—"

"You mean after having slept around so much?" Caissa asked as she picked a bag of cheese-powdered chips from a white wire shelf. They had stopped in a brightly lit convenience store to get a snack on the way to the train.

Martin affected a wince. "Whatever. But what I was saying is that I think I've finally figured it all out. That the place I want to be is back where I started."

"In your mother?"

"No." He reached for her hand and grabbed her thin wrist. "With you."

She pulled easily out of his grip and brought her bag of chips to the counter. "In what sense did you start with me?"

"You were my first love. In college, at least."

She paid with a five. She hadn't drunk too terribly much, but Martin was wobbly. "I'm surprised you even remember me from college."

"The heart's a muscle like any other. It has a memory of its own. I can't forget what we had."

She grabbed her change and shoved it into her purse. "We made out once at a party. That's the story of your first great love?"

He sighed and nodded. "That's where it all began for me." He followed her out onto the street. Other drunken amblers were about, heading for further bars or home. "If I'd been as suave back then as I am now, we could have had something. You don't know how much it killed me when you wound up with Mike. I mean, everyone else in the world could see what an asshole he was, but you just swallowed all his shit. And that metaphor totally makes sense. Which is why you should kiss me again. Reset the clock. Or the cock. Or whatever. That metaphor doesn't make as much sense. Maybe it's not even a metaphor. But still." He looked to her pleadingly.

"Stop," Caissa said, and they both did, stepping towards a storefront window to clear the sidewalk for other pedestrians.

"Look," she said. "This is us." She opened her chips and held the bag out to him. He took one.

"Yes," she said. "See. I am a girl who shares her chips with you. I am not a girl who kisses you."

"You slept with Walter, right?"

"What does that have to do with anything?"

"Nothing, just . . . I mean, at that party freshman year—"

"Okay." She sighed, stopping him from going any further. "I am a girl who kissed you once almost twenty years ago. But I am not a girl who will be kissing you anymore."

His eyebags were sagging with drunkenness, but he nodded. "Okay." He took another chip. And after a few more chips they walked on.

He did try to kiss her when they parted at the subway station. She was letting him go in for the good-bye cheek kiss, but he went for a last-second swerve. His lips were on hers for a moment or two before she pulled away, but she didn't return his pressure, and her mouth remained firmly shut the entire time. She gave him a look.

"Whoops," he said. "I forgot."

Judas did not kiss Jasmine that night, but he thought about it. He thought about what had happened between them at Walter's place, and wondered if he should have been taking her back there to watch Chester rather than back to her own place. And he thought about getting revenge on Caissa for being out with Martin. Though even in his drunken state he realized this was ridiculous and that she probably wouldn't have cared. He thought that maybe Caissa could just be his ideal love after all, and Jasmine could be his actual one. Except he didn't love Jasmine in any actual sense. He just found her attractive and had a slight desire to sleep with her again. He admired her nose, but that was no foundation to build a relationship on.

By night's end, the point was moot, as he was too wasted to try anything. Or at least he was too wasted to judge his chance of success; she hadn't mentioned anything at all about their connection the other night. But more important, Jasmine was so wasted herself, tripping on her heels, that Judas felt a need to get her safely home that overrode any desire to kiss her, much less to try anything further.

"Thanks for talking," she said at her door, fumbling in her purse. "I really think you're someone who could help with everything." She frowned. "Not Martin and me. Just the movement and all. You know?"

"It was fun."

She nodded but didn't abandon her frown. "I'd kiss you good night, but, as you may have noticed, I have a smelly tooth." At least that's what he thought she slurred as she pulled her keys out of her purse and, after a few seconds' fumbling, managed to open the door. She turned around once she was in the entryway. "Call me." She smiled and held her hand in a shaka sign—keys gripped in the middle—up to the side of her head.

Judas smiled back and hoped she'd make it safely up the stairs.

He woke to the sensation of a buzzing palm. He'd slept with his phone in his hand. A text message from Caissa: "Sunny day. You up for a walk or something?" It was 11:06. His head ached, and he wanted a shower, but he texted back to say he'd meet her in the park down by the water in half an hour. He threw on some clean clothes, deodorant, and splashed his face in the bathroom sink, but a shower really would have helped. He was sweating alcohol by the time he found her—green dress with small white polka dots—sitting on the park's cement steps and eating an ice-cream cone. Cinnamon, to go with her freckles.

"Hey," she said as he sat down beside her.

"Hey yourself."

Across from where they sat, four boys in black were standing on rocks and posing for photographs against the backdrop of tourist boats and the Manhattan skyline. The sound of trains rattling across the Manhattan Bridge reminded Judas of the night he and Caissa had first met.

"Sorry I couldn't come out last night," she said. "I thought Martin was having a crisis."

"He wasn't?"

"It's all relative."

Judas nodded for lack of anything to say. A breeze came off the water, and they both watched as one of the boys in black jumped in the air and tried to perform a scissor kick, struggling against the tightness of his jeans.

"Oh, look," Caissa said, pointing at an airplane flying low out over Queens. "A nine-eleven."

Judas followed its flight with his eyes until it disappeared behind a building. "You said something about a walk?" he asked as she crunched down on the last bit of sugar cone.

"Sure. Wanna walk along the water?"

They headed back to his neighborhood, and as they strode along the promenade they discussed all manner of things. They discussed Chinese swordplay novels in general and Judas's pet translation project in particular; Caissa's hard time getting started on her book about Guyana and her dad; Judas's crooked finger; Caissa's lack of fulfillment and her vague desire to become a woodworker; a supposedly great place to get pizza that neither of them had tried; an idea that she had for a young adult fantasy novel; the fact that Judas suddenly realized he couldn't recall eating anything solid in over sixteen hours; olives; national varieties of pickled cabbage; other types of pickled vegetables, and where to buy them; how bad Caissa was at therapy; the relative merits of New York and Northern California; the importance of getting out of the city on a regular basis despite how great it was to live there; farmers' markets; and the lack of any idea what to expect in Bloomington. Yet there were also a good number of things that they failed to discuss, such as their relationship (if it could be called that), Martin, Jasmine, or when Judas would be coming back.

"The other night I had a dream that you were supposed to have my pen," Caissa announced near the end of their walk. As she spoke, she reached into her purse and from it produced a perfectly ordinary black-ink ballpoint.

"If only I'd been the one to have that dream about you, this would all make perfect sense." He accepted the pen and shoved it into his right pants pocket.

"Write me."

"Like a letter, in an envelope?"

She shrugged. "Make it a postcard if that's all you can manage."

• • •

From the Journal of Jasmine Green

I am feeling: hurt/lonely/maladjusted. Those words are the first that come to mind, but they do not quite express the way I feel.

I feel empty. I feel devoid. Nothing can touch me. I can stare at the spot in front of my face forever and think of absolutely nothing and yet not get bored. It's like zazen. I mean, I can just be not thinking of anything, sort of, which is weird and probably not true, but I can just stare and I won't be able to tell you what I was thinking about.

The sunset is beautiful. I will try to draw a picture of it.

[She draws a picture here that I won't even attempt to replicate.]

I love the way parallel lines come together in the distance. The above is a picture of the sun setting over Grand Army Plaza, as seen from a corner of Prospect Park, where they're building the Tower of Ideological Apocalypse for the big SOFA event next month. I know it's not that good. I have never been coordinated of the hand and eye.

The trees in the park are more textured and layered than I usually recall. Green is everywhere, my namesake, despite the onset of autumn, but brown and red and yellow enter the palette as well. Browns and reds and yellows. Not separately, but all together. I never understood this principle when I'd watch painting shows on PBS as a child. There is one broken, dead, old tree standing not far into the park. It reaches tragically toward the sky, cracked/twisted/deformed as it approaches.

I feel the world as I stretch out through it. Martin is right now nursing a hangover. Gabriel is smoking alone. Judas is inside of an airplane and his seat is Yale blue. None of this makes any difference, I suppose.

Another word that comes to mind: crepuscular.

I don't know what any of this has to do with anything else, but every time I think my circlings around the way I feel are getting close to the center, I just end up flying tangentially off into infinity.

Judas is probably somewhere over Pennsylvania right now, or somewhere further north. I mean "farther north," unless I am being metaphorical. He is going to Indiana. I found out from Martin, who, strangely enough, answered when I phoned. Perhaps Caissa has gone there, Judas following her, and her absence makes Martin's heart grow fonder of me. I didn't ask. Martin said he couldn't talk long. He said he'd spoken to his sister about me. And his friends are tired of hearing about me. He said he doesn't know what he's doing right now. I don't know if that's just more of his bullshit or what. But he said he wants to talk later. I don't know if I want to. That's not true. I want to. But I don't know if I want to want to.

I feel my molecules disperse
and flow throughout the universe.

It's a pleasant sensation as the sun sinks directly below the street and renders me orange, like a turned leaf, and kind of blots out most everything else in that direction. I have nice thighs. My thighs are not just thin—they are athletic. Even in the warmth of orange I can tell. Even with little red dots from having sat in the grass (grass pimples), I can tell. I wonder if Martin has ever truly appreciated my thighs. I feel funny. I think my molecules are starting to drift away from one another. I'm not quite sure what that means. I don't know what I want to do. I've never had any nervous breakdowns to speak of. I'll know I'm having one if I ever start to act the way I feel like acting right now.

PART TWO

BLOOMINGTON

Writing, he'd come to see, was the spiritual disease of which it considered itself to be the cure.

—Alexander Theroux, *Darconville's Cat*

Adam Spillwater woke with a weight on his chest and a pressure against his forehead. Lump had come to nuzzle him into consciousness and remind him that she needed her morning num-nums. "Mrao": a fuzzy alarm clock. Good thing, as he had to teach this morning, and the LED on his bedside bookshelf was just sitting there blinking at him in bewilderment. He must have slapped it too hard when going for the snooze. He grabbed his cell phone from the shelf beside him and checked the time. Shit. There would be no planning of lessons this morning. His own fault. He'd always liked to request early teaching slots since the students who signed up for them usually either were serious about the class or dropped out when they discovered they couldn't wake up in time for it. But lately Adam had been suffering from this latter trouble himself.

He disentangled from the sheets, stood, and scissored two fingers between his bedroom blind slats to see if it was drizzling out—it was, a slight mist, sky the color of nonfat milk—before trudging to the kitchen to pour Lump her quarter cup of dry food. She raised her rear for some affirmational scratching and started to chow. Adam obliged her with his right hand while with the left he tested the relative fuzziness of his throat. Palpable scruff, but he wasn't up for shaving, and he hardly had time; besides, the hair on his face was getting long enough to give the throat some cover. When Lump decided she was sated he let her out the back door. She balked for a moment at the drizzle, looking back at him over her shoulder, before darting off across the unmown lawn; Adam watched her disappear into the neighbors' bushes. He grabbed some clean black boxers and a matching V-neck tee from the clothes dryer in the kitchen nook, took a swig of orange juice from the carton in the fridge door, swallowed a handful of dry-roasted peanuts from a jar he'd left on the counter the night before, and then padded to the bathroom to piss, rinse his face, brush his teeth, and otherwise ready himself for the day ahead.

He found the drizzle outside was welcome once he went out to meet it. It was fairly light, helped to wake him, and gave a silent excuse for the unkempt state of his curly hair. Though as he walked to campus—no sidewalks this part of town—he had to be extra careful of all the undergrad drivers barreling along heedless of the road's rain-released oils. His sweatshirt was clinging to him, and his jean cuffs mud-caked, by the time he reached Ballantine Hall, home of the English and creative writing departments and host to the class he taught this semester. Legend had it that the building, made from the same limestone as the Empire State, was shaped like a tube of toothpaste in deference to a long-ago Colgate grant, but Adam thought it looked more like some sort of three-dimensional diagram—triagram, he supposed—of a four-dimensional object: jutting out in places where it wasn't supposed to in order to illustrate analogous twists upon an unknowable axis—like Dalí's *Crucifixion (Corpus Hypercubus)*. Workers in the lower courtyard were busy tearing down the Apocalypse Tower that SOFA activists had put up the previous week; it turned out that the university press release and work permits they'd shown to have it put up in the first place were fakes. Adam hoped his books weren't water-damaged in his backpack, but at least his socks felt dry inside his shoes.

The clock on the ground floor of the building told him he still had ten minutes till class and one of the elevators stood open: enough time to head up to four to check his email. Just as he pressed the button, a secretary from the English department—among the younger, with a soft face and a butch haircut—asked him to hold the door, which he did, but then she gave an embarrassed smile when she stepped in and saw him. He figured the embarrassment must have sprung from her being a little late for work, and they rode together in silence, parting ways as soon as the doors slid open.

The English grad lounge was known as the Work Room, so called after a surname rather than any activity that might take place within. Bound dissertations lined the wall opposite the window, and a few fabric-worn chairs surrounded two tables layered, like the bottoms of birdcages, with magazines no one wanted to read. The main draw of the place was a row of computers along one wall, old and slow but hooked up to a printer with free paper and ink. There weren't many other early risers here today: just Lauren Schmetterling, a Victorianist who not only had a nice ass but also favored thongs and low-rise jeans (though these attributes were somewhat tempered by her googly eyes), and Bethany Seraglio, née Sara Elizabeth Jones, a medievalist who might have been pretty if she weren't always dressed in outfits better reserved for the live-action role-playing she was so fond of.

LARPing was actually relatively popular in Bloomington, at least in part because it was the home of one of the only folklore PhD programs in the nation. And strangely enough, this was also what had made it one of the first sites of SOFA activism, since so many of their early stunts had involved a similar sort of imaginary politics.* Adam had even interviewed Bethany for his piece in *E*, though he hadn't managed to get in her pants.

"Hey," he said as he entered the room. The two women made only the briefest eye contact with him before rising to leave.

He logged on to the computer that Lauren had left behind, her chair still warm, and after some finger-tapping page loads he made it to his inbox. Four unread emails: student with a bullshit excuse for having missed a week of class; something from the department head that he didn't open; an invitation to a party at the house of another fiction writer, Sherilyn La Mush, an overachiever who'd already been published in *The New Yorker*'s debut fiction issue before she even applied to the program, and who'd just placed a second story in the same magazine and wanted to celebrate; and a reminder from himself that he needed to pick up this guy Judas from the airport at four P.M. today—a fact that had somehow slipped his mind

* I would also guess that this had something to with why the Bloomington Apocalypse was both less effective and less destructive than most of the others (Oakland being the most obvious example of the opposite extremes): the core of the local SOFA movement was accustomed to the "playing" part of "role-playing."

to this point. He checked the bottom right corner of the computer screen: three minutes to go till class. He logged off, picked up his bag, and dropped downstairs to the third floor, trying to time his steps to arrive at the door to his room just as the distant clock tower finished chiming; a couple of his students, both male, were standing there in the hall, pointedly not going in to take their seats.

"So, class is canceled today?" one of them asked. Keith something: a freshman on the swim team who seemed only to have enrolled in Adam's class on the assumption that creative writing would be an easy way to pass the university's composition requirement. Adam looked from the boy to the door and saw that a jagged half-sheet torn from a yellow legal pad had been scotch-taped to the clouded window, block letters in thick red marker asserting the affirmative to Keith's question.

"Apparently so," Adam said. The two students waited a beat before disappearing down the hall. Adam opened the classroom door and peered in to confirm that it was empty, and then he walked back upstairs. Perhaps he should have opened that email from the department head after all.

"Antipathy" wasn't the right word for the emotion that Adam felt towards Nick Buenaflor, head of creative writing. But the feeling was mutual, and it had been born at their first meeting two and a half years prior. Adam had fallen in love with Bloomington on his first drunken visit during college, having come to see a band that he also loved, and for that reason alone it was his first choice when applying for MFA programs. By the time he met Buenaflor, he'd already sent in his application, and he knew admissions were based almost entirely on the writing sample, but he figured it couldn't hurt to introduce himself to the faculty. So early one morning he drove down from Chicago (where for the three years since finishing his BA in Ann Arbor he'd been working whatever day job would have him, all so that he could devote his evenings to writing) and stopped by unannounced during Professor Buenaflor's office hours, which he'd looked up beforehand online. The conversation had started out harmonious enough, Buenaflor telling Adam all about what a great department it was, and how happy he was that Adam was interested. But discordant notes began to sound as soon as he asked Adam to tell him a little about himself.

Adam went through his outside interests, his early influences, how he fell in love with Rabelais and Burton—all of which Buenaflor nodded along with politely—then concluded with, "I love lists. Which is what most writing is though anyway, right? More or less disguised? A list of things that happen to a list of characters, with a list of ideas about those lists, all prettied up." He laughed. "Not to give too much away about my writing sample, since I know that's supposed to be blind."

Buenaflor blanched, but what he said next was meant as a kindness.

"Have you considered that perhaps this isn't the right department for you?"

"What do you mean?" Adam asked, fluttering lids over eyes that were suddenly dry.

Buenaflor spread his hands in something like a gesture of supplication. "It's just that most of the teachers and students here practice a more naturalistic style than what you're describing. I hope that my readers will overlook any list-like aspects of my prose, focusing instead on character and emotion. So this isn't a value judgment—I'm not saying that my approach is right and yours is wrong—but I'm just not sure what we would have to offer each other. Have you considered some place like Brown?"

"But you haven't even read my stuff yet." Adam's tone was pitched towards whine.

There hadn't been much more to discuss. But somehow, despite this, Adam had been admitted to the program, the other three professors on the committee giving him scores that pushed him marginally over the line. Out of embarrassment, perhaps, Buenaflor had been uneasy around him ever since. His email on the morning of the canceled class was to the point, though the point wasn't exactly clear. It read, in full, "Perhaps we should discuss this in person. Please stop by my office. I'll be around all morning."

Adam had still been in shock from that initial encounter with Buenaflor when he met-cute with Selah Park. Squinting down at a text message, she bumped into him on the steps that led up out of Ballantine's courtyard, where he'd paused to rub his eyes; the sky immediately began to hail. He looked at her, blinking, taking in the brief image of a round-faced Asian girl with chin-length hair that was red black and slightly wavy rather than blue black and straight, and he was promptly struck in the forehead by an almond-size stone. Feeling somehow responsible for his daze, Selah offered him joint use of her umbrella—they were headed in the same direction—and after she'd babbled for a while in aimless apology, they began to converse.

They hit it off right away, despite the apparent lack of much in common. Selah was about to start the second year of her master's program in Uralic and Altaic studies, which Adam had never heard of before, and she likewise hadn't really heard of most of the fiction he admired, though she said she thought it sounded interesting. They were both hungry at least. She was from California, and so she suggested that they head to a place near campus that served passable "California-style" burritos. He realized he was smitten when, moments after finishing his burrito, he felt compelled to run to the bathroom just to look in the mirror and make sure there were no bean bits caught in his beard or teeth. After lunch, they'd stayed on for lattes at the café downstairs.

The sun reappeared in the late afternoon, and—though they didn't hang out into evening—they exchanged phone numbers, Selah promising to drive up to see the Art Institute of Chicago with him that weekend. She didn't mention that she would need to borrow a friend's car to do so, which spoke to the level of her own infatuation. In any case, she followed through on her promise, the date was a success, and after that he'd driven down to Bloomington to see her pretty much every weekend that followed, especially after he was officially accepted to the creative writing program, as that gave him the excuse of looking for an apartment. He became an expert in the art of timing drives to album lengths.

They took things slowly at first; they slept together a few times before they ever had sex. But when Adam still hadn't found a place by July, with the semester set to begin in the end of August, Selah sent him an email suggesting that they rent a house together. Her apartment was small, with walls that a few passes of sandpaper would have rendered translucent, and houses rented pretty cheaply in Bloomington. Besides, she wanted a pet, and her apartment manager didn't allow them, and they'd recently said they loved each other, so it sort of made sense.

Adam wrote back with perhaps a bit too much enthusiasm: "Yes. This is a good idea. I don't know why I didn't realize it before. But we should totally live together. I want to be with you all the time. I love you as I love the smell of linden, tobacco shops, freshly baked cookies, or old suits. I love you as I love the sight of Chicago after too long away. I adore you with my mouth. I admire you with my eyes. I venerate you with my loins. I want to know every time you've lain in bed sad, happy, in love, filled with whatever ecstasy of emotion, over a song, a crush, an idea. I want to know every time that you thought the world would end. I want to know every time that you've felt elated. And living together will give us a chance to get to know each other with that level of intimacy."

"All right, I'll start looking tomorrow," she replied.

With Selah in charge of the search, a place was soon found, and thus in a relatively short amount of time they'd gone from seeing each other on weekends to living together. Which marked the shift to when they started to take things quickly.

The MFA fiction program was set up so that each of the four main professors led the workshop once every four semesters, ensuring that over the course of two years the students could experience the full range of viewpoints that the program had to offer. As luck would have it, Adam's first-semester workshop had been taught by Buenaflor. When he finished his first piece for class, he went out to the couch and asked Selah if she would read it over for him. He'd never offered to show her any work before, and she'd never asked to see any.

She looked up from her laptop where she'd been reading about some celebrity scandal. Her hair was tied up above the back of her head like the scroll of a cello. "I was just about to start reading for class," she said.

Adam tried to frown, but nuance of facial expression was lost in the thick red blond of beard. "You don't have to edit it," he said. "I just want you to glance over it; let me know your immediate reaction."

She widened her nostrils and eyes, took a deep breath, and snapped her laptop shut. "I don't know." There was no uncertainty in her tone. "I'd rather not."

"I see," he said, rising from the table and trying to sound gentle. He went over to sit beside her on the couch. "Well."

She pulled away from his attempted shoulder rub. "What if I don't like it?" she asked. "What if I think it sucks? Or worse, what if I'm just underwhelmed, no strong reaction either way?"

Adam nodded. "That's fine. If that's how you feel, I need to know that. I mean, I trust you. And I'm not so fragile that I'll completely fall apart if you don't like something of mine."

She shook her head. "No. That's not it. I'm sorry. Maybe *you* could take me not liking your writing, but I don't think *I* could take it. Something so important to you. Not yet. I'd think less of you, and I don't want that."

"Oh," he said. And the conversation ended there. The next day, he brought Lump home from the animal shelter as a special surprise. He knew that Selah wanted a cat, and so just before she got home he'd put Lump—short for Fatty Lumpkin—into a picnic basket in the bedroom with a trail of rose petals leading to it from the front door. Selah's delight at this was only slightly overshadowed by her outrage at what she called the "animal cruelty" of keeping a cat in a basket for five minutes.

So let's get this out of the way: Adam and Selah eventually broke up. They lived together for a year while she finished her master's, towards the end of which she applied for a history PhD program in California, to work on a project about a Nazi expedition to Tibet before World War II. The plan was that they would spend a year living apart, trying the long-distance thing, while he stayed in Bloomington to finish the coursework for his MFA. But it was only a matter of months before she announced that it wasn't going to work and made the breakup official.

"This game is starting to seem cruel," she'd said over the phone one Wednesday night; it was already Thursday morning for Adam. "Rather than going around the board with you again while we try to take the last of each other's money, I think it would be better for me to just step outside and play some tetherball. At least for a while."

"I don't know what that means," Adam had replied. But he did. He just wanted her to say it. He could hear her breathe deeply on the other end of the telephone line.

"I think we should break up," she said.

And in the nausea that followed, he could hardly believe that he had ever wanted her to say such a horrible thing.

He didn't recall much of how that workshop discussing his first piece had gone. He still had the document he'd typed up from the notes he'd taken, but now he read it as loaded with hidden significance regarding his relationship with Selah and could hardly relate it to the story he'd written at all.

From Adam's Notes

They would have me believe that "plot" is a four-letter word. That I am imposing artificial structures onto the chaos of life—isn't that what art means? *I imagined a structure that would support us when in reality there was none. There was no meaning, no story in which we twisted together like elegant plot strands. There was only the chaos of moments in which we found ourselves occupying the same space without the coincidence of it meaning anything at all.* Also, they say my story is aesthetically—rather than just politically—bad because I use the word "Gypsy" to describe a Gypsy. *Of course it was in her nature to wander.*

They would have me set more modest goals. Accept limitation. *Why couldn't I enjoy what we had for what it was? Neither of us was the end point for the other, but I wouldn't let her be anything to me if she wouldn't be that. I never met her in the place where we naturally should have settled. I was always jumping fences.* Illuminate a small corner of the world, a corner I know well, and make the reader empathize. *But how could I have expected her to empathize with someone as alien as me?*

However, *Lolita* asks readers to empathize with a pedophile and murderer even as he is simultaneously held up as an object of abhorrence, and the ease with which we as readers are able to acquiesce to this request is what makes the book so great. We go beyond the place where we believe our limitations to lie, and we become fuller humans in the process. *I was obsessive. I can see that now. Beyond the bounds of reason. A hairy ape. Possessive. Bribing and cajoling. And lo, she has gone to California.*

So: empathy yes, limitation no. *I thought I had it all figured out.*

Idea for illuminating this shitty corner of the world—too middling to even be a corner: man standing on back porch, underarm stains on a white T-shirt, beer in hand at noon, yelling at his dog, an imprecise German shepherd. "If you don't shut the fuck up I'm gonna come out there and give you something to bark about, you stupid bitch!" *I am this man, misdirecting my anger, lashing my whip without looking down to see the beast that lurks in the pit beneath my own arms.*

Adam was reading meaning into these notes that hadn't initially been there, he knew. But it was a habit that he'd learnt from Selah, so it seemed appropriate. If she were here, and he'd pointed to the notes and said, "These are about us," she would have known exactly what he was talking about.

She had always valued hidden connections, like the fact that Adam's grandmother was named Harmony—which sounded like the Korean word for "grandmother"—and the sense of unspoken understanding that could be felt between two people who shared the perception of a secret pattern. For the sake of such sense alone, she would carry on whole exchanges with him while a toothbrush garbled all of her words beyond recognition, or make privately cryptic comments to him in the middle of group conversations, or post music videos on her Facebook wall that were slantingly relevant to some recent event and then wait to see which of her friends displayed the proper reaction. Adam knew never to ask questions in these moments, even when she was at her most mysterious. In the early days he'd just tried to project a false sense of understanding, though eventually he had learnt to attune himself to the frequency of her irrational leaps. It had become something that they genuinely shared, and that was why it pained him so to recall how, in the moment that she had ended things, he had professed not to understand her at all: "I don't know what that means." Thinking back on it now, it was hard for him not to see this sentence as a personal betrayal of her, denying the significance of what had passed between them, and thus in some way retroactively justifying her decision to leave him.

He hadn't slept well since she'd left. As a writer, he knew he was supposed to be able to transmute his pain into its own salve through the alembic of art. And yet he found that all of his attempts in that direction tended to vacillate between the two equally unhelpful extremes of the literal and the absurd. Either dry recounting of the facts—"Selah has left me. I am sad"—or automatic writing that resulted in crap like these meaningless SAT analogies that he'd half-consciously been scribbling on any page that passed within reach of his pen. For example:

Woe is to Me as:
A. Cloud is to Sky
B. Dream is to Skull
C. Boy is to Bush
D. Horse is to Plain

The problem was, he decided, that he wasn't in touch with his feelings. Looking at the two sentences "Selah has left me" and "I am sad," he couldn't quite see the connection between them. It would have been too much to say "I am sad *because* Selah has left me," as that would denote a sadness that was an essential component of any state of being in which Selah had left him; it precluded the possibility of him ever being happy again, since the fact was that she *had* left him, and that fact would remain. Better just to let the two sentences stand on their own without any connection between them.

Furthermore, a part of him felt guilty that he even wanted to use his pain over Selah to inspire him. It felt as if it would be a betrayal not only of their relationship, but also of the honesty of his pain. In the past he'd been good at drawing meaning from intense experiences, but he was coming to feel that a more sensitive writer would be able to find intensity everywhere. The best art is actively engaged with the world, he told himself. Sensitive artists always have something to write about, because they are able to find the depth in any situation, not only in the big, heavy drama of life. Adam worried that his way of relating to the world was too blunt. That is, even if a great novel came out of his breakup with Selah, he worried that he'd never be able to write anything else as good unless he broke up with another girl or had some similarly traumatic experience. And so he was paralyzed.

This had all gone on for about a year before he decided that it was a problem that might need addressing. Rather than consult a therapist about the trouble he was having dealing with the breakup, though, Adam elected to analyze himself and his problems through means of his own devising—unconventional though they were. He knew that Freud was outdated and that everything in the psyche didn't always, necessarily, come down to sex, but in dealing with the loss of the person he'd been sleeping with, he reasoned that sex would at least be a good base from which to launch his psychological explorations. So, vaguely inspired by the proximity of the Kinsey Institute, he decided that he would turn to porn.

He'd never really watched porn before. He'd found some *Playboys* in his father's sock drawer when he was a kid; he'd occasionally stayed up late in the hope of catching some simulated sex on pay cable; and he'd seen roughly five minutes of one hard-core film with a group of friends in high school—his most vivid memory of this was a fly that wouldn't stop buzzing around the male lead's asshole—before convincing everyone else that they should go out and try to buy some beer instead. Which, in retrospect, might help explain why he had this unhip, quasi-puritanical feeling that there was something gross about it. A small part of him, though, wondered whether his feeling of grossness might not be masking some more deeply hidden urge, and in the name of greater self-awareness he decided to make the sacrifice.

His methodology involved seeking out different sorts of

porn and recording his reactions, both positive and negative. He hoped that, once he had enough data, he'd be able to get some statistically accurate answers about his mental state: to read his fundamental neuroses and quirks in the numbers. His last two girlfriends had been Asian, for instance; did he have a fetish that he was unaware of? By comparing his arousal level (AL) when confronted with Asian porn to his AL when confronted with black, Latina, or Caucasian porn, he hoped to find out. And after he'd been at it for a while, he began to hope that he might be able to find varieties of porn to answer nearly any question he might have about himself. Simulated incest porn might reveal latent familial tensions; BDSM might reveal hidden feelings of helplessness or megalomania; gay porn might reveal previously unsuspected sexual identity issues. The possibilities seemed limitless, and he threw himself into his work with unbounded enthusiasm.

In short, his findings hewed fairly closely to his initial hypothesis. Yet he did find one unexpected factor that caused AL to skyrocket: narrative tension. Videos yielding the highest AL invariably had plots. Not just premises either, but stories with actual dramatic arcs. It wasn't enough that a housewife ask the plumber to lay some extra pipe unless there had been an earlier scene in which, say, the housewife and her husband were eating breakfast, talking about how the plumber was supposed to come fix the sink that day, and then the husband left for work but forgot his wallet, so that when the plumber and the wife started going at it, the viewer's (in this case Adam's) tension was heightened by the thought that the husband could come back and discover them at any minute. "Forbidden love" ranked highest, thematically, with a particular emphasis on prohibition and transgression, followed closely by "final night together," with "makeup/reunion sex" coming in a distant third. Breaking "forbidden love" down even further, story lines in which the prohibition involved issues of authority seemed to contribute an unexpectedly large amount to overall AL, especially considering his largely negative reaction to BDSM. But boss/employee, teacher/student, warden/prisoner, etc., were all found among the highest-scoring scenarios.

If things had gone according to plan, he would have carried out this experiment for a full month. But around the two-week mark, something happened that distracted him from his original goal: he recognized one of the girls. Or at least he thought he did. And it seemed to be a girl who was a student in his class. Allison Rose.

Adam did not think of himself as a perv of a teacher. That is, at least, he tried not to consider the attractiveness of his students when he taught them, or even to talk about how hot they were with other men in his department, though he'd heard plenty of his colleagues carry on such conversations. He preferred to think of his students as intellectual rather than sexual beings. But seeing this girl who looked so much like his student in the context of this video provoked strange thoughts. For one thing, it had to be her. The resemblance otherwise was just too uncanny. She played a student who was repaying a tutor with sexual favors after he had written her term paper for her, and the tension of the scene was heightened by intercut shots of a professor grading her paper and beginning to suspect that it might not actually be her work; Adam imagined this was part of a longer movie in which the professor would eventually have a scene of his own. After multiple viewings of the video, he couldn't help but indulge certain fantasies.

The way she would move her pelvis before her pants even came off, indicating that she *wanted it*. And not just sex. The way she kept looking at the camera, it was clear that she also wanted to be watched having sex. She wanted to be the object of fantasy. She wanted to be jerked off to. And it was the imagining of this desire that really got Adam excited. But still, he was pretty sure he'd maintained a border; he hadn't thought such fantasies had intruded on real life at all. Well, except for one drunken night when he'd sent the girl a "friend" invite on Facebook. She still hadn't accepted—which he took as a bad sign, since he was fairly certain that most of his students were much more diligent about Facebook upkeep than they were about class work. But now, even though there was nothing more than this Facebook invite to suggest any degree of inappropriate behavior, he began to worry that somehow this was the matter over which his class had been canceled and which Professor Buenaflor wanted to see him about. And yet, in this worry, he was completely mistaken.

The actual situation was this: one of Adam's students was gay and had recently come out to his parents. Sitting in a chair across a cluttered desk from Nick Buenaflor, back where he'd been two and a half years earlier, Adam wondered at first what his student's sexuality might have to do with him.

"Your reading list, for one thing," Buenaflor said. Peering down through the lower half of his bifocals at a printed email, he read aloud: "Oscar Wilde's 'The Nightingale and the Rose.' Paul Bowles's 'Pages from Cold Point.' David Sedaris's 'Something for Everyone.'" Buenaflor looked up. "Need I say more?"

Adam shook his head and spread his hands. "If you have a point to make . . ."

A nod. An exhale. "It's nothing to do with me, you understand. But the boy's parents took this straight to the university president himself. A family with connections." A pause. "These authors all were, or are, homosexualists."

"Wait, yes, those three, but that's not all we read. 'The Balloon,' by Donald Barthelme, is on that list. Faulkner's 'A Rose for Emily.' Hemingway's 'Hills Like White Elephants.' Updike's 'A & P.' None of them were gay. Hell, Hemingway was a homophobe. But even if my whole list had been all gay, all the time, I still don't see what the problem would be."

Buenaflor nodded sympathetically. "It's just that Jim's parents maintain that he wasn't gay until he took your class."

"What?" Adam couldn't repress a disbelieving smile. "I could tell he was gay from the moment he walked into my class."

"Oh?" Eyes widening.

Adam took a moment to think and sigh. "I mean, I assumed."

"So it didn't set off any alarms for you when he turned in a story for class about a college student coming out to his parents?"

"No." And after a further moment's thought this seemed a triumph. "Exactly. I mean, half of what these students write is thinly veiled autobiography. You know that as well as I do. So especially after that story, why should I be surprised to find out he's gay? I'm more surprised that he hadn't come out to his parents before he wrote the story."

"But regardless, you praised this story. His parents have seen the copy you returned to him, with your handwritten comments."

Adam nodded. "So what? It was a good story. The material may have been a little trite, but he made it fresh."

"Some might interpret your comments as a trifle *too* encouraging."

Adam was silent, but he hoped that the intensity of his stare would convey his sense of indignation.

Buenaflor raised one hand to rub the porous skin on either side of his nose. "In the story, the main character has a crush on one of his instructors," he said. "If your defense is that the story was likely autobiographical, you must have realized how delicate, not to mention inappropriate, the situation might be."

"Well," Adam said, "the story also ends with the closeted professor committing suicide, so forgive me if I didn't think it was completely based in fact, much less about me."

Buenaflor again widened his eyes, looking to Adam as if for appeal. "Look, I know we've had our differences, but I'm on your side in this. I'm just laying the situation out for you; you have to realize it's all quite beyond me. The boy's parents are upset. They're pulling him out of school and sending him off to a camp in Utah to help him with what they call 'his problem.' We're lucky they're not suing us."

"Let them." Adam was shocked at the volume of his own voice and took half a moment to modulate it accordingly. "I mean, I'm not a lawyer, but what pretense would get more than a second glance in court? The fact that I allowed their child to write a story about homosexuality without alerting them to the fact? I don't think it'll stick."

Buenaflor shook his head. "That's not the point. It doesn't matter whether they have a case or not. The president doesn't want the bad publicity. A family with influence. In his eyes, it's bad enough that we have the Kinsey Institute here."

"So what, you're canceling my class?"

Buenaflor crumpled his face like a wet coffee filter. "No. Of course not. I just wanted to talk to you and tell you what the issue was. To let you know that there was an issue."

Adam bit his lip. "All right. I appreciate that. Knowing what a ridiculous system this is." He nodded. "So that's it then?"

Buenaflor breathed deeply before answering, and then let a sentence out in one breath. "Well we'll have to pull your current syllabus and you'll need to have a new one approved with the department before your next class." A pause. "You can base it on the old one, of course, just removing any material that might seem questionable in light of recent events."

Adam didn't know how to respond.

Home again, he tried to put the encounter with Buenaflor out of his mind, as he needed to focus on preparing for Judas's arrival. Tidying wasn't much of a problem; he was generally a neat person, and he hadn't been using the kitchen much, so he just gave the bathroom a quick scrub. Though it only occurred to him belatedly that there was also Judas's room to consider—the guest room—changing the sheets, rearranging the boxes in the closet to make space for any luggage Judas might have. Boxes which, some of them, still contained belongings of Selah's, as she hadn't originally planned on leaving permanently. Also the recycling to deal with. He counted: eight wine bottles and twelve beers, the weekly pickup still a day away. He didn't want to look like an alcoholic, so he'd have to get rid of them before Judas got here. But he didn't have time to drive them all the way out to the recycling place on South Walnut, as the airport was in the opposite direction. After a moment's thought he decided to just throw them into paper shopping bags and take them to the dumpsters behind the College Mall shopping center. And while he was out, he reasoned, he could stock up again, since he was running a little low and it would be rude not to have anything for Judas when he got there.

He made it back home with a few minutes to spare before he had to take off again for the airport. He paused a moment at the door to consider how depressed he was: not just about Selah, but also about all the other looming suckiness in his life. This gay student thing was just the culmination. An objective correlative. Then he headed out to the car and put on the album *Architecture and Morality* by OMD, which he knew would get him most of the way to Indianapolis, unless there was really bad traffic.

Adam waited for Judas at the baggage claim wearing a red sweatshirt—as had been previously agreed upon—though he felt too warm in the controlled airport climate. He'd arrived at roughly the same time as Judas's flight, and the first bags were falling onto the carousel as he walked up to it—dumped from a conveyor with a steady, lurching regularity that reminded him of Lump coughing up hairballs. He was mesmerized by the rhythm until Judas startled him with a tap on the shoulder.

"Adam?"

Adam turned. His first thought was that Judas looked like a weenie. Not a hipster weenie as he'd expected—pale skin, boxy glasses, unkempt black hair, tight jeans and sweater; rather, Judas's complexion was on the ruddy side, no glasses, his hair short and dirty blond, and his blue flannel shirt hung loose as if he'd recently lost some weight or just didn't put much effort into picking out the right size—but a weenie nonetheless. There was no other word for him. He had this fresh, clean-shaven look—kind of like *Rip It Up*–era Edwyn Collins, though older, and maybe with the smugness of Andy Rourke from the inside cover of *The Queen Is Dead*—that immediately put Adam off.

"Hey, thanks for picking me up. And thanks for hosting me. You are Adam, right?"

Adam nodded. "Yes, Adam." He offered a right hand to shake, but Judas held up his own to display two middle fingers taped together and splinted, thus prohibiting the pleasantry. Even through the tape and gauze, Adam could see that the ring finger was discolored and unnaturally bent.

"What happened?" he asked.

"I fell."

Again, Adam nodded. This struck him as a personal message: "Be careful, or you might cause permanent damage." But also, in the back of his mind: "Ring finger severed as sign of relationship's end, like Selah off to California: note to self for future use."

"Well, we should head out to the car," Adam said. "My half hour's almost up."

• • •

Judas kept quiet for the first few minutes as Adam navigated out of the airport and onto the freeway, but then—once it seemed that they would have a relatively straight shot for a while—he tried to engage Adam in some basic small talk. He started as casually as possible—thanks again for picking him up, inquiries into how long the drive would take, etc.—and then moved incrementally on to more personal topics. Like what Adam's piece for *E* had been about.

"You were in the first issue, right? How'd you even hear about *E*?"

"I'm not totally out of the loop. I mean, I knew someone. But yes: first issue."

"Do you have a copy? I'd love to read it."

"It wasn't very good. I think they just needed to fill a few pages." He reached down and turned off the OMD, which had just finished "Souvenir" for the second time. "The theme of the issue was 'Evolution,' and I wrote something about SOFA and the evolution of activism. You know, like gaming social change and stuff. It was pretty much a college freshman-level piece, but Gabe Stilzkin seemed to think that my sense of humor made up for the shallowness of my thought."

"Yeah, sounds hilarious."

Adam turned to Judas and whispered, "Weenie."

"What?"

"Oh, sorry." Adam turned his eyes back to the road. "Been living on my own lately. Get to talking to myself."

A moment's pause. "I know how that is."

"Or my cat."

Judas nodded. "That's cool."

"I mean, not really. Not like that, how it sounds. My girlfriend and I both used to talk to our cat. You know, just in the way you do. Not like you really think that a cat can understand you. Well, your tone maybe, but not your words. Though my cat's pretty smart. She knows her name. But it's not as if I started talking to her because I'm lonely."

Judas nodded again. "That sucks. She left you, then? I mean, not to pry."

Adam squinted and shook his head. "I let her out this morning. But she always comes back in for dinner in the evenings."

"I meant your girlfriend."

"Oh. Oh yeah. I was kidding. Well, no, I wasn't, but I guess so. That is: yes, she did leave me. For California."

"Yeah?" A little too enthusiastic. "I'm from California."

Adam clucked his tongue. This confirmed his opinion that Judas was one of the enemy. "Not that California is my enemy," he said aloud. "She didn't leave me *for* California. She's not dating California."

"Right." Judas looked at him with what might have been a wary glance. "But so your piece was about SOFA? I'm kind of vaguely interested in them myself." He was thinking of Jasmine. "So what was the gist of it?"

Adam shook his head. "It doesn't matter. I wouldn't write the same article today."

"What do you mean?"

"I was just kind of naïve about them before. But you can read it if you want. I have a copy. You know, since that's all they paid me. *E*, not SOFA. But you knew that, right? You know everything."

"What?"

Adam hesitated a moment. "Sorry," he said. "Seriously, I'm not usually this weird. Or incoherent. Or out of it. My mind's just elsewhere. I'm having an off day. The president of the university basically thinks that I turned a student gay."

"What?"

"One of my students came out to his parents, and the president of the university blames me. So I'm preoccupied and sleep deprived and sort of babbling. And no, I'm not sleeping with the kid. Or gay myself."

"That's crazy."

"I know, right?" Adam let out a long breath. "So yeah, my mind is kind of elsewhere. They canceled my class today, and now I have to come up with a new syllabus. I'm thinking I might just have my students write simple sentences without ever combining them. No content for the rest of the semester. Since, you know, I wouldn't want to influence anyone with an *idea* or anything. But also I thought these girls were treating me weird this morning—fellow graduate student girls—and now I know why. It's like I have this stigma for something that: a) I didn't do, and b) shouldn't be stigma-worthy even if it were possible to do such a thing. It's ridiculous. And it's frustrating." He glanced over at Judas's broken finger. "And I think I might be an alcoholic." Adam bit his lip. "Sorry. What? I'm just kidding."

Judas took a breath and looked at him. "That's cool," he said. "I'm not gonna judge you or anything."

Adam frowned, reached over, and pulled a new CD from the glove compartment: *Music for the Masses.*

Judas did read Adam's piece on SOFA that afternoon when they got back to the house. There were no major revelations in it, but it clarified some of the vagueness that had remained in the aftermath of his own research. Like how the social-change website he'd found was a way of crowd-sourcing organizational goals and thus building a larger support base—making each member feel as if he or she had an equal voice in the overall direction of the movement—even though Viv as charismatic leader tended to tack on his own larger goals as addendums to whatever resolutions were reached by consensus. When he was done reading, Judas wondered how Adam's views on SOFA could have soured any further since the writing, as the piece in general came across as generally negative; but then he recalled that Adam seemed to have shit attitudes about pretty much everything, and he wondered no further.

Adam, for his part, considered his change in attitude a simple outgrowth of a bit more research. He'd been excited by SOFA when he first heard about them. They'd seemed as if they were a fun, playful twist on the usual variety of social movement, which he'd enjoyed at least for the entertainment value. And that had been pretty much what everyone else had thought, too. So when he'd begun writing about them, though, he'd felt compelled to take a slightly more negative perspective, if only for the sake of balance. But then the more he'd learned, the less enchanted he'd become. He began to see that they were more SLA than OWS. While he'd liked the idea of impostors posing as representatives of the mainstream social order so as to discredit them in the same way that law-enforcement agents had periodically masqueraded as protestors—like a few months ago when SOFA members had dressed up in suits and given television interviews in which they pretended to be openly evil investment bankers—he was slightly disturbed to learn that SOFA had actually initiated a policy of enrolling young members in police academies or grooming them for public office: essentially creating sleeper agents.* To Adam, this smacked a little too much of the sort of tactics that had been employed by the forces that were theoretically being fought against. The end seemed worthwhile, but he wasn't sure that it justified the means. Regardless, he didn't give it too much thought either way. He wouldn't have been an active participant in the movement, even if he'd fully endorsed it. His time, as he saw it, was better spent drinking.

Part of Adam suspected that his suspicion that he might be an alcoholic was just a way of trying to make himself seem more interesting: that telling Judas about it was a misguided attempt to sound mysterious and cool. But another part of him suspected that this skeptical analysis of the situation was just the alcoholism's way of trying to hide itself. Regardless of which of these choices represented the truth, he was able to decide that —while drinking every night was not the sure sign of a problem —the desire every night to drink *was* a problem. He no longer felt in control of himself, but rather felt that he was slave to some mildly destructive urge. He was destroying his liver with alcohol, just as he was destroying his idea of sex as an expression of love with porn. But even if the latter preoccupation

---

* People often paint the SOFA Apocalypse as an exercise in pure chaos, but they ignore the fact that it was a carefully orchestrated chaos. In Brooklyn, for instance, real police officers, some of whom were SOFA affiliated, clashed with fake, and neither the impersonators nor the impostors had any way of recognizing the other. Viv preferred not to know all of the details himself in order to prevent the plan from ever being completely unraveled.

hadn't proven as useful as he'd hoped, at least the former was helping him to be more productive in his writing.

He was supposed to be working on his thesis this year, but instead he'd recently started working on a book that he had no intention of using for that purpose. He had tentatively titled it *The Anatomy of Drunkenness.* Whenever he got drunk he'd just start typing. Topics covered thus far included types of drunks (mopey, sentimental, violent, sleepy, quiet, sloppy, etc., with various subcategories), types of drunkenness (on beer, on red wine, on white wine, on sparkling wine, on gin, on tequila, on happiness, on love, on power . . .), famous drunks (writers and politicians, mostly, though he tried to make space for every profession and even for fictional characters), the drunkenness of American Indians, the drunkenness of dwarfs, the drunkenness of Asians, the drunkenness of fathers, symptoms of drunkenness, the pleasures of drunkenness, the pains of drunkenness, the aftereffects of drunkenness, feigned drunkenness, cures for drunkenness, false cures for drunkenness, the history of drunkenness, the absurdity of Indiana's alcohol laws, and so much more. Throughout, it was littered with favorite quotes on drunkenness, from the likes of Rimbaud and Sartre to Kerouac and Douglas Adams. For an epigraph he was considering "Ask a glass of water."

That night, once Judas had thrown his backpack into a corner of the guest room without even bothering to open the closet door, Adam suggested various things that they might do to entertain themselves. Order pizza. Watch a DVD. Play some video games. Go check out some of Bloomington's famous sights, like the courthouse from *Breaking Away*, or the Steamy Bench. But in the end they decided to go to a bar. Nick's English Hut, on Kirkwood, was a long, dark, wooden establishment, built on two floors, where Adam insisted that Judas try the fried mushrooms. They found a table upstairs, and the music was loud enough that they didn't have to worry about how awkward the conversation might otherwise have been, with just a few perfunctory comments shouted between them.

Almost everyone in the bar was very white, except for a Nigerian boy and a Filipina girl at a table of folklore grad students, and some flat-iron-fried, chemically tanned sorority girls at a table across the room, who were wearing boots that gave them feet like Shetland ponies. The atmosphere was a bit fratty in general—a television in every corner showing all available sporting events, boys wearing either crimson and cream or cycling jerseys—but just as the waitress was bringing Adam and Judas their first mason jars of Newcastle, the table beside them was filled by a group from the English department.

"Adam! How are you?" Martha Saroyn, standing beside his chair as her three friends—two girls and a guy—sat down. Adam had met her in one of the lit classes he'd taken (Time and Temporality in Romantic Literature) in his halfhearted pursuit of an MA to go along with the MFA. He'd always found her cute in a nerdy way, auburn hair and glasses, but he'd still been with Selah when they'd had their class together, so it hadn't ever gone much further than observation. Also, she was now roommates with Sherilyn La Mush—the MFA student who was throwing a party to celebrate her most recent publication in a day or two—and Adam's complex feelings about Sherilyn only made his feelings for Martha harder to parse.

"I'm okay," he said. "How are you?"

"No," she said. "I mean, I heard about you and your student. I can't believe it. That is so unfair."

He sipped his beer and nodded. "Yes," he said. "Ridiculous might be a better word."

"Who's your friend?"

Adam looked at Judas, who was looking back at him with eyes expectant.

"This is Judas," he said. "He's only in town for a few days."

"Hi." Judas gave a slight wave with his crooked-fingered hand.

"You guys should join us. We're going to play Sink the Bismarck."

"Uh . . ."

"Sure," Judas said.

Sink the Bismarck was a local drinking game involving a bucket of beer and a small glass that floated (or didn't) in the middle. The goal was to add beer to the glass without sinking it, as otherwise you'd be obliged to reach into the bucket to retrieve it and down its contents. Which, if you were trying to get drunk, wasn't entirely bad, but Adam had always been mildly disgusted at drinking from a bucket into which everyone else had been dipping their fingers. He pulled a pen from his pocket and scrawled onto his napkin:

Liver is to Pickle as:
A. Bush is to Burn
B. Bridge is to Bid
C. Brain is to Fry
D. Monkey is to Chill

Then below that he wrote, "Nobody moves, nobody gets hurt." Judas, having taken the seat directly beside Martha, was chatting with her affably between turns. An affable weenie, Adam thought, noting that the two women whose names he hadn't caught were fixing their eyes on Judas with far more interest than they granted him. He was stuck at the foot of the table, between Judas and Martha's male friend, whose name turned out to be Alex. Dark hair, dark eyes, pale skin, tight jeans, boxy glasses, and a white collar poking out from beneath his cornflower cardigan, like some odd cross between a Bunnyman and a Housemartin.

"I heard about how they're making you change your syllabus," he said to Adam at one point. "You're right that it's ridiculous, but I grew up in this town, and it really doesn't surprise me at this point. I'd probably have been lynched if I grew up anywhere else in this state, and I'm only halfway joking."

Adam was starting to feel the beer in the form of a frozen forebrain, and it took him a squinting moment to process what Alex had said and respond. "Oh, you're *that* Alex!" He finally nodded. "Now I remember. Martha totally wanted to have sex with you before she found out you were gay. She was basically stalking you. She would come into class and tell me about her latest Alex sighting, where she'd followed you across campus, or about some half-encounter she'd had with you in the Student Union, usually peppered with details of all the things she wanted to do to you."

Alex smiled. "Yes, and it's made her an energetic friend. So you know her through class?"

Adam glanced over and saw that Martha was giving him what he took to be an interested stare, but before he could respond to either it or Alex's question, Judas tapped him on the shoulder to inform him that it was his turn.

"Bottoms up," he said, dumping the last inch of the pitcher into the glass in the communal bucket, going above and beyond what was required to sink the Biz. It was the culmination of a progressive lack of caring. As the game had gone on, Adam found himself putting less and less thought into his glass-filling technique. Not intentionally trying to sink it before this, but he'd told himself that the alcohol in the beer would kill any finger germs, and he was here to drink, after all. And so this final dumping was more the abandonment of pretense than a statement of purpose. The six of them had been through half as many pitchers, and it seemed ridiculous to play anymore at the idea that they didn't all want to get drunker.

As Adam guzzled, Judas pulled out his cell phone and looked at the time: 11:30.

"I need to make a call," he said.

"You sure?" Adam asked, suppressing a burp. "Can I save you from a drunk dial?"

"In case you hadn't noticed," Judas said, "I was winning tonight. I had the pints I ordered for myself, but I didn't take a single sip of your finger-soiled beer." Rising from his chair, he indicated his splint. "It would have been kind of awkward, anyway," he said, and then he descended the stairs, presumably headed for the street.

"Well fuck," Adam said, though he didn't know why.

Judas had meant to call Caissa, but once he was outside he decided that it would be too much to call her on his first night away, so instead he dialed Gabriel Stilzkin, just to check in with someone back in Brooklyn.

"Complications have arisen" were the first words out of Gabe's mouth.

"Such as?"

"Errors of communication. Fundamental misunderstandings of basic realities. Dude doesn't have a new book out after all."

"What?"

"Don't piss your pants or anything; not all is lost. He did actually announce a new book, but he just hasn't released it yet. And supposedly he wants to release it in English and Chinese simultaneously, so the situation remains pretty much the same, aside from some minor logistical issues."

Judas nodded and tried to take in how these facts would affect What He Was Doing with His Life and, as he did so, pictured the process as something like the dough of reality being pressed into discrete strands through the sieve of his mind.

"Also, it's not a novel," Gabriel added.

"What?"

"Nonfiction. At least I think so. It has something to do with SOFA, according to internet speculation. Turns out dude is Viv LaRevolution's dad. It was kind of ambiguous, but that would explain the supposed connection to Hal Auerbach and the rumor that *Brother* was going to put the book out. That guy is basically Viv's minister of propaganda."

"So this whole thing is pointless? I moved to New York for no reason?"

"Yes to the latter, not necessarily to the former. I mean,

everything we know about dude is kind of hazy, but realizing he's connected to Viv LaRevolution at least gives you more of a lead, right?"

"Why is it that everything seems to come back to SOFA?"

"I don't know, maybe because it's the only thing dominating the headlines lately. Don't you ever read the news?"

Judas shook his head.

"Anyway," Gabriel said, "who's to say dude won't be impressed by your tenacity when you find him? Seems unlikely, but worth a try, maybe."

"So I should keep looking for him?"

"Yeah, sure. I mean, he could still be a big deal if all of this shit comes together. We wouldn't want to miss out on that, right?"

He shook his head again. "No, I guess not. Have you heard from Caissa lately?"

"Not really," Gabe said, and then he laughed. "I mean, dude, aren't you over being smitten?"

Judas wondered briefly if he should be.

The next morning, Adam woke expecting a hangover, but all he had was a numbness. He came into consciousness gradually, trying first to recall the specifics of the night just finished, and only then giving thought to the situation of the present day. He knew that they had gone to another bar, the Video Saloon, after Nick's. Lump had been waiting at the front door when they made it home around three or four. They'd taken a cab together, and Judas had paid. So Judas was presumably asleep in the spare room, despite the fact that Martha had given every indication of wanting him to sleep in a different bed; she had ended the night by making Adam swear on the health of his penis that he would bring Judas to Sherilyn's party, and she made Judas swear on the health of Adam's penis as well. Adam knew all of these facts, but he was filled with the sense that something had been forgotten—that something was missing.

He plodded out to the kitchen to find that Judas was already up, had set coffee to brewing, fed Lump, and was crouching down to pet her with his non-injured hand as she ate. She was purring.

"Hey, sleep well?" Adam asked, scratching at his neck scruff.

"Yeah, great, thanks." Judas stood and grabbed a half-empty mug from the countertop. "I hope it's all right that I rummaged around your kitchen to make the coffee."

Adam narrowed his eyes and then grabbed a mug for himself out of the cupboard. "Of course, no problem," he said once he'd filled it with coffee and a splash of milk. "So, what are your plans today?"

Judas would be spending the whole day out at the Tibetan Cultural Center, doing interviews for the article or whatever that he was working on for *E*—Adam hadn't asked him much about it. But this left Adam with the day free to get some work done without having to worry about entertaining his guest. He had two student stories he needed to read before class the following Tuesday, and which he didn't want hanging over him all weekend. Also, he'd have to figure out how to shoehorn the story discussion in with the material that he'd been planning to get through yesterday. Though that material was from the old syllabus, so maybe he could just skip it. Besides, he also hoped to do some writing of his own, so immediately after Judas closed the door behind him, Adam googled some words that he was pretty sure would yield a high AL, got his masturbation over with quickly, and then found the student stories in an ever-growing pile of papers on his desk.

The first story was about a girl who goes to a party, meets a boy, and doesn't get date-raped, though something in the way that the boy acts makes her consider the possibility, thinking that a weaker girl than herself would definitely have been taken advantage of. Adam jotted a few notes about the language, added some missing punctuation, underlined the two places where he found compelling connections between ideas, as well as the one place where he found a striking if muddled metaphor (the narrator described her vagina as "a halved walnut, but no one had ever cracked the shell"), and then made a few careful remarks about what was at stake in the story. He paused for a moment before closing the pages and thought about yesterday's drama with Buenaflor. At least this was a story about having *not* been raped, so he supposed he was in the clear as far as not needing to report anything to the department or the police went.

The next story was by a student he liked, but he found himself disappointed by what he read. It was called "Players," and it was divided into two sections titled "Game" and "Postgame." It was basically the events of a date related in the style of sports commentary, though the language was balanced in such a way that it didn't call too much attention to the general conceit. "It's a wonderful night here in Bloomington, for what promises to be a beautiful match," went the first line, though a few lines near the end of the "Game" section went a bit over the top in Adam's opinion (e.g., "She's at her door, only a few seconds left on the clock, and he goes in for the kiss. A slight flinch, but she's smiling, and . . . Oh, a swerve, she plants one on his cheek! Can you believe that nonchalance? What an upset!").

It was a hard story for Adam to critique. He didn't want to discourage the kid from trying new things, but he wasn't sure how to suggest greater aesthetic consideration without coming across like one of the enemy. On the one hand, he admired him for trying something outside of the realm of the usual received wisdom of minimalist realism, but on the other hand the conceit never seemed to justify itself, and so—however subtle—came across as little more than a gimmick. Which was exactly the sort of stigma that nontraditional fiction had long struggled to overcome. A story actually had to be about something *beyond* itself in order to merit the indulgence of, secondarily, being about itself. Adam's own *Anatomy of Drunkenness,* for instance, was actually about his pain over Selah's departure and his attempt to use alcohol to anesthetize himself. He hadn't ever consciously realized this before, and suddenly he wanted a drink. He decided to look at Selah's Facebook page instead.

This wasn't an activity that he indulged in often. Not because it was too painful, but because it made him feel a little creepy. He hadn't been able to tease out exactly why it made him feel creepy—they'd been intimate with each other for about two years, and she had never deleted him as a friend, so surely he was allowed to look at her pictures and status updates—but it usually made him feel that way nonetheless. All of these people he didn't know, all of these people who now overlapped with the sphere of her life, sharing experiences that he, Adam, was no longer permitted to share. They smiled at barbecues and held sausages on skewers, sweated together on wild Californian treks, smirked at dimly lit parties while holding glasses that were crafted to hold their particular drinks. Adam wasn't of this world, Selah's world, and knew that he never would be again. But he punished himself with her pictures nonetheless, clicking through until he found one in which she was framed alone, leaning against her kitchen counter, her nipples making perceptible protuberances in the surface of her aquamarine tank top, and then he pulled down his pants and masturbated for the second time that day. After that, he was able to concentrate for a while on his own writing.

While he was out at the Tibetan Cultural Center, Judas was fed a few tidbits of information that were, at the least, interesting. He wasn't sure how accurate any of it was, but people here certainly knew who Drolma was. He didn't talk to anyone who had ever actually met the man, but there was a general consensus that he had lived in Bloomington at some point, albeit briefly, and that while he was a vocal proponent of Tibetan independence, he hadn't actually taken part much in the doings of the local Tibetan American community. And there seemed to be a small amount of resentment over this latter fact.

"I don't think he even really writes his own books," one shriveled and hunched old man opined. "And I think he married a Chinese woman. That's the real reason his books are all in Chinese—not for any political reason, despite who his son is. He reads books in Western languages, and she helps him translate them into Chinese. Or she did before she died; that's what my cousin told me, anyway."

"But he's published books since then. How's that possible if she died?"

The old man nodded. "I imagine he thought ahead. Probably has a whole box of unpublished manuscripts tucked away somewhere."

Judas recalled the similarity between the single Drolma book he'd read and the Magnus Valison novella, but then he also took into account that this man went on to claim that in addition to being apolitical, Drolma was also a crypto-neo-Nazi and a Maoist sympathizer. So he wasn't sure how much credence he should give to any of the things he said.

"Well, thanks for your time."

Judas got home just a bit before dusk. He chatted with Adam for a few minutes without relating much about his day beyond the vaguest of summary—"I need to go back tomorrow, but it was a promising enough start"—and then he said he'd probably better hit the shower if they were going to go to a party, especially if they planned to walk.

"Oh, right," Adam said. "Sherilyn and Martha."

By the time that Judas was out of the shower and dressed, though his hair was not yet dry, Adam had his laptop out on the dining room table, an online video interview with Sherilyn La Mush queued up and ready to play. In it she explained that even though she could have gone pretty much anywhere she wanted, enrolling in the Indiana MFA program was an attempt to reconnect with her roots—she'd been reared in the state—and to hone her craft in a setting that seemed "more authentic than the sterile factories of Columbia or Iowa." Besides, she'd already lived in Boston, Manhattan, London, and Los Angeles, so she was looking for something a little quieter: a place that would give her the freedom to fully devote herself to her novel.

"Gross, isn't it?" Adam said when it was over.

"What do you mean?" Judas asked. "Isn't that why you're here, too?"

"You don't think she sounds pompous?"

"I don't know. Why are we going to her party then?"

Adam shook his head. "Never mind. I'll let you finish getting ready."

In addition to publishing a second story in *The New Yorker*, Sherilyn had just signed a two-book deal. At twenty-nine, she was already a lawyer with an Ivy League degree; she'd interned at *Harper's*, the *Paris Review*, and *The New Yorker*; and she was rumored to be on the short list for *Brother*'s annual "30 Under 30" list—Hal Auerbach himself had interviewed her in *Sister*. So though it might have been tempting to attribute her success to the striking angles of her face and figure, or to her dark, vaguely exotic looks—her orchidaceous lips—Adam couldn't say that her success was entirely without merit. But then that was part of his problem with her. He didn't think that success should be about *that sort* of merit. Youth, professional accomplishment, connections, appearance: these were all supposed to be beside the point; the writing itself was supposed to be all that mattered, but he hadn't been that impressed with the story he'd read.

It hadn't been bad, of course—she was a competent prose stylist—but here and there clichés crept in, along with specious leaps of thought, readerly pandering, two factual errors and one grammatical (which could plausibly be attributed to one of the characters, if he was feeling generous), faux erudition, and an emotionally manipulative climax. On the other hand, he wondered if he would have read closely enough to notice all of these things if it hadn't been for the outside factors that he thought were supposed to be beside the point. That is, if Sherilyn had been a plain-looking fifty-year-old who had slowly honed her craft in small literary magazines before her virtually unreviewed debut collection became a bestseller based purely on word of mouth, would Adam have scrutinized the story with the same intensity? Probably not. So wasn't it possible that some of what he felt was exclusion and jealousy? And not just jealousy of the literary success, but also of those other, supposedly meaningless considerations?

Yes. If he was honest, yes. But then he was actually lucky that he didn't have those things, he told himself, because he could see himself being easily seduced by them—giving himself over to the idea that he really was as special as everyone would be making him out to be based on these trivial factors. He knew that it would be easy for him to invest in the fantasy that he was an Important Writer and a Meaningful Cultural Figure. The same way that he clung now to the idea that what really made him special was his unique vision—that whether he was writing or not, he saw the world with a writer's eyes, felt the world with a writer's heart, found meaning and connections in everything and could take it all apart and put it into words that he could then hone to remove all such imperfections as he had found in Sherilyn's work. His value came from the purity of what he did: self-worth rather than external affirmation. Though of course he didn't always feel that confident in himself, so again this might just be sour grapes. And even thinking the words "sour grapes," couldn't he have made up a better metaphor of his own, or pulled from something fresher than Aesop? At least it wasn't as bad as some of the reanimated corpses of metaphor that Sherilyn had resorted to in her story —no, now he was trying too hard, and he groaned aloud; Judas called from the guest bedroom to ask what he'd said and then walked out to ask if he could use the computer for a few minutes before they left. Adam nodded, and rather than mull on all of this more, he simply reflected that sour grapes were at least useful in making wine—groaned at himself yet again—and then went into the kitchen to pour himself a pre-party glass.

Judas checked his email first—nothing of note, but he clicked on each message until nothing in his inbox was marked as unread—and then he logged on to Facebook and went straight to Caissa's profile to try to piece together what she'd been doing with her life over the past few days. It offered only the scantest of clues: she had attended the release party for a literary quarterly; she was now friends with three new people, two male, whom Judas assumed that she had met at said release party; she had indicated that she would be attending the Brooklyn-based SOFA event next month, which, he noticed, her sister, Marfa, was one of the page creators for; an older friend, also male, had posted on her wall that he was going to be in town and wanted to catch up, and she had commented about how excited she was and that she would set aside some time for him on Monday; and she had posted a video of a Patti Smith song that he had trouble reading any subtextual messages into, try as hard as he might to think that it might be about him.

"Are you just about ready?" Adam asked from the kitchen, having just finished his second glass.

The two of them arrived at Sherilyn and Martha's place early, each bearing a bottle picked up at a liquor store along the way.

Judas had brought a zinfandel, emblem of California, whereas Adam had brought something with a monkey on the label and 14 percent alcohol content. Sherilyn and Martha were still preparing hors d'oeuvres in the kitchen, and the door was answered by a burly, bearded Shakespeare scholar named Matt, who modeled himself on both Harold Bloom and Falstaff.

"Welcome!" he bellowed. "The festivities have only just begun!" He waved one arm at a table containing a bowl of chips and salsa where two other literature grad students, both guys, were discussing an ambiguous encounter with one of their female professors, and then he stood smiling for a moment before heading back to join them and plunge his hand into the chip bowl. Besides these three, a few of the MFA poets—men and women alike—were in the kitchen helping to assemble cucumber sandwiches, but it looked crowded enough in there as it was, so Adam and Judas just brought their bottles over to the drinks table, and Adam poured them each a glass from an open bottle of pinot noir.

"Interesting crowd," Judas said.

Adam took a deep gulp of his wine. "Things'll pick up."

They did, if slowly. Although it seemed unlikely that there would be an outbreak of dancing any time soon, Martha momently came from the kitchen and put on a classic hip-hop mix—choices that were meant to be popular rather than obscure displays of her cutting-edge taste—and Judas went over to talk to her, leaving Adam alone to contemplate an artful, black-and-white eight-by-ten nude photograph that Sherilyn had taken of herself and framed on the wall above the drinks table. But more people arrived in twos and threes, some of whom Adam knew, and the party population eventually reached the critical mass at which, with alcohol as a catalyst, he was able to overcome his social anxiety and start to unselfconsciously react with those around him. At some point he found that he was even having a good time. And then, about two hours in, the mass of bodies directly in front of him parted all at once and he caught sight of Sherilyn, the celebrated literary wunderkind herself, making concerted eye contact with him. Perhaps he should go over and talk to her—congratulate her on the story. She raised her glass. So, yes then. He awkwardly broke off his conversation with a colleague who'd decided that he wanted to give up fiction for science writing, and he made his way over.

"I heard about what happened," she said. "With your student. That sucks."

He nodded and leaned in to speak quietly over the music. "You know, whatever. But congratulations on your story. What's it about anyway?" He'd never been this close to her before and was surprised to find that she was almost his height.

"Thanks, yeah, I'm sorry I never had the chance to workshop it with you. I mean, I really think you would have been the perfect person to critique it. From everything I've heard about you, at least, I could have used your perspective. I wish I'd got here a year or two earlier."

Adam was flattered that she'd heard anything about him at all. "I wish that too. I'd have loved to have you read some of my stuff. You being the next big thing and all."

She tried to roll her eyes, and Adam understood that this was what she was going for, but it was far jerkier than the platonic ideal of an eye roll: a staccato up, left, right. "I know, it's kind of ridiculous, right?" she said to go along with this motion. "But I'm more embarrassed than anything else about all the attention. I mean, God, did you see that interview with me they put up on the department website? I come across as such an ass."

"I don't think you're an ass."

"Yeah, well. It's just that you get this one little piece of clout and they treat you as if you're some sort of authority, and for a second you start to believe it, and so you end up coming across as all pontificatory, you know?"

He nodded.

She laughed. "But then if you start worrying too much about that shit, it gets even worse. It becomes like this false modesty thing, where you're like, 'I have to pretend I'm not as great as everyone thinks I am, otherwise I'll seem like I'm full of myself.' But then that ends up being the real sign that you've bought into your own hype, when you feel like you have to hide it."

"Right."

She bit her lip and looked genuinely thoughtful, and Adam felt an unexpected sympathy for her. "It kind of paralyzed me a little, when I finally figured it out," she said. "But eventually I just realized that I couldn't let that sort of thing rule my life, you know? I mean, if someone asks me a question, even if it's a question that comes from their assumption that I'm something more than I actually am, I've decided I just need to answer it as well and as honestly as I can. Or if they treat me a certain way, even if it comes from a wrong place, I just need to react as who I actually am, without any second-guessing. And, you know, if they have a problem with that, then they can S my D."

Adam nodded for what seemed like the fortieth time. "That's great, though. I mean, it's good to learn that lesson early."

"Yeah," she said with a long exhale, turning her glance up towards the corner of the room. "But I'm getting pontificatory again, aren't I?"

"Not at all. So what did you say your new story was about, then?"

She looked him in the eyes again, but this time she looked somehow more deeply, and for once she was the one who nodded. "Right, see, that's what I'm talking about," she said. "You read my first story, so I know that you're going to look at my new one in relation to that. You have expectations about who I am and how I write. And I can't help that, I guess—I mean, there's nothing I can really do about it—but I can't let it bother me either. So yeah, you know, the new one is completely different from the first one. But then that's a choice, too. I mean, do I deliver a known quantity and position myself as a niche writer, just doing this one thing well, over and over; or do I risk alienating my established audience by trying something new? It's like, that question is always there, but it's a question that you can't let yourself worry about. Or it's a decision that you have to make without worrying about all of the repercussions, at least with regard to that particular question. I mean, you have to make the decision for entirely separate reasons."

"I think I understand," Adam said. Honestly he was starting to feel a bit buzzed at this point, and his understanding consisted mostly of parroting her words in a slightly different order: "It's something that you have to decide on for reasons of your own."

"Right!" Her jaw dropped a little, casually, and her eyes

opened wider. "I mean, you've been writing longer than I have, and you must know all of this already, so I don't know why I'm spouting this shit to you. But it's just been on my mind recently, I guess. And now this party, and I have to feel like an ass all over again for having it. Like I'm throwing it to celebrate my own success, when I'm worried that everyone who shows up might be jealous. Even though I've decided not to let outside perspectives alter my decisions, it doesn't mean I'm not aware that they exist. But whatever, you know?" She finally looked away from him. "The party was Martha's idea, anyway."

Adam shrugged. "Yeah, I think everyone here is just as happy for you as I am. No need to worry, really. But you still haven't told me what the new story's about."

She huffed and tried again to roll her eyes, to similar effect as the last time. "God, you should know what a tough question that is to answer. Where do I even begin?"

"I don't know. I guess I've always thought that was the difference between novels and short stories. That a short story is a thing where you can tell someone in one sentence what it's about."

"Huh. I've actually always kind of thought the opposite. But it's an interesting challenge, I guess." She nodded. "I mean, what would I say, if I were really pressed, and I had to distill it down to a single sentence. You know, not communicate what the story does, but tell you about the process through which I hope it manages to do it." She laughed. "It's hard, though. I'm just so close to it, I guess, it seems to need a lot of context."

"Sure," Adam said. "But I've got time for context."

She smiled wider. "Well, then I guess I have time to explain it to you. Have you seen my room?"

He paused for a moment as possible futures branched before his mental eye. "No, I don't believe I have. But I'd like to."

Nothing romantic, at least of a physical nature, happened between Adam and Sherilyn while they were in her bedroom that night. They simply sat and talked. Or, rather, Sherilyn talked and Adam listened. She told him about her new story in *The New Yorker* and the real-life experiences that had informed it.

"If I actually have to summarize it in a single sentence, I guess I'll say that it's about Ludwig Wittgenstein lacking the words to express his love for a young Cambridge mathematician. But that makes it sound pretentious, you know, when for me—even though it's about a language philosopher—it's not really about language or philosophy; it's about the emotional core. I mean, to be totally honest, even though I obviously don't expect anyone else to get this, for me it's about my twin brother, Isaac."

As mentioned in the video on the department website, Sherilyn La Mush had been reared in Indiana, though she was also a second-generation American of Algerian extraction; her father had brought the family to Bloomington so that he could take a job teaching French literature at the university. Monroe was one of the few liberal counties in the state, but it was still Indiana, and during the 1980s being perceived as Arab had been second only to being perceived as Russian in terms of garnering the ill will of locals. The La Mush family was of mixed descent and didn't obviously share much in common with the likes of Khomeini, Arafat, Gadhafi, or any of America's other Islamic enemies, but the parents spoke with accents, and there was an undeniable if vague exoticism to the family's looks. So, throughout childhood, both Sherilyn and Isaac sat balanced on a narrow fulcrum of social acceptability, and, by late junior high, they had each fallen to opposite sides.

Sherilyn had been pretty and cheerful: on the weekends she would watch movies or go clothes shopping with her friends; she dressed fashionably and kept current with popular music, and she got A's in all of her classes without ever appearing to care or try. Isaac, however, was quiet, with a sickly cast to him; he perspired, so that he was sweaty all summer and clammy all winter. For fun, he liked to stay in his room and read science fiction of the 1960s; and the height of his extracurricular activity was to join the math team, which was where he met his only friend—a boy called Jo Hannah, whose name probably went a long way towards explaining his own social awkwardness. She didn't spell these things out to Adam in quite so much detail, but the shape she gave him of the story was a fractal from which he could imagine finer iterations.

"My brother and I were always really close," Sherilyn said. "I know it's a cliché that twins have this intense bond, but he and I really did, even when our lives were taking totally different tracks. He would come sit on the foot of my bed in the middle of the night, and I'd tell him all about which girls liked which boys, and who was fighting with whom. Or I'd tell him the plots of all the movies I'd seen. I swear, sometimes I would take longer than the movie itself to tell him every little detail of what had happened. I think that's where I got my start as a storyteller, actually; it made me want to make up my own stories to tell him. But he would just sit there and listen, and laugh or smile or cry with me, the ideal audience, and he never really needed to say much himself, but we just had this sort of intuitive harmony. I mean, I think I knew before he did that he was gay. So when he started to tell me about some of the stuff he was doing with Jo, I basically already knew it all, but I still waited for Isaac to tell me about it. Which, I don't think he was keeping anything from me, but I don't think he even thought there was anything to tell me until something really major happened. And, you know, the two of them both being pretty awkward, that took a while."

As Isaac told it, Jo had been the one to make the first move.

"Sometimes I get so horny I scare myself," Adam, in his drunkenness, imagined Jo saying, just as the tension was mounting towards the inevitable lights-out session of them sitting across from each other and talking through masturbation, telling each other what they were doing and what it felt like as they did it, and then trying to climax at the same moment. "Sometimes I get so horny that I think I probably couldn't even control myself. Like, not just that I have to masturbate—though that's what ends up happening, sometimes even when you're not around. But that if someone else were there who wanted to have sex with me, I'd have sex with them, no matter who it was. Like, even a fat girl."

Isaac nodding. "I know what you mean." And he did. "Sometimes I feel like I'd have sex with a fat girl too. I just wish I knew what it would feel like for my dick to be in something besides my own hand."

And so, over the course of an hour or two more of discussion, they would have managed to bolster each other's confidence to the point that—just for the sake of curiosity—they decided to give each other a blow job, Isaac volunteering to go first, swallowing all of Jo's cum even when Jo tried to pull away.

Sherilyn paused but she didn't look away from Adam's eyes. "Isaac told me that they'd done some sexual stuff—he didn't go into the details—but what happened next—well, it was kind of long and drawn out. I mean, the details don't make a good story. Things were awkward between the two of them, and then they stopped hanging out. Isaac was depressed. For the first time he started to show an interest in the music that I listened to. But mostly it was just the darker, gothier end of the spectrum. He and Jo hardly spoke to each other throughout our junior year. And then, I don't know."

"What do you mean you don't know?"

"I mean no one knows. I have my theories, I guess. But in November of our senior year, Isaac and Jo were both found dead in the back of Jo's dad's flower-delivery van. With Jo's dad's gun. They called it a double suicide. But Jo was the one who shot Isaac and then himself." Tears had filled her lower eyelids.

"Oh my God. I'm so sorry. I was really hoping that wasn't where this story was going. I mean, that's horrible. And I'm especially sorry to make you go through this in the middle of your party."

Sherilyn looked down and grinned a little, which went a long way with those lips. "No, it's okay. It's actually a huge relief to talk with you. It's nice to be honest with someone about the fact that this story in *The New Yorker* means something to me, and it's not just an excuse to throw a party, or another line on my CV. Though it actually makes me feel embarrassed about this whole thing now, like I don't even want to be here. I don't know." She looked back up at him. "But I feel as if you understand, and that's kind of nice."

Just then there was a knock at the door, and Sherilyn's grin spread as she wiped away her tears. Looking at her long dark lashes, it occurred to Adam that she was a girl who would never need eyeliner.

"I guess I should probably answer that," she said.

Adam nodded. "Right."

Sherilyn got up and opened the door to Judas leaning against the outer frame with one elbow raised above his head. "Hey, somebody said you might be in here," he said, looking at Adam.

"Yeah?"

Judas stuck his tongue in his cheek for a moment before answering. "Yeah, and I just wanted to tell you that I might take off. And see if you wanted to come with me."

"You're going home?"

"No, I think I'm heading to another party. There's a kid here who says he knows a Tibetan girl who's got something going across campus, and he thinks she might be able to help me out with my thing. And I think it's kind of SOFA related, so maybe it'd be worth your while, too?"

"I already wrote that article. But you know how to get back to the place on your own?"

"I think so, basically. Are you going to be out late? Or can I just call you if I get lost?"

"You should go with him," Sherilyn said, putting a hand on Adam's upper arm.

Adam looked at her. "Well, I don't want to just leave you like this. We were having a good talk."

"Yeah, I didn't mean to interrupt anything," Judas said, casting a glance around the room.

"We can talk more later," Sherilyn said to Adam. "We should have a drink some time. In fact, I insist on it. I really don't know how I managed not to meet you before this."

"Okay." Adam nodded. "Or, you know what, you said you didn't really want to be here anyway. So I know Martha's throwing this party for you and all, but why don't you come with us instead?"

Judas stood dumb in the doorway. Sherilyn bit her tongue. "Yeah," she said. "Why not?"

The walk across campus—past the bright-lit limestone buildings and through the darkened, twisting paths of Dunn's Woods—was quiet. Sherilyn asked a few polite questions of Judas while Adam said mostly nothing; he preferred, instead, to seethe in silence at the fact of Judas's presence, resentful of each uttered pleasantry. He wished he were walking to this party with Sherilyn alone, even though Judas was the one who'd told them about it.

"So," Adam said when finally he condescended to speak. "Are you dating anyone, Judas? Because Martha seems kind of into you."

Judas took a moment to answer though his mouth hung slightly ajar in the interim. "Yeah, I don't know," he said. "I'm not really seeing anyone, I guess."

Adam shrugged. "But I guess you're leaving in a few days anyway, so the point is probably moot."

"When are you leaving?" Sherilyn asked.

"I don't know," Judas said, turning his head to squint through the darkness at Adam. "I've been stupidly buying one-way tickets. Not planning ahead."

"Once, when I was a kid, I left my favorite doll in a playground sandbox," Sherilyn said. "When I realized what I'd done, I ran crying to my mom, and I said to her, 'I'm so stupid.' She was making cookies, and right away she rapped my hand hard with the wooden spoon. 'Don't ever call yourself stupid,' she said. And then she rapped her own hand, just as hard, to show me that she wasn't being malicious. Which is just to say, you're not stupid for buying one-way tickets." She flashed a smile at Judas. "So don't say that about yourself. You're just living in the moment."

Adam sighed aloud. "Where did you say this party was again?"

"North . . . Walnut, was it? Up around 11th or 12th. We'll supposedly know it by the searchlight." He pointed to the sky. And through the tops of the trees, Adam saw that—indeed—the clouds were illuminated with a spectral white.

"Well, okay then," he said.

The light above was all the more visible because no lamps illuminated the grove; navigating the path required a mix of prior knowledge and keen night vision. Judas had neither, but he stuck close to Sherilyn. The light at the far end was thus a blessing and a curse, relieving him of his sightlessness but also of his need to hew to her side. He was about to say something, make some excuse for further proximity, when the three of them were stopped by a young man in the uniform of a campus policeman.

"I'm going to have to ask you for your IDs, and for you to hand over any drugs or alcohol that you may have on your persons."

"I think you need a search warrant for that," Adam said. "Or something. Not that we have anything on us. Other than IDs, which I don't think we're obliged to show you."

The guy nodded. "Right, but with that excuse you've just given me probable cause. Hand over the drugs."

"You're not a cop." This came from Sherilyn.

"What?"

"You're not even a campus cop. Who are you trying to fool?"

The young man looked abashed. "Sorry," he said. "I'm just trying to foment unrest. Against the real police, you know."

"Right. Well, next time try to find some marks who aren't already unrestful." She pushed forcibly past him, and Judas and Adam followed.

"How'd you know he was fake?" Adam asked.

"I didn't. Just a guess." And Adam knew then that he must find a way to sleep with her. He only regretted that the party they were heading to was so far from either of their beds.

In the time since he'd been an undergrad, Adam had largely forgotten what such parties were like; just as he, Sherilyn, and Judas walked through the front door into a living room lit only by Christmas lights hung a few months ahead of season, a balloonish boy was hoisted up for a keg stand, resting his legs on the bannister of an upward-leading staircase behind him for support. Farther in, girls wearing tube tops and too much eyeliner clustered, either around boys or in places out of the way —off to the side—a few moving minimally in time to overloud music; a boy in a blue vest and beanie, who reminded Adam inexplicably of himself, sat in a wooden chair beside the stereo, studiously programming an MP3 player and periodically taking gulps from a glass of some amber liquid. As the party went on, Adam would find that he approved of this young man's song selection, though something in the party's general tenor suggested to him that few else shared this appreciation; it was a dance-y enough set list, but it was heavy on British New Wave and post-punk—from an era when all of these kids had still been glimmering preconceptions.

Back toward the kitchen, what had once been someone's parents' dining room table—now scuffed from years of beer pong and less savory practices—was arrayed with cheap liquor of every variety. No wine, but a Styrofoam ice chest beneath the table supplemented the keg in the room up front. Adam could tell by the expression on Sherilyn's face that she was having second thoughts about having come here.

"Not quite what I was expecting," he said, before she could voice her own objections.

"Maybe it will be fun," Judas said. "Remind us what it was like to be young and stupid."

"I thought I told you not to call yourself stupid."

Judas smiled. "Well, only when it's by choice."

"Maybe you should try to find the hostess," Adam said. "That's the whole reason we came, right?"

"Yeah, but let's get a drink first." A pause. "Or maybe you've had enough?"

"No. I could use another."

Judas grabbed a beer from below the table, gave Sherilyn a nod, and went off to search for the party's hostess.

"Weenie," Adam breathed.

"What?" Sherilyn asked.

"Oh, nothing. Just something that I remembered."

He took a tumbler from the kitchen counter, some half-melted cubes from the Styrofoam cooler, and poured himself a cheap Irish whiskey. He was resolved to forget himself tonight—to forget Selah, and to live more within his body than within his mind. Perhaps Falstaff back at Martha's party was onto something after all.

"Can I get you something?" he asked Sherilyn.

She shook her head. "No, I just want to sit. My feet hurt from walking all this way in these shoes." She was wearing heels that didn't look entirely unreasonable to Adam's undiscerning eye, but he took her at her word and ushered her over to an empty burlap couch. Had there been light, he was sure that they would have observed motes of dust flying out from the cushions as they plopped down next to each other. A small glass table squatted beside the armrest, already crowded with cups and cans, but Adam nonetheless managed to find a place for his drink on a cardboard coaster adorned with the SOFA logo. He never knew how to feel about the fact that SOFA events were so popular with his students, whom—by and large—he found to be politically apathetic. He assumed that they must just be going to see the bands that had attached themselves to the movement. Or, as he'd written in *E*, more generally for the game factor that aimed to make social protest fun.

"I probably shouldn't have snuck out like that," Sherilyn said, disrupting his drunken thoughts. "Especially for this.

Martha's going to be pissed. And not just at me. Alex was supposed to show up later."

"What, Alex can't come if you're not there? That's not your worry. Tonight is about you, and you should do whatever makes you happy."

"Yes, but now my feet hurt. And I'm already thinking about the walk home." She clicked her tongue against her two front teeth. "I'm having regrets about having come here."

"We can take a cab home together. And until then, put your feet up." Adam patted his lap. "I'll give you a foot massage."

She looked at him slantwise before saying okay, kicking off her shoes and complying: turning sideways on the two-cushion couch, peaking her knees, and placing her feet across his mid-thighs.

"They're probably pretty dirty," she offered before he laid hands upon them.

He shrugged as he began to pinch and wiggle her toes, starting with the little one on her left and moving up to the big of that foot, before working his way across the right one in opposite order. Her toes were cold to the touch, and he tried to rub them into warmth.

"So why have you been such a mystery?" she asked, allowing her eyes to close.

"What do you mean?"

"Well, I know you're already in your third year and everything, but I know a lot of the third-year students. And I know you were in workshop, but everyone says you kept pretty much to yourself even then, and no one's really seen that much of you since. So was it just your secret, or was there something more to it?"

He cocked his head to the side, taking a moment to recognize the first few notes of the song "Marquee Moon" by Television before he answered her. "No big secret," he said, moving his thumbs up to the undersides of her arches. "I guess when I started here I was just concentrating on a new relationship—being part of a couple for the first time in a long while—and then the breakup kind of eclipsed everything for another long while after that. I probably should have been more social for my own sake—it would have been a healthier way to deal with it—but I figure you can't force that sort of thing, and I was sort of doing the best I could with what each day brought me. I'm only now getting to the point where it's not affecting every little thing I do." He stopped because he worried that he was beginning to slur, and also because he realized that he probably shouldn't be talking so much about his ex right now.

"I didn't even know you'd been in a relationship," Sherilyn said, opening her eyes again. "I somehow assumed that all of this was new."

"All of what? Like you and me?"

She tilted her head from side to side in a sort of reclining shrug. "No, just everything you've been going through. I thought it was all new. I didn't know it was part of something larger."

Adam wrinkled his forehead as he moved his palms up around the dead skin on her heels. "You're losing me."

Her feet tensed and her eyes opened wider. "I don't know, I guess it all just has to do with how little I know you. But I mean, I just assumed you'd been outed against your will or something."

His hands stopped moving. "What?"

She pulled her knees in closer to her torso, and he let her feet fall from his hands. She shook her head. "I'm sorry. I must have misunderstood something. I guess it's good that we're getting to know each other tonight."

His forebrain was numb, and he paused a moment before speaking, fearful that the question he was about to ask was something that he would only ask in a drunken state—knowing it was something he could never take back—but eventually he overcame such filters and spoke. "Wait. Did you think I was gay?"

"I guess?" She sucked saliva through the sides of her mouth. "I mean, you hooked up with one of your male students, right?"

Adam was too drunk and flustered to do much more than sputter.

"God," she said, wincing and turning fully now to place her feet on the floor.

"No." He pronounced the word mechanically, not clearly in response to her. "No. I did not hook up with one of my male students. I can't believe that's the rumor going around. And I can't believe that you thought I was gay."

"I'm sorry. It's just what I heard."

He took a deep breath. "My AL is actually less than zero in that category."

Now it was her turn to say "What?"

"Nothing." He shook his head. "It's no big deal, just . . . just I don't happen to be gay." He paused to give himself a last moment before the next thought escaped his mouth. "But, I mean, I know this is our first time hanging out and everything, but I thought you and I sort of had a connection."

"Yes. That's true. And I'll stop apologizing for this, but I guess I just thought our connection was about you being gay and able to sympathize with me because of my brother. But you know what, I've had too much wine tonight to even think about this." She made a buzzing sound with her lips. "I know I just said I'd stop apologizing, but—I'm sorry—do you think you could call me a cab?"

He nodded. "Sure." As he spoke the word, a despair came over him that was only partially due to the extreme amount of alcohol in his body. "Let me see if I can go find someone who knows the number."

She put her palms to her eyes as he rose from the couch, and then his whole world turned red, shot through with sparks of white. A warm gush of blood to the head, or maybe from it; he didn't know.

"Are you okay?" Sherilyn asked.

"I'm fine," he said, standing where he was, not wanting to move. And then, as the starry red wash over reality began to fade, he saw something through it that seemed like a sign: his student, Allison Rose—the one he'd fantasized about—descending the staircase bearing a bottle of absinthe—he knew it was absinthe even before he saw it up close. She looked lovely, glowing with reflection from the most beautiful hues of Christmas light, her eyes wide and wet, brown hair down and bouncing off her shoulders as she stepped. Forgetting the task at hand, he approached her.

"That's real absinthe, isn't it?"

"Mr. Spillwater," she said, looking down at him from the second-to-last step of the stairway. "What are you doing here?"

He smiled and shrugged. "Just trying to have fun on a Friday night." He was taking care to speak slowly in order to counter the clumsiness that alcohol had bestowed upon his tongue. "How about you?"

"Um, same, I guess." He noticed that she had a way of slouching as she spoke and then straightening again once she'd finished, and he wondered what this said about her character.

"That looks like real absinthe," he said. "Or at least it's not the shit they sell here. Where'd you get it?"

She squinted at the bottle in her hand as if it were a strange shell that she'd found half buried on the beach, with a hidden mollusk possibly still curled within. "Yeah," she said, "I met this guy when I was in Spain, and I told him I liked licorice. So he brought this over for me. He's here somewhere."

"Oh? You were in Spain? That's where I did my year abroad when I was an undergrad. Where in Spain were you?"

She cast a glance around the room behind him and stepped down from the final step of the stairs. "You know, in the north or whatever. With the Basque and stuff."

"Right. That's a kind of dangerous place, isn't it? I was in Barcelona, myself. Which is nice. But I hear it can get pretty crazy up where you were."

"Um, I guess, but seriously, why are these people rebelling against fucking Spain? It's not like they're living in Korea or Iran or wherever. I mean, it's a totally nice place."

He bit his tongue. "I guess that's true."

"Besides, real-world violence is so two seconds ago. We're supposed to be attacking headspace or whatever now, right?"

"Ideaspace. Right. But so you've never had absinthe, then?"

"It's supposed to be good?"

"I don't know." He cocked his neck from side to side in lieu of a shrug. "I've never had the real stuff. I mean, it is. Supposed to be good. I even kind of like the fake stuff. But there's more to it than that. Wormwood. I've always wanted to. In fact, I've already started writing a short chapter about it in my book. There's a special way of drinking it. Do you want me to show you how?"

"Um, I was just gonna take a shot."

"Okay." He nodded. "I can do that. Let's go get something to drink out of." He then led her into the kitchen, where he proceeded to rinse out some used shot glasses that he found in the sink.

"So you never accepted my friend request on Facebook," he said, pouring out two drams of the pale green liqueur.

She sighed. "Yeah. Sorry. I've got like two million friend requests, and I can't even deal with it. Plus, I was going to wait till the end of the semester, you know, because a friend of mine totally got caught lying to her professor about why she was absent from class? Because they were like Facebook friends, and the professor woman saw the shit the rest of us posted on my friend's wall about how drunk she was, and how she had trouble getting up the stairs, and my friend had just told her that she was sick or whatever? So yeah." Allison laughed. "But I guess you've seen me here now, so there goes that, right?" She started to lift the shot glass to her mouth, then paused. "But wait a second, aren't you worried about contributing to the delinquency of whatever?"

He shook his head. "I don't think I have much to contribute."

"Hah, okay. Well, cheers."

The taste was a bit harsher than he expected—probably why you were supposed to mix it with sugar and water. Though he did love the taste of anise.

"Wow," he said. "I probably shouldn't drink enough to feel the effects of the wormwood. Too bad."

Allison's face was wrinkled. "Hmm, yeah, I don't know. It's no Jägermeister. Anyway, good to see you, but I'm gonna go outside and have a cigarette."

"Cool. Maybe I'll join you."

Judas, meanwhile, had been luckier than he could have expected to be; Karma, the party's hostess—only halfway smashed—not only knew who Jigme was, but she even had a cousin in Southern California who knew roughly where he lived.

"Yeah," she explained. "I guess he lived there in the eighties or something, and he recently moved back? My cousin's a book nerd, so she was all excited. She says she met him at a party and they slept together, but I don't believe her." She laughed. "I mean, I don't know why she'd even want to. But, you know, there aren't many famous Tibetan writers besides the Dalai Lama or whatever, so I guess it's kind of a big deal if you're into Tibetan pride and stuff."

Judas then managed—over the course of fifteen minutes or so—to get the girl to take him up to her room, find her laptop, boot it up, and get her cousin's contact information for him. "Thank you so much," he said once he'd written everything down on the back of flyer for another SOFA party that was happening later that month, and which was the only paper that she had at hand. The writing was a bit shaky due both to his splint and his alcoholic buzz, but he wrote slowly enough to make sure that his handwriting was at least legible.

"All right, glad I could help or whatever," the girl said. She was already walking through the door to head back down to the party.

"I suppose I should head back down to the party myself," Judas said aloud to no one. "I should go down and celebrate this unexpected stroke of good fortune by drinking with my newfound friends."

"Where's Adam?" Judas asked Sherilyn once he found her. She was sitting on a couch, leaning over to force her feet back into a pair of dark blue heels.

"I don't know," she said, not looking up. "He told me he was going to find the number for a cab, but then he just kind of disappeared."

"You're heading out then?"

She nodded while she wriggled her foot the last few millimeters down the back of the shoe. "Yeah," she said, as if in afterthought.

"Huh, okay. Well, I got what I came for. Why don't we try to find Adam, and we can all head out together?"

"Sure," Sherilyn said, still not meeting his eyes, but nonetheless rising to join him in the search.

Judas thought it best to check the crowd around the drinks table first and then up front by the keg, but neither was to any avail. The party's hostess, however, was just finishing a keg stand of her own as they approached.

"You haven't seen our friend, have you?"

"Old dude like you?" Karma asked, wiping her mouth. "I think he's out front with Allison and Pepe." She indicated the door.

The scene outside was a bit hard for Judas to fully comprehend at first. A tall, skinny boy in a Spanish soccer jersey—presumably Pepe—stood in front of an old Chevy in the driveway, making quick, violent gestures with a lit cigarette as he spoke to Adam, who was leaning against the car's hood, blank-faced, with a cigarette of his own hanging drunkenly from the corner of his mouth. A brown-haired, anime-eyed girl of about eighteen years stood between them, closer to Adam, but looking with maximally widened eyelids at the boy. Her expression was a mix of fear and awe. The boy was smiling as he spoke, but his anger gleamed like starlit braces.

"What's going on?" Judas asked, approaching. Sherilyn hung back.

"We are just working out some arguments," Pepe said. "It is nothing that is concerning to you."

"We aren't arguing about anything," Adam said, pushing himself up from the hood of the car and looking to Judas. His cigarette fell to the ground as he spoke, landing cherry-side down and immediately extinguishing the ember. "There's nothing to argue about. I was just having a cigarette, and Pepe here—"

"To you, I am Jose!"

Adam nodded. "Pepe here came out and started getting jealous because he saw me take a swig from a bottle of absinthe that he bought."

"Look, we were just about to head out," Judas said to Pepe. "I mean, I apologize for my friend, but—"

"Dude, I don't need you to apologize for me." Adam spoke with an audible slur. "In fact you should apologize *to* me for even thinking about apologizing on my behalf."

Judas was tempted to slap either his own forehead or Adam's. "Fine, whatever, but maybe you should apologize to him yourself then, and we should all just leave."

"Yeah, sure. But not until you apologize to me first. You should both apologize to me."

"No," Pepe said. "Enough. It is too late for anyone to apologize to anyone else. Just answer what I have asked you. Have you tried to make the moves on my girl, you fag fucker?"

Adam shook his head. "Shit, man, I already told you!" And then, as he spoke, he caught sight of Sherilyn, standing over by the door, and something like clarity came into his eyes. The muscles in his face relaxed, resigned. "This is a misunderstanding," he said, extending a hand to Pepe. "We should all be friends."

"Yes," the Spanish boy nodded. "We will all be friends. Please allow me to acquaint you with my friend the floor!"

"Pepe, no, he's my teacher!"

There was a flash of brightness in his eyes, though very little in the way of physical sensation as the fist connected with his face, and then the next thing that Adam could recall was Allison Rose, leaning over him, cradling his head, and saying, "Oh my God, Mr. Spillwater, are you all right?" He felt that he was lying on cold concrete, both literally and figuratively.

The others were all presumably standing somewhere nearby, but he couldn't see them from where he lay. All he could see was that Allison's thick lips were rough, with bits of skin peeled back. But they weren't dry. She must have licked them, and —nothing to lose now, already punished in advance for such a transgression—he tried to bend his neck up for a kiss. She shied away, wincing at his bloodied mouth.

"God, what the fuck?" she said. She lowered his head gently to the ground. "Are you trying to give me AIDS or something?"

Adam closed his eyes for a moment and stared at a floater shaped precisely like the profile of Alfred Hitchcock, and he heard Judas's voice say, "Easy, there." And though he didn't realize it at the time, this was but a small part of a larger intervention that ultimately spared him a kick to the ribs. Adam opened his eyes in time to see Allison rising to head back into the party—Pepe's arm wrapped around her shoulders—but Judas and Sherilyn were quickly at his side.

"Can you stand?" Sherilyn asked. "Did your head hit the concrete?"

A light mist had fallen at some point, and Adam was staring up into it. "I think I'm okay." He reached a hand behind his head to feel for a lump, and in doing so recalled that Lump was still outside.

"It's getting late," he said.

Moaning only a little, then, with support from his newfound friends, he stood and turned his face back up to the moistness of night: a haze in the sky to harmonize with that which was in his mind. In that moment all he knew with any certainty was that it was time for him to head for home; he had to let his cat come in to sleep.

PART THREE

BERKELEY

Shallow natures dream of an easy sway over the emotions of others, trusting implicitly in their own petty magic to turn the deepest streams, and confident, by pretty gestures and remarks, of making the thing that is not as though it were.

—George Eliot, *Middlemarch*

Remembrance is a funny thing—though it was only when I felt my face smash against the wet grass that this thought occurred to me. By "remembrance" I mean both memory and recall: the things we bury in the river-bottoms of our minds and the moments at which we dredge them up by choice or chance. Our memories form the stories that we tell ourselves about how we came to be who we think we are—which is funny, because even though we're the tellers, it's still sometimes hard to know how we should interpret these stories. What are the major themes? Just how reliable is the narrator? What do we make of the things that we remember yet choose to ignore, as opposed to the memories that we find ourselves visiting over and over like ancestral shrines? Or what of those thoughts that come upon us whether we'd have them or not? What do our habitual remembrances have to say about us?

I'll give an example of what I mean by "habitual remembrance": at any moment, the word "Mesoamerican" is apt to pop into my head. I don't know why. I have never been particularly fascinated by the United States' southern neighbors, linguistically or culturally; growing up Sino-American, I already had enough to worry about between the country of my descent and the country of my birth. But I'll be standing there washing the dishes, squirting soap onto a wet sponge, and, suddenly: *Mesoamerican!* Resonating in my skull. Does this word hold some hidden meaning for me? When I was reading a lot of William S. Burroughs in college, I guess I developed a bit of an interest in the Maya, but I never did any deep research on the subject. And I went to Tijuana once when I was a college freshman, but that wasn't exactly a life-changing experience, despite the fact that it's the closest in my life I've come to really getting in a serious fistfight. Still, there it is: *Mesoamerican!* It's not as if I have a choice in the matter; I just can't stop the unbidden recall.

That's a bit of a random example, I know, and I mention it mostly as an admission that I don't have memory as a concept completely figured out. I'm still working through it, trying out theories. Like, I had this idea recently about how, in superhero comics, there are often these important moments in a character's life that the story keeps coming back to: events that are told over and over, kind of in the way that certain formative memories recur in real life. Origins are good examples, but that's not the extent of the phenomenon. Getting bitten by a radioactive spider and failing to stop a robber who later kills your uncle makes for a powerful memory, but so does your maniacal archnemesis dropping your girlfriend off of a bridge while you fail to save her. Extreme examples, sure, but it occurred to me that real life has these moments too in a way, and the stories we tell ourselves about ourselves keep coming back to them. In my experience, these tend to be the embarrassing moments: finding out that the laptop box you bought from the charismatic criminal outside the bar contains nothing more than masonry, for instance, or even just getting caught in a blatant lie by someone you're trying to impress. And it's also embarrassing—to say the least—if you do something that costs the life of your uncle or your girlfriend. But the thing is, these moments can make you strive to be a better person. So I guess that's my theory for the moment: embarrassing moments define us. They're the ones we're stuck with and that keep coming back even when we don't want them to.*

Perhaps I should offer something more concrete to illustrate my point. I work in a used-book store: Shakespeare & Company, on Telegraph and Dwight. I've worked here for twelve or thirteen years, but there are two particular days of my employment that stand out more sharply to me than all the others. The more recent was less than a year ago, so I guess it has an obvious reason for being fresher, but that's not the only reason. I mean, it's also a memory that makes me cringe, coming back when I least expect it, and I know that even if it gets less frequent, it's still going to keep coming back just as strongly for years to come.

It was like this: a girl came into the store just as it was time for me to begin my lunch break. She was attractive, Asian, about my age, and dressed in a comfortable-looking hoodie. Attractive girls come into the store all the time—this is a college town—so that fact in itself was nothing special. But then she came up to the counter and asked if I could recommend a good book

* This is—not incidentally—part of the theory that was behind the founding of SOFA: that embarrassment can be a tool for change.

to her. Haruki Murakami immediately popped into my head. *Hard-Boiled Wonderland and the End of the World*, to be specific. But I didn't say this out loud because I was afraid she'd think I was being racist—like, we were both Asian, and so I thought she should read an Asian book.

"What sort of stuff do you like?" I asked.

"Well, I just read this book by Haruki Murakami—"

"That's amazing," I interrupted, realizing as I spoke that she would have no reason to believe me. "I was just thinking, 'Haruki Murakami.' We should have something by him. Or, you know, if you like him you might also like *The Crying of Lot 49* by Thomas Pynchon. Let me see if we have that."

As it turned out, we had neither, nor could I immediately find anything else that might suit the image I had formed of her taste. And then one of my coworkers came up to remind me that it was time for me to take my lunch break, so I had to walk out of the store while the girl was still browsing. It could all have ended there—and in that case I would never have cause to recall this day—but a friend from school happened to be passing by the entrance to the store, and he and I wound up spending a few minutes talking, catching up. I couldn't tell you what we talked about; on that score, my memory is not clear at all. My mind was stuck on the connection that I'd felt with this girl in the comfortable hoodie. And though I may not have consciously known it at the time, I think I was probably only talking to this guy from school as an excuse to wait for the girl to leave the store.

In any case, when she finally came out, I let her walk about a block before I gave my friend a quick farewell and trailed after. I tried to keep my distance. It was early in the afternoon, and perhaps she was on her way to have lunch somewhere, I thought. Then I could act as if I'd just randomly chosen to have lunch in the same place, recognized her from the store—what a coincidence—and she would suggest that we eat together . . .

She paused on the corner of Telegraph and Channing, though the white light of the walking man was lit. I stopped too, half a block down, in order to avoid catching up with her. I looked through the window of the fetish/head shop that I found myself standing out in front of, and I scratched my temple with two fingers in order to obscure my face in case she decided to look back my way. An older black woman, with closely cropped hair, lacking lower teeth, spoke to me—"Spaney change?"—a phrase that took me a moment to decipher. I simply shook my head. I can recall all of this with perfect clarity. When I turned back towards the girl from the store, though, she had already progressed across the street, and a red hand was flashing at me not to follow.

I followed regardless. She was about a block ahead again, and by the time I reached the corner where she'd paused, the icon of the red hand had stopped flashing and a flow of cars was impeding my progress. I tried to keep an eye on her as she threaded through the crowd on the next block, and—catching a lull in the traffic—I dashed across the street after her. Then, in my confusion, she was gone. I lost sight of her. I came to the crowd that she'd moved so easily through—apparently some sort of loiterer's convention—and tried to make my way to the other side, but it was denser now, and I had to go around, stumbling in the gutter; then, as I stepped up onto the sidewalk again, I saw her coming straight back towards me.

"Oh, hi!" I said, with a quick wave, and I tried to walk past her as if it were all just a coincidence. A different sort of coincidence than before. Not like me thinking of Haruki Murakami and her speaking his name immediately afterwards; I meant now to assure her that "this means nothing" rather than "this must mean something." She moved to block my way, though, and I felt my face flush with the blood of embarrassment.

"Were you following me?" she asked.

"No, I—I was just going to lunch," I said. "I mean, why? Are you hungry?"

She breathed a laugh, hardly audible, then walked away. Now, I hadn't had any real thoughts of lunch with this girl; it was just a playful fantasy. I don't know what I was thinking, actually. Just the desire to keep her in my sight—to keep her real in the universe as bounded by my solipsism, or to keep her available as an object of my fancy. I don't know. But I do know that the embarrassment made me realize something: that no matter what the reason was, I didn't want to be the creepy sort of guy who followed girls on the street. And so this memory has come to define a small part of who I am. Or at least it's led me to realize something about the person I don't want to be.

Selah wrote a letter about this event in her journal, though she didn't send it. She didn't even tear out the pages on which she wrote it:

> Dear Adam,
>
> A bookstore clerk followed me up Telegraph Avenue today. I finally read the book you gave me for the

plane when I first came out here (I really liked it!), and I went to see if they had anything similar. This clerk was trying his hardest to help me. It was kind of sweet how disappointed he'd get when he couldn't find the book he was looking for. And I thought he was actually cute while we were in the store, even though my low-level self-loathing usually leads me to steer clear of Asian guys. I even sensed the chance that my feelings for him might develop into a silent, fruitless crush: that I might have gone back in a week or so to see if he was working again, never speaking to him on any subject other than books, and abandoning the whole thing if he tried to start such a conversation with me. But then the "following" thing was just too weird. Creepy. Skeezy. Still, in a way, I suppose that it was nice to be skeezed over. Or at least it was nice to know that someone thought I was worth the skeezing.

Love,
Selah

One of my problems is, if I try to tell a story, I can never tell it straight, starting at the beginning and progressing steadily to the end. First I have to tell you about what made me think of the story in the first place, or what was going through my head when the events of the story happened. Or then I have to go back and tell you how I met the person whom the story involves, and how that led to an earlier incident which will ironically flatten a wrinkle in the fabric of the story at hand. That is to say, I feel as if—to really get the full significance of any story—you need to get all of the context and tangents first. To me, a story told straight is little more than a trussed-up list. And if there's no more to it than that, I have to ask myself why it's even worth the telling. And the reason I can't get to the point is because the points I try to make tend to lie outside of those strictly defined by the function of the facts at hand—like the foci of hyperbolas rather than the vertices.

Which is all just to say that I'm going to focus on Judas for the moment—at least get the basic details out—even though he's not really the point of the story as I see it; my memory just keeps bringing me back to him. The stench of someone's Lapsang souchong tea in a café, half the tracks that my iPod deals out from its shuffle: I guess the logical explanation here is that he was my roommate for a good long while, and so he was around often enough to make me associate him with a lot of things in my life. But there's more to it than that. He may not be the point of all of this, but I don't think he's many transformations away from it. Whatever the justification, though, he's pretty involved in everything that happened, so as a practical matter he's not a bad place to start.

As I mentioned, he and I were roommates, and that's the main thing to know. We met at the end of sophomore year. He was in an Asian studies class I was taking, and I noticed him right away. He stood out a bit since he was one of the white dudes—the assumption being that he and the others were just there to steal our women—but we were also both comp lit majors, so we kind of hit it off. We hung out a little over the summer, played some basketball together, and then junior year we became roommates. We were friends as well as roommates, I guess, but friends of a strange sort. Not best friends. We had long conversations, and we encouraged each other's geekier tendencies, but we also sort of wound up moving in different circles; we didn't always invite the other out on Friday nights; we fought over the silly things that roommates fight over—our biggest battle was over ice trays. But I guess on top of the friendship, we were also kind of casually dickish to each other.

I never thought much about the fact that I had crooked, discolored teeth, for instance, until Judas pointed it out. And even then, perfectly unselfconscious, it took me a while to realize that he was serious. When he called me unusually hirsute for a "bucktoothed Chinaman," I thought he was just appealing to a stereotype about my heritage. And when he called me "teabag mouth," I thought he was just talking about the amount of tea that I drank. I mean, he almost never used my actual name, so these epithets hadn't struck me as anything particularly out of the ordinary. He couldn't properly pronounce what my parents had called me in Chinese: Long Deting in Pinyin. And though my confirmation/English name is Thomas, he never used that either.* Usually he resorted to wordplay to come up with things

---

* Magical mottoes are a longstanding tradition among those who take the practice seriously; Aleister Crowley called himself Frater Perdurabo, for instance, among other names, when he was composing magickal works. Perhaps that had something to do with why I felt the need to alter my Chinese name into something slightly more Anglo for the creation of this book: to forge a new personality for myself devoted purely to this one intent. But it may also have had something to do with Judas's nicknames for me.

to call me. He'd start with, say, "Longdongo," shorten that to "Lodo," expand it back to "Long Duck Dong," and then spend a week calling me "Ducky" before swerving unexpectedly two steps to the left with "Jon Crybaby." So it wasn't until I told him about my crush on my coworker Karen Catchall, and he responded by saying that he couldn't imagine how I ever got any women, considering my crooked, discolored teeth, that I began to take such comments seriously.*

There had been a time when Selah couldn't wait for her roommates to leave the apartment. She would sit there perched on a stool at the kitchen bar, trying not to chew her cuticles as the two of them went about their morning routines, unable to think of anything but their eventual absence.

"What's the word with Chad?" That would be Amelia, head wrapped in one red towel with another around her torso, resting flamingo against the kitchen doorjamb.

"Chad?" Rebecca would answer, coy, wrinkling her nose but not looking up from the Arts section of the *Chronicle* as she stirred granola into her yogurt.

"Isn't that his name? That drug dealer guy you went out with last weekend."

"What?"

"The one who made you meet him all the way up in Richmond then didn't even ask you to spend the night?"

"Oh, Mark! Where'd you get Chad? He's not a drug dealer."

* For most of human history, the majority of people have had bad teeth.

"Then what is he?"

"He sells Adderall to EECS majors. Maybe a little weed, but that hardly makes him a drug dealer."

"Actually, that's exactly what makes someone a drug dealer. So I guess you're seeing him again."

Selah admired Amelia's skinny arms as she reached high into the cabinet to grab a cereal bowl.

"He said he might come to a party with me this weekend. Here in Berkeley. But today I'm going out to lunch with Jeremy."

"Intern Jeremy?"

"Business Jeremy."

Rebecca was an assistant editor at the UC Press—at twenty-three, one of the younger—and Selah understood that she'd been juggling two Jeremys. Business Jeremy was forty and sold ad space in the Cal alumni magazine. His cube was in the back of the building, but they'd hit it off during cigarette breaks. Intern Jeremy was twenty-two and worked one cube over from Rebecca. He was a former cross-country runner and didn't smoke. Selah took all of this in and even offered a few comments, but all she was thinking was *When will you leave?*

It took another ninety minutes for both of them to get out the door, which gave her three hours before she needed to be at work herself. She spent about thirty seconds in further chewing of her cuticles and then went into her bedroom, pulled a glass pipe from the jewelry box atop her dresser, and packed a bowl of weed. Once she had smoked it, she lay down on top of her covers and tried not to think of anything at all.

Karen Catchall worked at the bookstore with me. She started as a clerk the year after I graduated; she was still a senior. I was beginning to settle into the job, had just made the move up to manager, and I finally had enough hours, at a scale far enough above your average bookstore employee, to afford my half of the place with Judas (rent-controlled), buy the occasional CD from Amoeba down the block, and still set aside a little in savings. That is, I was self-sufficient for the first time in my life.

Karen was pretty tall for a girl. Five foot nine, according to her driver's license, and at one point she mentioned that her boyfriends in the past had all been six foot or over. That night at home, I measured myself on a doorjamb to make sure that I still made the grade. She was pale also, though not in a sickly way like a few of the other employees. Unblemished by so much as a tan, I should say. Freckled, yes, but I never considered those blemishes. Straight brown hair, not quite black, but stark against her skin. And how do you describe the beauty of a face? Symmetrical? It was that. Vibrant green eyes, a balanced and proportional nose, lips that protruded just enough. I don't know. I thought she was the prettiest girl I'd ever met, at least, and I don't mean that in just a rhetorical sense. I honestly couldn't flip to a better-looking girl in the Rolodex of my memory.

Now, I don't mean to suggest that my attraction to her was purely physical. There was something in her manner, too—an aloofness—which was definitely a factor. Which perhaps says more than a little about me, desiring most that which seems hardest to obtain. Forbidden fruit or whatever, like having an allergic reaction to mangoes but being unable to resist the sweetness of the flesh. Though that's still not the whole story either. But then I guess it's hard to say what the whole story is. I mean, it's something that I've given a lot of thought to—what ever attracts me to anyone? But it's a question to which there's no easy answer.

But Karen was definitely funny, and I think that was the main thing. Anyone who works retail will inevitably start to make fun of the customers a little, but Karen had a genius for it, like, with this one young student who'd been telling homophobic jokes to his friend while they were shopping: "Oh, you're getting *The Faerie Queene*? I would have figured you more as a Faulkner fan. Like, 'The Bear.'" The guy's only response had been, "It's for a class." Her humor was never truly malicious, though; it was more as if she were illuminating the absurdity of life, as illustrated by the examples of these ridiculous people—she was an anthropology major, after all. Still, when she got going, I'd sometimes find it hard to keep my laughter under control. And being the manager, that was kind of a problem, since I was supposed to keep up appearances.

Being her manager also complicated any prospect of a romantic relationship with her. Even though we got along pretty well—I think it's fair to say that the way in which we joked might have been considered flirtatious, and sometimes the two of us would grab lunch together—I wasn't sure that I'd ever be confident enough to actually ask her out on an unequivocal date; if she turned out not to be interested, it would have made things pretty awkward, so it was something I'd have to be certain of beforehand. But then Judas came by the store one night while she and I were closing up, and he suggested that we all go out for a drink together. Karen said she was up for it, and so I said, "Why not?"; it seemed like a way to do something vaguely date-like without actually having to ask her out, even if Judas had to be there too.

Anyway, we all went out to a bar just down Telegraph. These days we probably would have headed over to Shattuck, but Telegraph was a more vibrant area back then. It's always had its gutter punks and its mentally atypical street folk, but it also used to have a far greater share of students, and ex-hippies who had turned to respectable middle-class citizens (albeit with far-left-leaning politics), and part of Berkeley's charm used to be how all of these groups would mix. A kid with spray-painted hair, in a black leather jacket with a white anarchy symbol, busking outside of a bookstore could actually draw customers in rather than turning them away back then. But I'm starting to lose the thread.

So, more to the point, once Karen had had a few beers, she started to show signs of actually being into me. She was polite to Judas, sure, but I was the one whose ex-girlfriends she asked about, and my jokes were the ones that really made her laugh. And afterwards, as we walked her back to the boardinghouse where she lived, she told us about a project that she was working on for a class: an anthropological study of the California Peace Action group, which was pretty active back then; which—it now occurs to me to specify the timing of all this—was right around the time that the U.S. had decided to invade Afghanistan. But she asked me if I wanted to go to one of the meetings with her that weekend for field research. And there was a pause of at least two seconds before she invited Judas along too—almost as an afterthought. I took all of these things as propitious signs, and when Judas and I talked about it at home that night, he basically concurred.

"You should ask her out," he said. "She's totally into you."

"Maybe. But I just want to be sure. I mean, I don't want a sexual harassment suit or anything."

"Whatever, dude. You're thinking way too hard. Besides, if you don't ask her out, I might have to make a move myself. She's pretty cute."

I hardly took his words seriously at that point.

Selah worked at a bakery in Rockridge, one of Berkeley's more yuppified areas, bordering Oakland, dominated by shops and restaurants that weren't quite as upscale as those to be found in the Gourmet Ghetto up on Shattuck, but surrounded by a nicer residential area. She was only now beginning to get a sense of all the city's different neighborhoods: how they fit together. She'd come out here the previous summer for her PhD while Adam finished up his MFA back in Indiana, and at first it had seemed as if the long-distance thing might work out—as if everything would be okay. With summer classes she could finish the coursework in a year, and then she could head back to Indiana to work on the dissertation. But then he started suffocating her with his constant calls, making plans to live frugally so that he could fly out to see her once a month . . . and it had all gotten to be a bit much. She had her own life to live. So after a few telephonic fights, she'd made up her mind that he and the Midwest were not for her; California was where she was meant to be—where she'd been reared—focusing on her work rather than on having a boyfriend.

Actually, if she were being honest with herself, it had never seemed as if everything would be okay. Even when they'd lived together, she'd had this constant, implacable feeling that could only be called fear, though she was never certain what that fear's object was: uncontrollable tragedy, perhaps. Or failure. Or just her "true self," which might have been what she was talking about when she referred to her "low-level self-loathing." A fear that, at root, she was a bad person—whatever that might mean—and that Adam would discover this truth. Though this fear only intensified, actually, when she moved back to California; her family was about five hours to the south of her, in Santa Barbara, and she was even more afraid of them discovering the truth about her than she was of Adam. To distract herself, she'd focused on her studies, doing all of her class reading for the first time in her life. Yet when the reading was done, the only option left to her was to go out to parties and bars with other graduate students: to get drunk and make out with random guys. When she woke on the ensuing days, an immense guilt would overtake her from below like an inverse Paraclete, starting in her bowels and moving up to her head—but the threat of such morning remorse was never enough to curb her evening activities, so it had largely been to avoid this sense of guilt that she had broken up with Adam. She was still trying to reconcile her feelings.

In the meantime, she liked working in the bakery. She didn't really need the money, as she had a teaching stipend, but it was nice to have a little extra, and she liked that it forced her to get out and mix with the world. Plus, she had a thing for frosting. Not that she particularly liked to eat it, but she thought that a well-frosted cake was a thing of beauty; it was something she took pride in making. She enjoyed the smoothing most, and she could stare at a blue sea of sugar-cream punctuated by pinkish-white shells for fifteen minutes without a blink—particularly on days like today, when she was high and business was low. Or slow. It took her a minute to realize that someone was asking her a question: an old man, probably in his late eighties, holding a loaf of super-seeded rye. He was dressed all in beige, from his felt hat to his raincoat, even though it was a beautiful afternoon outside: clear skies and low seventies at the coolest.

"What sort of a name is Selah?" he asked, squinting at the tag that hung from a lanyard around her neck; she hated the fact that Max made her wear it. She'd heard this question in various permutations since the day she started kindergarten, and she'd long since tired herself of all the possible answers. *It's a family name.* True, in that she was a member of her own family. *My parents had just moved here from Korea; they couldn't spell "Sarah."* Also true, as far as it went, though it had nothing to do with why they'd named her Selah. *It's Hebrew.* An evasion that usually caused people to drop the subject in confusion. These days she'd settled into a flat delivery of the long, boring truth.

"My parents are religious," she started, but then the man interrupted her.

"That explains it all. My parents were atheists. They named me Baby. That's what they put on my birth certificate, anyway. Descriptive and to the point. The youngest of ten. My brothers and sisters called me Buster, though, and the living ones still do. Or sometimes 'Bussie.' But I don't want to get too familiar."

Selah blinked. "Is that what you call yourself? Buster, I mean."

"No." He shook his head, smiled. "When I was ten I chose my own name."

"And what was that?"

He half opened his mouth and inhaled, as if to think for a moment—as if it hadn't been the natural question for her to ask. "Call me Stu," he finally said. "Not Stuart, just Stu. I was ten when I chose it, so I didn't want to put on airs. So. Is that your work?" He indicated the blue-and-pink-frosted cake at which she'd been recently staring.

"Um, yeah. I mean, it wasn't my design. But it's my handiwork."

He smiled. "There's a lovely curve to your shells."

From the way he said it, Selah wondered if this was meant as some sort of innuendo. *Am I supposed to sleep with this man?* she thought.

She looked down at his aged hands, which somehow suggested silkworms to her, as he held out a five to pay for the rye. Sometimes Selah felt as if she were elderly herself, and not just in the relative way that women nearing thirty do; she felt as if she were old in spirit—that she had more in common with an octogenarian named Baby than with people her own age—and that she could only shake her head at the youthful folly of her peers, even when it was something that she participated in herself. Of course, when caught in the undertow of other emotional tides, she had a tendency to romanticize her childhood, yearning to be as cool as she'd been when she was seven, and in these moods she would seek out the unfiltered wisdom of any children whom she came into social contact with. So if she averaged these feelings out, she figured that she was actually supposed to be middle-aged, but what all of it seemed to come down to was that she just didn't want to deal with the reality of being a young adult—worrying, for herself, about a life that lay in front of her—so she indulged in imagining the extremities on either side.

"Nice to meet you, Stu," she said after a long pause.

He just nodded at the truth of what she'd said, put his change into a rubber coin purse, and left. Alone in the store then, she shoved a few mini cupcakes into her mouth. They were delicious.

I should mention at this point that the responsibility that I felt as store manager—the sense of propriety that kept me from openly asking Karen out on a date—only extended so far. In fact, in some respects, I guess I acted in direct opposition to the duty with which I'd been invested. Which is to say that, shortly after I was promoted, I started to steal a little from the store. Not money, just books. And not even a lot of books, but still. It's not an excuse, I know—my definition of morality is acting honestly when no one is looking, and from that point of view, I suppose I just wasn't that moral of a person at the time—but I still think it's worth the clarification.

The first book I stole was before Karen started working in the store, and it was sort of an accident that I even stole it. It was a first/first of *Infinite Jest*, with William T. Vollmann's name missing an "n" on the back-cover blurbs. The owner had marked it at our standard price—two-thirds of whatever the current paperback was going for—but I thought it might be worth more, so I took it home to look it up online. It just sat on my desk for a few weeks, though, and I kind of forgot about it. And when I remembered it, I realized that I wouldn't mind owning it. And I told myself that I would pay the store back the amount that the owner had paid out for the book, and that would make it okay. But then somehow I just never got around to that. And after that, the justifications grew slowly less elaborate.

The most expensive book I ever stole, and the one most relevant to the story at hand, was called *Hodge's Ars Magica*. The book was kept in a glass case otherwise filled with nothing rarer than twentieth-century signed firsts. My boss had picked it up cheaply at an estate sale, not knowing anything about it but guessing that he could at least turn a profit since so much of the store's business came from Berkeley's New Age hippie crowd, not to mention professors and students with an interest in anything obscure. When he couldn't find any information about it online, though, he priced it at seventy-five bucks based solely on the fact of how old it was; recall that this was in 2001, when the internet wasn't quite as comprehensive in its cataloging of cultural ephemera.

I don't know what attracted me to the book exactly. Probably just the fact that it was old. When I was a kid, my favorite book in the house was a beat-up black hardcover of *Hamlet* that my mother had read in high school; I don't know if she actually read it, but she'd used the flyleaf as a lipstick blotter. I didn't read the play until I was in high school, but I loved to hold the book itself, to stare at it, just for the aura of ancient knowledge that it projected. So it was with *Hodge's Ars:* its marbled endpapers, hand-cut pages, and the dentelle border on the leather binding meant more to me than whatever text it might contain.* Though I did actually start reading it within the first few days of bringing it home.

Hodge's basic idea seemed to be that magic is just a convenient method of putting names to principles and actions that, whether we understand their workings or not, achieve desired effects. In his view, Voltaire missed the point when he wrote that "certain words and ceremonies will effectually destroy a flock of sheep, if administered with a sufficient portion of arsenic." In Hodge's view, the arsenic could be seen as an essential component of the spell, and the fact that sheep could be killed by arsenic without the "words and ceremonies" did nothing to discount the fact that the spell itself was effective. The arsenic was just the natural basis of the supernatural work. In Hodge's view all problems came down to the language in which they were couched.

If, for example, we take it as a given that such abstractions as "intelligence," "language," "communication," and "art" in some sense exist, and we decide to group these abstractions together and label that grouping with the collective name "Mer-

---

* I think another part of my love for old books might stem from the fact that modern books just don't have the same sort of impact. There was a time when people didn't know what to make of novels, for instance; *Robinson Crusoe* and *Pamela* seemed dangerously real. The secret that Viv learned from Bendix and the *Ars Magica*—particularly from the footnotes, in which Hodge, after the fact, comments on and explains the magical intention of his book—was precisely this: how to make one's own fiction seem dangerously real. Like a mime turning to attack the crowd with an invisible knife.

cury"—as in the Roman god—then we can say that Mercury also, in the same sense, exists. Those who value language and art, then, might choose to devote themselves to Mercury through a daily ritual of reading and writing, and in return they might be blessed by him with greater knowledge or communication skills. To make magic work most effectively, though, Hodge argued that you have to externalize the internal. You can create your own god, but then you need to send him out in the world to watch over you. Which isn't as hard as it sounds. Just like smiling can make you happy, worship can make you believe.

These ideas held a certain fascination for me, and the more I read of Hodge's arguments, the more they really seemed to fit with my experience of the world. I mean, I know it sounds a little ridiculous to say I started to believe in magic, but I guess after reading Hodge's book I just had a broader understanding of the word than most people, and looking back at my life I could see certain aspects of it in a more magical light. For instance: it may be hard to believe, but back in college I was actually pretty good with the ladies. It's cliché, I guess, but I think it mostly came down to confidence. Like, if you seem confident, then the assumption is that there must actually be something cool about you that inspires the confidence. And laughing off missteps is a lot more attractive than openly obsessing over them. But even before I figured out that the direct approach was best, I still had this thing that worked for me. It's kind of weird, and I don't recall how I thought it up, but basically it went like this:

Preferably at a party—though it could also work when out at a bar—I would start talking to a girl I was interested in, and if the conversation didn't kill the interest, I would call her "Kelsey Grammer." As in, "So, what's your major, Kelsey Grammer?"

I don't recall if Kelsey Grammer's TV show was even still on the air the first time I did this, and if it was, I wasn't a particular fan. I think I just liked the sound of his name. In any case, the desired effect was that the girl would then ask me why I had just called her Kelsey Grammer, to which I'd reply, "Why don't you come into my room and I'll explain it to you?" And if the girl went along with this and didn't just think I was some weirdo, everything else was pretty simple.

So, once we were alone, I'd explain to the girl that I'd only called her Kelsey Grammer to make her curious about why I'd called her Kelsey Grammer, and thus, hopefully, to get her alone in my room with me. And this exposure of the trick was itself the final part of the trick. Well, sometimes I'd also explain that it had been sort of a joke, only playing as if I were trying to seduce her in this absurd way, when really I just wanted to amuse her (and to amuse Judas, who knew about the joke; I don't think I would have done it if I didn't know that I had an uninvolved audience who was completely in on the joke). But most of the time I'd just end with the exposure of the trick. And curiosity having been resolved, we would find ourselves alone after all. And more often than not the girl would be amused enough that she would want to make the most of our privacy. Decency dictates that I should stop here in this recounting of such escapades. But I guess my point is that all of this seems to me to be as good an illustration of "magic" as any other I've ever heard about. In the same way that Dumbo's feather was a magical talisman—it really did allow him to fly—"Kelsey Grammer" was a magical incantation for me. I didn't understand all of this at the time, but after reading *Hodge's Ars,* I came to see it for what it was.

I mean, I've never been one of those Berkeley hippies who worships Gaia or whatever—I'm a pretty rational guy, all things told—but if I'm going to make any headway here, I'm going to have to say it plainly at some point: once I had learnt a little of what it was actually all about, I realized that magic may very well be fiction, but this doesn't mean that there isn't also a certain truth to it. Magic is fiction that asserts its own reality; it makes itself real, or at least it refashions the real into its own image.* Just because you're the one who invents a god, for example, that doesn't mean he can't still smite you. And as ridiculous as it sounds, I guess that's one of the points that I'm trying to get to.

When Selah got off work, she found Amelia home from class, lying on the couch and reading some art magazine. It was unusual for Amelia to be home at this hour; her schedule was pretty light, it's true—she was a philosophy grad student, and she paid her share of the rent with a few modeling jobs each month—but her "beau-friend," as she called him, was an artist, and he had an apartment/studio in the Mission where she

---

* Not to say that magic is by any means a shortcut; direct action is still required to achieve any desired material results, as the SOFA Apocalypse so recently demonstrated; actually kissing a girl is the final and crucial component of any spell designed to achieve the result of kissing a girl. But magic can just be another way of approaching the work that needs to be done in order to solve a problem. The best way of explaining it that I've found is to say that magic may work within the imaginary space that makes love poetry possible, but that the poem itself is the only thing that has any chance of actually wooing a woman.

usually spent the parts of her day that didn't require her to be in the East Bay. So Selah didn't actually see her at the place that often, except in the mornings over breakfast or when she was arriving home late at night.

"Hey," Selah said, and after a reciprocal salutation without much more offered in the way of dialogue, she went into her bedroom, shut the door, and sat down at her desk, which faced out a window that gave her an unobstructed view of the apartment building behind her own. Selah on occasion saw, through windows, people walking around naked or having sex—which always fascinated her in a detached, anthropological sense. But the opposing curtains were mostly closed to her at the moment, and the open ones showed no one home. So she just pulled out her journal and wrote another letter to Adam.

Dear Adam,

Last weekend, I went to a cocktail party with my roommates, a party for one of Rebecca's coworkers, at her apartment. Everyone was dressed nicely, but the cocktails didn't get much fancier than vodka and cranberry juice. I don't know why I went. I haven't felt like getting drunk lately, and sobriety makes such parties a bit absurd. A few cute guys hit on me, and each seemed as if he could have been interesting in his individual way if I had entered into the spirit of the conversation that he offered. But I somehow wasn't up for it; you know how bad I am at small talk. Which I guess is part of the reason I cheated on you so much: it was a way of getting affirmation without having to say much. But this weekend, even though I was willing on an intellectual level, I couldn't find the motivation actually to do anything. In fact, I feel as if—ever since I broke up with you—I've had this weird magical shield protecting me from men's charms. Please don't take this as a sign that I want to get back together with you, though; I realized the other day that part of the magical protection I feel comes from having let you go, even if I haven't found another man.

Instead, I have replaced you with the Southside. That is, I have replaced you with Telegraph Avenue and its environs. For company and conversation I have my roommates, of course. We live on Haste, not too far from Telegraph itself, which is sort of the Southside's aorta. But there's a masseur who lives in my building, as well, for times when I need a bit of physical intimacy. And the owner of the café where I used to do my reading for classes and where now I go to stare at an empty notebook in which I have yet to make a serious start on my dissertation—a fat Turkish man in his fifties—he talks to me over the counter, and he's there to give me hard advice in a way that you never would. "You are full of your own shit," he told me the other day. "You talk out of both sides of your mouth." I don't like to criticize you after the fact, but it might help you to know that you were always too nice—too soft. I didn't need my self-indulgence supported; I needed to be forced to face my problems. Also, the chefs here cook better than you ever did. Except for the Korean restaurant. I never go there because it's Korean. Or I went there once, and it was terrible. I suppose every relationship has its flaws. In any case, I want you to know that I've changed, and however flawed my current relationship is, I still don't think I could come back to you. Because it wouldn't be the same me coming back.

Which brings me to something that I've started to realize lately. Kind of a big revelation for me, actually, and one that's been kicking around my head for a while —though I haven't really put it into words before this. In any case, I only thought of it because of you, and it's something I wish I could actually say to you: I wish it could help you. But here it is, my big idea: the loss of a loved one is always pretty much the same. Or, that's not the realization, but it's sort of a corollary of the realization. But regardless of whether the reason you lose someone is because your love is unrequited, she leaves you for a neighborhood, or just because the person dies—and whether you're talking about a parent, a lover, or a friend —they're all sort of the same. The particulars allow for some shading of intensity, it's true, but the worst part is always the same. You feel as if you can't possibly get along without the person—and in a way you're right; the person you are at the moment that you think this is more or less defined by the attachment you have—but the hardpan truth of it is that time will make you into someone else, someone who *can* get along without that person, no matter how much you don't want it to. So the really traumatic thing in all nine instances—multiplying the three types of failure by the three types of relationships, though I don't mean to say that's the extent of the possibilities—isn't the loss of the other person; it's the loss of yourself. And it seems like the end of the world because it is—but only this world. The pain you feel—the pain that wakes you nauseated by your own gut-doubling sobs—it's the pain of birthing someone into another world. Someone other than the you who couldn't exist without that love. So, you know, for what it's worth: happy birthday.

In any case, it's strange to date a neighborhood. But I just thought I would let you know. I hope you have moved on as well. Bloomington is not the sexiest place, but at least she has a great personality. Speaking of which, I should probably visit soon. Not to see you —I don't want to falsely get your hopes up—but to do some research at the Tibetan Cultural Center. I think that might be what I need to get me kick-started again on my dissertation. I feel as if it's a commitment I made a long time ago because I thought it would make me happy, but that now I'm just sticking with it out of habit. Which is sort of how I felt about you, before we broke up. Whatever. In any case, I hope Bloomington is treating you well.

No longer yours,
Selah

P.S. Love to Lump.

After she finished writing, Selah opened the small, wooden jewelry chest that sat atop her dresser and pulled out the silver Buddhist talisman that her grandmother had given her when she turned thirteen. Her parents had allowed her to wear it because of the family connection, though they'd discouraged putting it on too often out of fear that it was an invitation to demons. Selah had always loved it, though, and now she clasped the chain around her neck and lifted up the false bottom of her jewelry chest to grab her glass pipe and her weed.

She didn't usually indulge while anyone else was home, but she somehow felt the desire tonight. In fact, she found that she was salivating a bit as she unfolded the foil wrapper that held the last, leafy nugget. There wasn't as much as she had expected, and a brief pang of paranoia led her to wonder if one of her roommates had been rummaging in her room to steal from her stash. But then she realized that these suspicions were absurd, and that if she thought rationally about the situation she would realize that she had known she was low when she finished smoking this morning. So she set aside such thoughts and packed herself the single bowl she had left, which pretty much wiped her out for the evening. She read the words of a book that she didn't care about while she listened to some wordless, electronic music, and she drifted around on the internet—between blogs and Facebook—and then she went to bed, happy at least that she had the next day off.

The California Peace Action meeting that I was supposed to go to with Karen fell on a Wednesday night. I'd asked her if she wanted to get an early dinner first, since the meeting started at 6:30, but then at the last minute I had to take a shift from my boss's son, whose car had broken down somewhere in the North Bay while he was out scouting books. So Karen and I had to revise our plans. Instead of taking the afternoon off, I was now supposed to work from ten to six, and then Karen was going to meet me in front of the store and we'd walk to the lecture hall on campus together; I told Judas that we'd just see him there. But anyway, that's how I wound up meeting Nicholas Bendix.

I was minding the store alone, and the only customer I'd seen for the past hour—a regular browser who rarely bought anything—had just left; so I was taking the opportunity to do a little shelving, and I didn't immediately see Bendix enter. He caught me off guard, actually, as I rounded the corner from Philosophy to True Crime: a pointy-bearded man in a black satin jacket, who wore his white hair bowl cut, somewhere between the style of an ancient Roman and an early Beatle.

"I think you have a book that I desire," he said, twisting his little finger into the conch of his left ear, which unduly disgusted me.* And, long story short, the book he was looking for was the *Ars Magica*. A friend of his from the Theological Union up the hill had seen it in the glass case and told him about it. Which understandably made me nervous. I panicked. At first I acted like I didn't know what he was talking about.

"Might you at least consult your log of books to let me know for what price it was sold?" he asked.

---

* Much of what is considered "proper"—chewing with your mouth closed, not farting in public, etc.—involves not reminding others that we inhabit bodies that must do things like eat, shit, and die. And, now that I think about it, that also demonstrates the importance of comma placement.

I was disheartened to learn that he knew of our rare books log.

"Just a sec," I said, and went to get the log from behind the counter. I made a show of flipping around for half a minute or so towards the back of the book, and then I just said, "Hmm, the entry doesn't seem to be in here." And that much was the truth, as I'd erased the entry right after I stole the book. "We must have forgotten to enter it. I think it was going for about a hundred bucks, though."

He squinted at me intently. "What did you say your name was?"

"Thomas."

"Well, Thomas, I thought you said you didn't know the book."

My tongue was exploring the insides of my cheeks in search of what to say. "I think I recall it now."

He stroked his beard and puckered his lips, looking at me like he was considering kissing me good night. "A hundred dollars; well, that's quite a steal. Perhaps the owner took it home to re-evaluate it? Might he have removed the listing till he brings it back to sell?"

"Um, I really wouldn't know."

Bendix squinted at me again. "So when is he supposed to next be in? I'd like to ask him of the book myself. Perhaps he might recall to whom he sold it. Or he could point me towards a fruitful path."

"You know, he's going to be out for a few days, I think. But I'll be talking to him soon, and I'd be happy to take your phone number and get back to you about it myself."

His pause seemed to dilate into infinity before me, as if I

were nearing the event horizon of a black hole, only asymptotically approaching the moment of my arrival. But finally he nodded and handed me a card with his name and number, which he pulled from a small metal case. "See what you can devise, and let me know," he said. And then he smiled.

Selah pressed the "End" button, sat up in bed, and pondered the meaning of the fact that her drug dealer's number had been disconnected from the cell phone to which it had once been tethered. This wasn't a completely unexpected development; he changed his number all the time, just as a precaution against the law. But he usually told Selah what his new number was going to be before he changed the old one. Which left her now in a quandary. Had he been arrested? Or, worse, had he abandoned her? Could she have offended him in some way: canceled an appointment for a pickup once too often?

"Fuck," she said. She was suffering from a migraine and really could have used a bit of weed this morning, even more so than every other morning lately.

She got up and walked to the bathroom with half-closed eyes to piss and take a painkiller that she knew in advance would be ineffectual. She had just flushed when she heard the sound of her phone ringing. *Can it somehow miraculously be him?* she hoped. But when she picked it up she saw that it was only Rebecca, calling from work.

"What's going on?" Selah groaned. "Did I forget to pay a bill? Am I supposed to meet you for lunch?"

"No," Rebecca said. "We didn't make plans or anything. But do you think we could, if you don't already have anything else going on? Meet for lunch, that is. My treat. You don't work today, right? Or is this one of the days that you teach? Because I think I left my cell phone in my bathroom, on top of the toilet, and I would totally be your best friend forever if you would bring it to me at work."

"Sure, I guess?" She winced at the pain in her head as she spoke. "Today's my day off. But let me just make sure it's here." She did, and it was, and they made plans to meet in a couple hours. It was already almost eleven. She looked at her unmade bed and groaned. But by the time she had showered and readied herself to go meet Rebecca, she had come up with a brilliant plan that made everything else seem like kismet.

What had that guy's name been? Chad? No, Mark. Yes, she found the name in Rebecca's phone and copied the number over to her own. Even if selling Adderall to college kids was the main source of his income, there was no way that an East Bay drug dealer wouldn't at least know someone else who could hook her up with some weed. She decided that she would give him a call after lunch.

For the rest of the day I was so preoccupied with the thought that Bendix was going to expose me to my boss that I almost forgot that Karen was supposed to meet me after my shift. I'd experienced another one of those embarrassing, defining moments that I was talking about earlier, and it was eclipsing everything else. I decided that I would bring the book back to the store the next day and call Bendix and say that I'd found it in the back room, and offer to sell it to him—but I couldn't help imagining all of these scenarios in which I was still found out: that he would come in some other time when my boss was there and mention the whole affair to him, or that my boss would notice that the new entry in the rare books log was in my handwriting instead of his. And I wasn't just worried about the fact that I didn't want my boss to fire me; I was worried that he would find out I was a bad person. And even as I was thinking this, it took me a while to realize that for him to find out that I was a bad person must mean that I actually was a bad person.

It can be hard to recognize the wrongness within yourself until you imagine it being exposed to someone else, but in those hours I felt as if I were staring in horror at the foulness of my own soul, through a magnifying glass, and that it was smoldering in the focal point. Further, I felt vaguely nauseated with the realization that—while in some token sense I didn't want to be labeled a bad person—I didn't have enough of an innate conscience to prevent me from acting badly when it served my immediate interests. Yet strangely I found this thought inspiring.

We come into this world as empty vessels, yet every moment that passes fills us with the sediment of experience, and animal spirits of every variety, good and bad, burrow their paths through this sediment, urging us to all manner of reaction to experience. Joy or jealousy at another's success. To fight or flee. To lie or tell the truth. And the spirits that we habitually indulge are the ones that grow strong. The ones that we allow to cut their paths early and often have an easier way to make through the sediment of years. Who could I be, I wondered, if I were the best me that I could imagine?

Mark—the drug dealer who had once been on a date with Rebecca, and who had said that he might attend a party in Berkeley that weekend—set up an appointment with Selah to meet him at his place in Richmond at six o'clock, which, even after Selah's lunch with Rebecca, gave her a few hours to kill before she could get anything to relieve her migraine. So when she got home, to distract herself, she pulled out her journal and started writing Adam another letter that she never planned to send.

> Dear Adam,
>
> I know it does you no good to read this (or to not read this, as the case may be), but I am not living the life I want to lead. I am trying hard to figure out what makes me happy, but so far all of my answers seem incomplete and provisional. They can all make me happy in the moment, but none of them seem to contribute to any sort of inner peace. They inflate my balloon, but with carbon dioxide rather than helium, and they don't even tie off the mouth. So all I have figured out is that I get fleeting joy from the following things:
>
> 1. Being adored by someone.
> 2. Having a crush on someone.
> 3. Pot and occasionally alcohol.
> 4. Sex.

5. Children, when they're opening birthday presents or just intensely enjoying themselves.
6. Amusing others with what I say.
7. Amusing myself with what I think.
8. Reading. Actively reading, and writing down my thoughts about reading, until the latent patterns of meaning that I faintly perceive are made perfectly apparent.
9. Praise from others about how smart or beautiful I am. Though, strangely, my family's praise doesn't do anything for me on these scores, while their censure stings unusually hard.

But I suppose that all of the aforementioned can also cause me anxiety, given the right circumstances. That is, I strive for these things and then feel uncomfortable when I receive them. Which is part of a larger problem that I've discovered about myself. My worst nightmares are often also my secret fantasies: I both worry and hope that someone is going through my journals, reading my emails, listening to me and writing down my best ideas, stealing them from me. There was a time when people thought of themselves as the protagonists of imaginary novels, read by imaginary audiences. Now it occurs to me that many people have become the protagonists of actual blogs, or at least feeds, read by actual audiences, instead. I don't know if this is good or bad, or neither good nor bad. Regardless, I don't blog, and I'm not very active on any social-networking sites, so I'm stuck in the old model: an imaginary protagonist.

Feeling like this is egotistical, but it's a curious sort of egotism. It's an egotism at a remove. A protagonist is not the subject at the center of the universe but rather the object, existing only in the consciousness of the audience. The reader of a story is primary, and the main character only secondary. A blogger, for instance, at least gets to tell her story and then instantly have readers hold her in her consciousness—which makes for a more immediate form of existence. But what does it say about me that you're my audience and yet I never send these letters to you? Does that mean that I only exist in the hypothetical consciousness that I imagine for you? It's confusing. So please let me know.

Love of a sort,
Selah

And then, when she had finished this letter, she supposed that it was time for her to get in her car and go.

It's not easy to maintain the right balance between thought and action—reaching that point where you're acting in the moment, and you know exactly what you're doing, but you're not thinking about it enough to paralyze yourself with self-consuming overthought. It's not easy, but it can be done. Drugs and alcohol are false shortcuts; they can help you to act more impulsively and directly, sure, but they also cloud any accurate sense of self-awareness, and what I'm talking about is living in a moment without being completely oblivious to what's happening within it.

I think lack of awareness is the problem that most people tend to have in striking this balance: living outside of their means or just generally managing time poorly—spending hours browsing the internet when they're supposed to be working. But overthought tends to be the bigger obstacle for me; trying just to do something, whatever that something may be—dancing, running, fucking—sounds straightforward, but I've found that the mind is capable of fighting you every step of the way in these things, twisting its strands of thought around you until its grip is tight enough to pull you up out of the action itself. If it's not worrying about how stupid you probably look to everyone else on the dance floor, then it'll start counting the beats, marveling at the polyrhythms that you've managed to attune the various parts of your body to, and then, in the very act of watching, it'll throw everything off and take advantage of the ensuing panic to reassert a bit of its customary control—which will then, of course, just fuck things up.

And if the situation is fucking instead of dancing, well, that makes it all the more awkward. Let's say it's the first new woman you've had sex with since the painful severing of a long and serious relationship. You're nervous; you've maybe made out a few times, but nothing more, and she's invited you to a party at her place where you don't know anybody else, and so you drink a bit too much—or more than a bit; you're pretty drunk. And even halfway through the party, when she's a little drunk too, and the two of you start to get unreservedly affectionate, making out in the kitchen and the living room, right in front of all the other partygoers, including at least two other guys that she tells you she has hooked up with in the past, still you're feeling nervous, and you take a shot of citrus-flavored vodka when she asks you to help her get rid of it. And so you're even drunker. But then around three or four in the morning, you find yourself still with her as she's ushering everyone else out the door, and she turns to you and says, "You made it. I feel like you deserve a prize." And you just say, "Well, I get to kiss you, right?" Because even then sex just seems so far outside the realm of possibility. But then she grabs the bottle of Irish whiskey that you brought with you to the party, and she suggests having one last drink of it, together, in her bed. "So, this is my bed," she says. "It's where I spend a lot of my time." And so the two of you kiss some more, and you start to undress each other, and she comments on the softness of your flannel and the fur of your arms. You note the niceness of her boobs, the way they hang, neither too small nor so large as to sag. And so you're just thinking, *This is it. I didn't know this could happen again.* Thinking about the situation from a distance rather than just experiencing it in the moment. That last Irish whiskey, it isn't doing you any good. But so then you start to feel so happy—this is something that you want so much—that you start worrying about making sure that you don't do anything to spoil it. And that just winds up taking you even further out of the moment. Still, things proceed. There's music in the background, her iPod on shuffle: some Mozart, some Neil Young, both of which embarrass her, some Neutral Milk Hotel, which doesn't. She pulls out a condom from beside her bed—which you only pause briefly to consider, that she'd have one at the ready—and you haven't worn a condom in years, but on it goes, and now it's really happening, finally, and it's good, it feels good, it feels right, and she's beautiful beneath you, holding you, together with you, in this moment. But your mind doesn't stay in that moment for very long. Because now you start to overthink what you're doing. You know what the previous girl liked, but this is someone new, and you don't know if you should err on the side of too vigorous or too tender. And so you start slowly and just kiss her breasts a bit as you move gently within her. She does have nice breasts, nicer than the previous girl's. But—oh no!—gently, that means you've already chosen "too tender," and maybe you should change things up. And you're still thinking of this when she lightly slaps your ass a few times and says, "You like fucking, don't you?" And so you say, "I like fucking you. I like being inside of you," which again might be erring on the side of too tender, but then she lifts her legs up farther than the previous girl—who was quite inflexible—possibly could, and you don't know if you should grab them in your elbows and bend them up even farther, or rest them on your shoulders. And so instead you flip her over, and she turns her head back and smiles at you with her blue-green eyes. Or eyes that are neither the midpoint of blue and green nor resolvable as either blue or green . . . But then, instead of getting up on her knees, she lies flat, which again is different from what you're used to. Still you slap her ass a few times, since she slapped yours, which might indicate that it's something that she likes. And she does have a nice ass. And for a moment you find that you're enjoying yourself again as you squeeze each cheek and slide into her from behind. But you're drunk, really drunk, and you're worried, and you don't know if she's having a good time or just feigning it—you have to trust her, right?—because she eventually turns over again and wraps her legs around you, pulls you hard into her as you kiss her, hovering over her face and staring into those blue-green eyes (what should you call them? bleen?), and she says, "Come for me." And you suddenly realize that you can't. That you won't be able to. The alcohol, the self-consciousness, the condom. Whatever the reason, you know in this moment that you won't be able to come. Not tonight. And you start worrying that she will see this as an inability to perform, and that it will mark the end of what you had hoped to be a budding relationship, and that only makes you more self-conscious and all the more unlikely that you *will* be able to perform. And this is the worst moment of your life. Or it feels like it. And so you eventually just pull out and roll over and make some awkward comment that you immediately wish you could forget. And soon you're both just lying there embarrassed. You don't say anything else for maybe half a minute; and then you lie, trying to use language to pave over the truth that your bodies both know. "That was great," you say. "Maybe we can try that again in the morning." And, thankfully, she offers a reciprocal lie. You consider offering to go down on her, then—not because it's something that you particularly want to do at the moment (even though you enjoy cunnilingus quite a bit whenever you manage to let yourself go), but, rather, out of the same, self-conscious urge that messed everything up in the first place. But no, that's too much: too intimate for a first time together. And so you say nothing, just lying there feeling embarrassed. Happy that this has happened, feeling that it was something special despite being less than ideal in the execution. But also embarrassed. In the morning, though, when you wake up and try again, the weight of the previous night's failure makes you overthink everything even more, and you once again fail to come—despite this never having happened to you prior to the previous night, and despite the fact that you're no longer incredibly drunk: no external excuses this time. And sure, maybe after fifteen minutes of mechanical passion you manage to trigger the desired physical reaction within her, but now—even though this is the thing that you were supposedly striving for all this time—it feels hollow. Or not just hollow, but as if there were a vacuum in the center of it.

Like when you were a kid and you were out at the corner store with your older brother, and your mom had given him money specifically to buy each of you something to drink, and when you got there you said you wanted a can of cola, and he said okay, seeming nice for once, and he went to the refrigerated section and grabbed an RC, your favorite, and brought it up to the counter and paid for it, but then walked outside without handing it to you, popped it open, and drained it all in one long, bullfrog-throated pull.

"Here you go," he then said, handing you the can, and he followed this with a long belch.

And so you had the can, which was technically what you had asked for—or at least close enough for your brother to take amusement at his own cleverness—but even though it resembled what you'd said you wanted, it wasn't actually anything like it at all. And that's the way mind and language can play tricks on you. Because you should have just been trying to have a meaningful relationship with your brother, and then he would have bought you the drink without your even asking. Or something. It's not a perfect analogy.

It's hard to avoid this sort of overthinking, though, which is why the longer route to enlightenment—or to finding the balance along the grass-blade edge of self-awareness—can actually be a little more reliable, even if it takes more dedication. Basically you just have to learn to take your awareness out of yourself—leave it floating above you. Because if you can't avoid it, you need to learn to control and focus it: get to the point where you exist within the repeated register of awareness that you're dancing or doing the dishes or whatever else without going any further. Or, when other thoughts do try to creep in to comment or just closely observe—which, make no mistake, they will—you can use your new mastery over your awareness to shut them down.

"No!" you can say. "Not now. I'm busy dancing. There will be plenty of time for thinking later, when we're walking home, remembering the girl we were dancing with, and wishing that she were still with us and that we would soon be fucking." Which, I suppose, can be painful enough.

"Now, you aren't what I was expecting at all," the man whom Selah supposed to be the drug dealer said when he opened the door.

She was standing out in the fluorescently lit hallway of his dingy Richmond apartment building; the door had felt hollow as she'd knocked, and the hallway carpet was imbrued with the smell of cigarette smoke. The guy standing there before her had an appearance that was simultaneously imposing and comforting: somewhat brutish in musculature and dress—wifebeater, baggy jeans hanging halfway down around his plaid boxers, and a snap-brim cap more commonly found on British cabbies than on Bay Area drug dealers—but friendly in his smiling face.

She'd somehow expected him to be black, but he was white. She wondered if this made her racist, or if it at least meant that her Californian Korean upbringing had had more effect on her than she'd realized. "Mark?" she asked after a pause.

"Yeah. Selah, right?" She nodded, and he smiled. "Becky never told me you were Asian. I figured from your name that you were Jamaican, or Guyanese, or something more reggae."

"She told you about me?"

He cocked his head in a kind of shrug. "Well, she never told me you were Asian. So what is it, then? Your name, I mean?"

"My parents are religious," she said. "Seventh-day Adventists, and they gave us all biblical names: my brother, my sister, and me. Mine's from Psalms. It supposedly means something like 'pause and reflect'—like you're singing a psalm, but then you come to a part where you're supposed to stop for a minute and think about what you just sang. Or whatever. I mean, no one's really sure about the exact meaning of the word." She felt a blush coming over her face, though the words were rote. "I actually lucked out, I guess, relatively speaking. My brother and sister got stuck with Simeon and Dorcas."

"Cool," Mark said. "Well, come on in."

"So how did you meet Rebecca?" she asked. The living room was all cheap IKEA: a metal-framed futon, a rickety wooden coffee table with a clean ashtray in the center, and a half-filled bookshelf with the fiberboard back hanging halfway off its nails; she noticed the mass of James Tutku Jones's *The Impermanence of Frailty* alongside the distinctive spines of Hal Auerbach's *Brother* and *Sister:* perhaps a complete collection. But no more than three people could sit here comfortably for any length of time. No TV, which surprised her, until she noticed the digital projector sitting on a platform opposite a blank white wall. Only two doors led from the room: one, she presumed, led to a tiny bathroom and the other to a tiny bedroom.

"I met Becky at a party," Mark said, turning the dead bolt. "I think so, at least. It's actually kind of hard to remember. Maybe we were in a class together. Have a seat."

Is he going to rape me? Selah thought, sitting down on the couch and fingering the Buddhist charm that hung around her neck. "So, you went to Berkeley too?" is what she said aloud.

He smiled at her again and walked over to the far side of the counter that marked where the living room area became the kitchen. "Yeah. I still do, as a matter of fact. One more year. Can I get you something to drink?"

"I'm all right."

He took a glass from the sink and filled it from the tap. She figured that he was in his midtwenties at least, if not quite as old as she was—old for an undergrad. And almost as soon as she thought it, he accounted for the fact by explaining that he had been a late starter on the education front, and that now he was trying to pay his own way through college—to make something of himself—after a misspent youth in which he'd been a tagger and a burglar, in addition to a drug dealer.

"Well, I still do a little tagging," he said. "And I guess you know about the drug dealing. But not much burglary anymore. Only in the name of SOFA. I'm like an activist, you know."

"SOFA advocates burgling?"

"Viv thinks you should live life as if the world were already the way you want it to be: take your desires for reality. So I live as if wealth were distributed in a more equitable way."

"You know him personally, or is that just some propaganda?"

"I do some work for him. But all you really have to do to be a member is to consider yourself one."

"Right. There is no god but Revolution, and Viv is its prophet."

"You're funny, you know that?"

"So what does SOFA actually stand for, anyway?"

"Many things to many people. The message is in the actions, you know, not the words. That's why I do what I do for him, rather than, like, getting out on the streets and proselytizing."

Selah silently debated whether or not it would be rude to ask him how doing the same things he'd always done was supposed to be taken for political action and simultaneously make up for a misspent youth, but then—again, before she could ask—he'd already answered.

"But anyway, the drugs are just how I'm paying my way. I'm planning to give it up as soon as I have my degree."

"And how does a degree fit into your big plan? I mean, why not just live as if you have one already?"

For the first time he looked less than comfortable. "Well, I'm mostly in it for the education itself. You have to understand the system if you're going to change it."

She nodded. "That's cool. I mean, you know, I'm not one to judge."

He took a sip of water. "So, you just need an eighth?"

She was thinking that it would be better to buy an ounce, since that would be cheaper, but then something else in her was thinking that it would be nice to have an excuse to see Mark again sooner. He was amusing. She wasn't into him, exactly; she knew that she would never sleep with him; but then she asked herself how she knew this. It wasn't that she found him unattractive, but he just wasn't particularly her type. Still, if there had been that unpredictable initial spark—which there hadn't been, so why was she thinking about this—he was someone in whose features she could have found much to admire. He had a nice smile.

"Yeah," she said. "I think an eighth should last me a while. I don't really smoke that much."

"Your call. I can give you a better rate on an ounce." He smiled again. "I mean, you know, I'm not one to judge."

She turned her eyes away only to turn them back immediately, looking at him again as if for the first time.

"An eighth should be fine."

He started to move towards the door that she presumed led to the bedroom, and he placed his hand on the knob. But then, before he opened it, he turned his head back to look at her. "I'm not trying to be forward," he said. "But do you want to fuck me?" He squinted his eyes at her slightly. "Because you've got a look like you want to fuck me."

She felt an apprehension equal parts terror and eagerness. Her breath caught in her throat, and her immediate instinct was to just get up and say, "I have to go." Instead she kept sitting there on his couch, staring at him as he returned her stare, and she took a moment to pause and reflect before answering.

"Maybe," she finally said.

I won't dwell on the details, but things didn't work out exactly as I had planned. At the California Peace Action meeting, I was preoccupied and inattentive, caught up in my own thoughts rather than engaged in the moment. And I was annoyed that Judas was hanging around, making Karen laugh, being charming and funny, cracking jokes about all of the fighting that was going on at the meeting, and distracting her from me. It really was kind of laughable, though, with all of the conflict over peace: all of these different groups crowded into a little amphitheater-style lecture hall, each focused on its own agenda rather than the mutual goal that had brought them together. They'd just voted to exclude a group called BAMN (By Any Means Necessary) from further participation in the coalition for being too extreme, and it looked as if Spartacus Youth would be the next to go.

"You're just treating the symptoms," the SY spokesman was shouting down to the coalition chairman, who was standing at a podium in the front of the room. "The only lasting solution to the core problem that causes this and every war is via worker's revolution, scrapping the current fascistic, capitalist state, dismantling the military-industrial complex, and starting over with a truly Trotskyist government, by and of the people." He really did speak in such trite stock phrases.

"I don't think violence is a solution to anything," the chairman murmured, leaning too closely into the microphone.

"Yes!" a young woman in the audience cried. "Men only shed each other's blood because they can't menstruate on their own!"

Before the Spartacus Youth spokesman could respond to either comment, the conversation was taken over by a man with a bullhorn arguing at unpleasant volume that the real issue here was that the war on terror was actually a war on minorities, and that what was therefore most pressing was the establishment of an independent College of Ethnic Studies within the university, as that would make it possible to expose the underlying ideologies that had led the United States into war in the first place. Viv LaRevolution was there, too—as I learned later that night—but this was back before he'd dreamt up SOFA, back when he was still using his dad's surname instead of making up his own. Anyway, I didn't notice him at the time.*

But so it went, with Karen taking notes, Judas cracking jokes, and me just sitting there as my mind bounced back and forth between annoyance with him—wishing he would just leave already—and the thought that Nicholas Bendix would soon expose me to my boss, and that I'd be either fired or arrested. At some point, around 7:30, as the coalition was trying to decide whether or not they should write out antiwar messages and fold them into paper airplanes that they would then launch from the top of the Campanile—which some viewed as littering and others viewed as ineffectual, arguing that instead they should do something big, like block Interstate 80 where it passed through Berkeley, and that they should do it tonight—I decided without any equivocation that I should leave.

"Do you have enough for your project?" I asked Karen.

She looked first at her notes and then at me. "Um, no, I should probably stay till the end of the meeting, just to see how this turns out."

---

* This meeting was a key moment in the history of SOFA in general and the Apocalypse in particular, not least because some of those causing the chaos were police stooges, which inspired Viv's own implementation of impostors and infiltrators.

"I guess I had a long day," I said. "How about you, Judas? Feel like heading home?"

"No way," he said. "This is far too fun."

I nodded, and I think in that moment I was just as annoyed with Karen as I was with Judas. I was fairly confident that she liked me, and yet she wanted to stay here with him and all of these other ridiculous people rather than leave with me. I knew this was an unfair, irrational sentiment even as I felt it, but it was nevertheless quite real to me, and in my distemper I rose as angrily as I could and said that I'd just head home on my own then.

"All right, see you later," Judas said.

Karen looked at me again, made eye contact, and I could see that there was something like confusion and sympathy in her eyes. "Are you sure, Thomas?" she asked. "I mean, I don't really think it can last that much longer."

"Yeah, my headache can't take much more of this."

She nodded. "All right. So should we give you a call when it's over? Maybe we could all go out for a drink or something."

It took me a moment to nod. "Okay. I think I just need to get a little rest, maybe some food in me."

And so I left them together, and I walked home alone, warmed by an inarticulate anger and embarrassment.

Over the course of the next few weeks, Selah started to see Mark quite a bit. On some level she knew, or at least felt, that she was making a mistake. And on another level, she felt that she had absolutely no idea what she was doing. But despite these being her dominant feelings, she nonetheless continued to see him. He had his charms, she told herself. He made her laugh, and he always had something interesting to say. More important, he had proven to be a sympathetic listener. Though as she thought this last, another voice rose within her head to say that sympathy was fine, and that she appreciated sympathy, but that his was the sympathy of a charmed snake, moving not to the music but to the rhythm of the musician. When he was kind to her, she was never sure whether he was lovelorn or just horny. But in the end it didn't matter, because he was satisfying some urge within her that needed satisfying, and he was making her feel something again after a few months of numbness. She tried to express this feeling in one of her unsent journal letters.

Dear Adam,

I've met someone, and I think I'm verging on happiness with him—at least a happiness of the fleeting, momentary sort. I know this can't last, but I think it's something I need to be doing right now. When I'm with him, I feel almost good, and that's a nice change of pace. A cat is probably happy when it's lapping up antifreeze. I don't want you to think that it's all about the sex, but I'd be lying if I didn't admit that that's a big part of it. I don't want to say that he's better than you in bed; he's just different, in a good way. You were loving and attentive, yes, but you also entered me as if you were entering a church.

Which is not to say that Mark is a perfect lover. I mean, sure, he can go down on me for hours, which is kind of nice. Now, I don't literally mean "hours," as that would get boring and probably start to hurt, but more like a long while, and the intensity of the pleasure is perhaps equal to the value of hours of labor. But his flaw is that he's so into knowing that he can go down on me for hours, and I can tell that he expects me to be impressed. I hope you don't mind me writing to you about this. Amelia would think I was trying to take her place as the roommate who talks about sex if I tried to tell this to her. And she would be angry if she knew that I had referred to her as "the roommate who talks about sex." So I still haven't told her or Rebecca that I'm even seeing him. I don't even spend the night at his place, just because I don't want them to realize that I'm seeing anyone seriously enough to do that. So let's make a deal: you never tell her I wrote that about her, and I'll never send you this letter.

Affectionately,
Selah

But what she didn't mention here was the most awkward part of her lovemaking with Mark, because she didn't know how to express it, even in an imaginary letter. There was something within herself that she was ashamed of, and which she hadn't ever really faced, but which somehow came out when they were having sex, and which was, perversely, an integral part of her enjoyment of the sex. It had started that first night, while she was confused, incredibly high on the weed that he'd sold her, and only sort of half believing that any of this was actually happening. He was heaving above her, his crappy box spring creaking below her, and he was staring straight into her eyes, and she'd just suddenly blurted out, "Don't look at me."

He didn't stop moving within her, but he screwed up his face a little and said, "What? You want me to stop?"

"No," she said. "Keep going. But just don't look at me. Imagine that I'm someone prettier."

He nodded a few times, his expression still confused, before he tilted his head upwards and closed his eyes.

"No," Selah said. "Keep them open. Just don't look at me."

He opened his eyes, and his expression was more confused than ever, but then he looked straight ahead, at the wall, and moved his hands from where they'd been massaging her breasts to place them lightly around her neck.

"Is that okay?" he said in a low voice, without looking down.

"Yes," she said. "Now pretend that I'm someone pretty."

"You're beautiful."

"No," she said. "Someone else pretty. She's beautiful. Not me."

He shook his head and tried to do as she requested.

Afterwards, he tried to have a conversation with her about it, saying nothing about how strange it had seemed to him, just trying to feel out if it was a normal thing for her. She was too embarrassed to engage with the issue directly, but then it happened again the next few times, and finally she broke down and started crying afterwards and asked him if he thought she was a total freak. They were lying in his bed, and he sat up and placed a pillow between his back and the wall behind him before he answered her.

"Viv says that freakiness is just emotional instinct unhindered by consideration of social norms," he told her, in one of those moments that made her wonder who he really was. "It's saying what you mean without worrying about what anyone else thinks. So you might be a freak, but I wouldn't say that's necessarily a bad thing."

She nodded and tried to take what he said for what it was worth. She was always surprised at his ability to slip back and forth between thuggishness and sensitivity, and she decided that this was one of the things that she liked about him. In fact, she should try to make a list of things that she liked about him, she thought. And this was also her way of averting her mind from the sort of self-contemplation that had scared her and made her cry.

When I got home, I made myself a pitcher of iced tea and sat down at the kitchen table to wait for Karen and Judas to call me. This was in the days before cell phones had become quite so pandemic, but I trusted that one of them would be able to find a pay phone or something. It was about eight o'clock, and I was still thinking vaguely of Bendix and the possibility of being found out as a thief. But now it was all tied together in a general stomach knot of doom from which I couldn't be bothered to tease the individual strands. I tried to distract myself by reading an article about the Dalai Lama in the latest issue of *Byner's*, but I couldn't concentrate, and I found that I was two pages into the fiction piece before I realized that I'd missed the note in the bottom of one of the article columns that had said "Continued on Page 88." So I tossed the magazine across the room, and I took a long gulp of my tea. I thought about Bendix, and I thought about getting up to read the *Ars Magica*, but instead I just sat there. I drank the entire pitcher of tea within half an hour, and I threw up about fifteen minutes after that—from too much caffeine, I suppose, or just too much liquid. When I'd cleaned myself up, I went in my room and lay down on my bed, with all of the lights off and my portable phone in my hand. I didn't plan to sleep. I put on some music and tried not to think. Soon, though, I was dreaming.

I dreamt of a future in which Judas and Karen were both living with me, and they were dating each other, and their happiness waxed in direct proportion to my misery. But then I recalled that I had a book of magic at my disposal, and I tried to craft spells that would transfer her affections to me.* In the dream, though, my spells were all crude and beside the point, and not at all like the methods actually described in *Hodge's Ars Magica*. I mixed my bodily fluids with her shower products. I stole her hair and nail clippings and made them into boluses that I would take as a daily medicine. I made our names into runes and twined the letters together, and I tattooed the resulting symbol onto the soles of her feet as she slept. But nothing

* In actual practice, when the problem is desire, sometimes the best magical solution doesn't involve trying to satisfy the desire, but rather trying to eliminate it, overcome it, or replace it with something else. The practice of magic is about asserting one's will, but will is not identical with desire. Revenge, for instance, can sometimes serve as a fair compensation for desire thwarted. Heathcliff, from *Wuthering Heights*, is perhaps the best literary example of a model magician, overcoming all obstacles by transforming himself into someone who no longer wants that which has been denied him and then accomplishing a compensatory goal through sheer force of will, letting nothing sway him from his path.

worked, and in the end I realized that I had only made myself reprehensible. And then, just as I was about to face myself in the bathroom mirror, I woke up.

The album I'd been listening to had ended, and I knew that it was exactly fifty-six minutes long. I lay there for a bit in the silence and the darkness before it occurred to me that I still had the phone in my hand, and that it definitely hadn't rung. I needed to distract myself, I thought. I rose from the bed and padded out to the living room. I thought about the bottle of Scotch in the cupboard but rejected the idea of drinking alone, and instead I sat down on the couch and turned on the TV. I was, of course, rather surprised to see Judas and Karen on the screen.

"I don't do any of those murals or shit," Mark explained to Selah when they were out at a bar in Berkeley one Saturday evening. An undergrad-type place, loud and crowded, as opposed to the more laid-back establishments that she tended to frequent with her fellow grad students. "And I don't touch anything that's owned by a real actual person: just corporate or state-owned property. That's one of Viv's rules. I do a lot of work for him."

"What sort of stuff?"

"Sigils. Propaganda. Messages for those in the know. Mostly though I just do my tag. I do that for me, I mean."

"And what's your tag?"

"Kernel."

She took a sip of beer. "Does it mean something?"

He gave a shrug that seemed to indicate that her question was somehow frivolous. "It's like an amalgamation of all kinds of different shit," he said. "I like Kern's fruit juice. My dad was a colonel in the navy. I went to high school in Kern County. But it's just too complicated to get into, really."

"Tell me about that."

"About what?"

"Growing up. Were you a military brat? What's in Kern County? What were you like in high school?"

He squinted at her and smiled. "Born, raised, and trapped? Not me; I lived with my mom. Bakersfield is in Kern County. I can take you there, if you want. I'm heading down in a couple weeks to meet with some associates of mine. Picking up some stuff for Viv. Big event next month, you know."

"And why does he need drugs for that?"

"Revolution is magic. Gotta get in an altered state to alter the state."

"So he's just another pothead hippie. That kind of demystifies things."

"No, it's not like that. He's cool."*

---

* Of course, as it turned out, Viv didn't intend the drugs for personal use; that is, they were to play an integral role in the coming Oakland Apocalypse, dosing civilians and police alike, but at this point the details of how were known only to Viv himself. "Apocalypse," of course, means little more than "revelation": literally "a lifting of the veil" so that man might see what's behind the maya. And yet as the final book of the Bible—sometimes known as the Apocalypse of John—deals in revelations concerning end times, the word has come to possess a more sinister connotation. I'm fairly sure that all Viv had in mind for the SOFA Apocalypse was to reveal the underlying machinery of social injustice in

Mark continued. "So anyway, in high school I was pretty much the way you see me now. Not a nerd, not a jock. Did drugs, but still got into Berkeley. I wasn't anything you could really put into words, you know. And I'm still not. Which I guess is part of why I decided to put it all into one word: the Kernel."

Selah sighed. She liked to imagine that Mark had depths, but she also felt that he was just being evasive here in order to come off as more profound than he actually was—and worse, that she had fallen for it by ever assuming that he had depths. So she had little patience for his conversation just now. There had been other instances when she had found herself sighing and wondering why she continued to see him, but some instinctual part of her had always answered that the fact that she continued to see him was evidence enough that she had good reason. On this occasion, though, she pronounced her doubt aloud.

"What are we even doing together?" Her doubts were exacerbated by having spent a good deal of the previous evening on Facebook, comparing herself with other women she knew and feeling sorry for herself, and Mark had been part of that sorrow. These women—most of whom she'd known at least since her undergraduate days—all had kids, careers, or both, while she was pursuing a useless degree focused on a dying country

---

a way that was dramatic and unable to be ignored, specifically by implicating all within it—liberals and conservatives, rich and poor—*embarrassing them*, and hoping that the inherent horror of the sight when they saw themselves would be enough to inspire them all to toss their shoes into the gears.

and would never have a child of her own if she continued to waste her time with guys like Mark. "I mean, it doesn't make a lot of sense, does it?"

He shunted his puckered lips to one side, squinted, and asked what, exactly, she meant by such a comment.

"I don't know. Just, I don't know how this could lead anywhere. You're who you are, and I'm messed up."

He nodded, with a look that seemed genuinely wounded. "Who I am. A drug dealer, right? An outlaw."

"No. I mean, yes. Or I don't know. But it's just not part of the life I imagined for myself. It's like I was on my way to the candy store and someone gave me a slice of pizza."

He looked her in the eyes until he was sure that her gaze was locked firmly into his. "I understand that. It's not an easy thing to deal with. Not part of the everyday reality that most people ever have to face. But it's also why you like me. I'm Han Solo. You like me *because* I'm a scruffy-looking nerf-herder."

"My God, I thought you said you weren't a nerd." She shook her head, but she also laughed, and this had been the response he was hoping for. But then her laughter stopped when she saw Rebecca and Amelia approaching from the bar, each with a beer in hand.

"Hey?" Rebecca said, a question. "Did you get my message then?"

"Rebecca! Amelia! What?"

"The beau-friend's band is playing in San Jose," Amelia said. "So we decided to have a girl's night."

"I left you a voicemail," Rebecca said.

"I must have missed it." Selah had seen the incoming call but hadn't answered because she'd been with Mark. "Glad it worked out, though. I mean, apart from the girl's night aspect." She motioned to Mark.

"Long time no see," Rebecca said. "What happened to you coming to that party?"

"Couldn't make it."

"Hi, I'm Amelia."

"Mark. Nice to meet you. Do you guys want to have a seat?"

Within minutes, Mark, Rebecca, and Amelia were laughing, but Selah was so filled with embarrassment that she could hardly focus on what was being said. She felt blood warming her face and hoped that she could pass it off as Asian flush. She didn't know why she should be embarrassed—because she had never said anything about him, she supposed—but then she had never said anything about him because she was embarrassed. Because he was a drug dealer, then, as they'd just been talking about. Or no, not quite that either. She wasn't embarrassed on his behalf; she was embarrassed because the fact that he was a drug dealer was a reminder of the fact that she did drugs.

Well, all three of them did drugs on occasion, but Selah knew that she kind of had a habit. Not that she was an addict, but she could have perhaps been classified as a pothead. She thought of what her mother would say, certain that it would start off with the abstractly practical—how immoral it was to support the drug trade when it thrived on a system of violence—but that it would end with talk of the devil. Because she couldn't listen, then, either to the maternal voice in her head or to the voices of the people around her, who all seemed to be having a good time and not judging her at all, Selah began to bray.

"Mark is a tagger," she said.

"A tiger? In bed?" Amelia asked.

"No. Well, yes. That too. Hah! I meant that he tags. You know, graffiti. He's an activist outlaw." She paused, but not long enough to stop herself. "But yes, he is also an amazing lover."

Rebecca laughed, and it occurred to Selah that she didn't know whether Rebecca had ever slept with Mark. Rather than backing off, though, she pressed on. "It's almost like his penis has a penis." At which point she was mortified that such words might be coming out of her mouth.

And so on: deepening her embarrassment with every word but somehow caught up in the absurdity of it all, as if she were daring herself to see just how much shame she could bring on herself.

"You know what your problem is?" Mark said to her later that night, after they'd finished fucking and she had dried her tears. She hadn't been able to face going home with Rebecca and Amelia after the way that she'd made a fool of herself in front of them, and so for the first time she had agreed to spend the night at his place. "You talk too much."

This criticism came as a shock to her. If anything, she'd always thought that she was too quiet, but the source of her surprise wasn't so much in what he'd said but in the fact that he had said it.

"I know. I kind of shocked myself tonight."

He shook his head. "I'm not just talking about tonight. I mean in general. You talk about your plans, and you talk about your problems, and you know what they are, but you never do anything about them."

"I know." She wanted him to shut up, but he kept going. He

had a muscular arm around her, and she felt suddenly as if she couldn't escape.

"Viv says that language is the enemy of action," he said. "You need to realize that there's no need to put everything into words. Open worrying can be a self-fulfilling prophecy. Act as if everything is the way you want it to be. The way you are now, you're kind of a pussy. And I don't mean that in a sexist sense. Just, you tattoo your insecurity all over yourself with needles of worry. And it's not an attractive tattoo, like a Maori one. Or a Mara Salvatrucha."

"Last night I dreamt that I was in a tattoo parlor, and the artist had his needle ready," she said, recalling. "But I couldn't decide what it would be or where it would go. Finally, the guy just asked me if I wanted it to be representational or decorative, and I couldn't even decide on that."

Mark nodded and squeezed her closer to him.

"You should get a tiger," he said. "On your arm."

The news was reporting that the California Peace Action coalition had decided to block Interstate 80 after all. Or some of them had. Others had decided to smash shop windows on Telegraph Avenue instead—presumably because store owners were cogs in the capitalist machine that had manufactured the war in the first place. Police were out in riot gear trying to quell the crowds. I saw Judas and Karen in a wide shot of the Campanile, where the coalition chairman was trying to emphasize that not all of the protest being done in the name of the coalition was being done on behalf of the coalition. Just some of it. But apparently there was chaos on the streets, and I hadn't even realized it.

It was probably a combination of my nap and the shock of what I'd seen, but I had one of those sudden, time-frozen moments in which everything becomes lucid and clear, and I saw exactly what I had to do. I've said that embarrassing moments define us by making us want to be better people, and as embarrassed as I'd been lately, I felt that here was a moment in which I had a chance to be someone better. I guess it was partially seeing all of these people out there fighting for something they believed in; even if I thought their methods were stupid, I still kind of admired their willingness to take direct action. And for my own part—though I wasn't so concerned with the ethics of the United States' military forays in the Middle East—the idea that the girl whom I had a crush on was out experiencing this night with another man was something that I felt strongly opposed to, and so I decided to launch a protest of my own.* It was at this point that I thought once again of the *Ars Magica*, and it occurred to me that the most direct sort of love spell would just be to rush out into the night, and find her, and kiss

---

* Everything is significant, and metaphor reveals this truth: realizing that one thing is like another is a tool that helps us put life's fragments into some semblance of order. It's easy to feel meaning beneath the surface of things, but metaphor openly exposes meaning. Internal drama, angst, job worry, unrequited love, etc., all add meaning to the day, though it's not always easy to see how. When you have a crush on someone, for instance, every misspoken word to that person *is* the end of the world.

her. And so I put on my hooded sweatshirt, and I rushed out into the night.

Selah was filled with shame when she saw Rebecca on the Sunday evening following the Saturday night out at the bar. She'd stayed on campus most of the day, nominally doing research in the library, but actually just trying to work up the courage to go home. By five o'clock she'd thought she was ready, but her stomach still overturned with nausea when she walked in and found Rebecca standing in the kitchen.

"So, you're dating Mark?" Rebecca asked after a "hey" and a few moments' awkward silence.

"Um, I've seen him a few times. I wouldn't say we're dating."

"You should tell him that. At the bar, when you were in the bathroom, he told me he was taking you home to meet his mom."

"Hah. Not exactly. He asked me if I would drive him down to his hometown so he can buy drugs off some old friends of his. If we're supposed to meet his family, well, he hasn't run that past me."

"Hilarious. How'd you guys hook up, anyway?"

Selah tried to chuckle, but it came out more like the sound of confusion. "I went to buy some weed off him a few weeks ago. We hit it off, I guess." She left out the bit about getting his number from Rebecca's phone, though she was fairly sure that Rebecca wouldn't have minded.

"Wow." Rebecca stretched the word across three syllables. "I didn't think he'd be your type."

Selah closed her eyes and inhaled, and then she opened her eyes again. "Since when do I have a type?" she asked "And how would you know it? And besides, why not? I mean, you dated him, didn't you?"

"Whoa, let's slow down there. I went out on some dates with him, yeah, but I never drove him three hundred miles to buy drugs. For one thing, though, I guess I never thought we would have the same taste in guys, since you're always telling me how sleazy everyone is. And, no offense, but I know your type because we have, on occasion, talked about guys in the time we've lived together, and all the guys you've ever even talked about have kind of been on the nerdier end of the spectrum, at least in comparison with Mark."

Selah's shame shot out with an unexpected recoil of anger. "Sorry, I guess I should have asked you for permission, right?"

"What, no, I don't care. I'm not criticizing you—you can date whoever you want; I'm just saying I'm surprised."

Selah watched her feet as she shuffled on them. "I mean, it's not like I'm ever going to meet any guys who wouldn't rather date you, anyway, so how does it matter whether or not it's someone that you've actually already dated?" She spoke these words with less anger than before, realizing as they came out that they were based more on a previously unarticulated fear than in any actual belief.

Rebecca laughed aloud before she answered. "Oh my God." She took a breath and laughed again. "You do know how ridiculous you sound, right?"

It took a moment for Selah to stop and hear what she'd said, because her internal voice was hardly audible just then, but after a few seconds she was able to laugh. "Yeah, I guess," she said. "I'm just sort of embarrassed is all."

"Embarrassed? Why are you embarrassed?"

"I don't know." She sighed before smiling. "I guess because I never thought that someone like Mark would be my type."

My apartment building was only about a block and a half from University Avenue, on Bonita, and as soon as I emerged from the foyer door, I could see that the night's unease was more extensive than the television had led me to believe. A police car was parked, lights reeling vertiginously, at the intersection of Bonita and University; officers with shields were lining the sidewalk, and traffic in the street was paralyzed by the pedestrian mass advancing glacially west, in the direction of the interstate. I turned the other way, up to Hearst, and then started running east, towards campus. The air had developed a dry but clinging chill in the time since I'd come home, and I think I started running more in order to warm myself than to make it to the Campanile quickly.

Shattuck was crowded too, but not as bad as University, and I managed to make my way across without slowing down too much. I couldn't understand how so many could have been swept up in something that had started at a seemingly ineffectual meeting of about fifty crackpots, but I didn't give it much thought. I was more concerned about getting to Karen and making the most of the moment, in order to manifest a reality in which she and I would be together.

I should probably say that, even at this point, I was not of the mind that Karen and I were "meant to be together" in some cosmically preordained way, or that she was in any way "the one" for me. She was just a girl whom I happened to have a rather sizable crush on, and with whom I thought that I was pretty compatible, and so I thought that she and I might be able to have a fun and perhaps "meaningful" relationship, however brief or lengthy. I don't think I was blowing anything out of proportion, or investing any more significance in the situation than was actually there. It's just that something had finally clicked within me about how I had this tendency to find myself in situations like this without ever doing anything to help them progress beyond the realm of fantasy—how I hadn't ever been active in trying to make good things happen in my life—and that this was something I wanted to change about myself. So Karen seemed like a worthwhile place to start making that sort of change, and I felt inspired by this resolution.

When I reached the corner of campus, I decided that it would be best to use the less-traveled paths, away from the major plazas. I ran basically parallel to the west side until I came to the eucalyptus grove, and then I pushed through a break in the bushes to run through the grove itself instead of sticking to the pavement. When I made it to the other side, though, I didn't have much choice except to head up a fairly major route that led pretty straight to the Campanile. Even from a distance, I could see that quite a crowd had gathered. Again, with more police officers, and when I saw them this time my mind turned back to Nicholas Bendix and the idea that had been nagging me all night about how my boss might somehow find out about my theft of the *Ars Magica*, and that I could thus, perhaps, be arrested.* But then, in the next moment—taken, I suppose, for a violent protester despite the fact that I was neither protesting nor violent—I was hit in the back of the head with some sort of billy club, and I fell face-first into the wet grass.

One consequence of dating Mark was that Selah began to smoke even more weed than she had previously been prone to. It wasn't that she smoked much with Mark—for a drug dealer, he was surprisingly abstemious—but the knowledge that she could replenish her supply whenever she needed to had made her a bit more prodigal with what she had. Also, she could afford more, since he gave her a slight discount, and she had developed the habit of discreetly pocketing any nuggets that she happened to find lying around. She wasn't even pretending to work on her dissertation anymore, and she had a hard time recalling the last day she'd even been on campus with 100 percent accuracy. But she didn't really notice these changes in her own behavior—or at least she didn't consciously register them—until she got so stoned one morning, at her own place, that she slept through her shift at the bakery and even slept through

* My fears weren't completely unfounded, either. When Bendix came back to the store, he made it clear that he suspected me of having stolen the book, and that he'd toyed with the idea of telling my boss. But then he wound up just chatting with me about my interest in the subject, and I agreed to bring the book over to his house in the hills to discuss it with him over tea.

Max's phone calls when he tried to wake her and ask why she wasn't at work.

"Fuck," she said upon waking, though she wasn't fully aware of why she was upset until she picked up her phone to check the time and saw Max's multiple missed calls. To further complicate matters, she still felt too stoned to call him and explain herself. She couldn't think of a plausible excuse, and she didn't think she'd be able to coherently communicate such an excuse in any case. "Fuck," she said again, and then she plodded to the kitchen to pour herself some orange juice.

As she wasn't sure what else to do, she decided to call Mark. But he didn't answer. She'd never known him not to answer before. Shit, he must be mad at her about something, or ignoring her because he was with another woman. She set the phone down on the bed beside herself and took a deep breath. Then —just as she exhaled—it rang, and she immediately answered.

"I was worried," she said.

"So was I, or at least I was starting to, but now it's clear that you're alive, perhaps you'd like to explain what happened to you today. Otherwise you'll need to start worrying about finding a new job."

The realization that the person speaking to her was Max, her boss, rather than Mark, her boyfriend—or that was the wrong word, she didn't want to use that word, but she wasn't sure what to call him—eclipsed the content of the words.

"Max," she said. "I'm sick."

"You were too sick to call and let me know that you were sick?"

"I tried to call, but I was asleep. I took too much cold medicine last night."

"Well, be that as it may, we have other problems. I don't like to say it, but you are a problem to me, Selah. I think you know this. Even setting aside your chronic tardiness of late, there's also the fact that we tend to lose more pastries under your watch than can be accounted for by the sales."

"I wouldn't call my tardiness chronic." And then she couldn't help giggling at the word choice. "I mean, I don't feel tardy."

Max sighed. "I don't have time for this." He hung up.

"Shit," Selah said. And then she pulled out her journal.

Dear Adam,

I want to write to you right now for real, but I think I am still *ein bisschen abgefickt* by this pot that I have smoked. I know you don't speak German, but neither do I, really, so that's okay. I think I might be fired. And Mark didn't answer my call. What should I do? I think I might be depressed, and that all of these external events might just be the world's way of physically manifesting my depression. Or I would think that, if I were solipsistic. But I'm not. I think that I need a break: to go away somewhere and to not think about my life.

In other news, why am I still writing to you? Shouldn't I be writing to Mark at this point? Or does this somehow relate to the fact that I am hesitant to call him my boyfriend, even though he wants me to go to his hometown with him next weekend?

Yr obdt svt,
Selah

P.S. Eighteenth-century stylistic abbreviations didn't kill the English language, so why should modern ones? C U 18r.

Setting her journal aside, she held her head in her hands and tried to think about what she should do next. She knew that it would probably be wisest to go to the bakery and try to make things up to Max face-to-face, but she didn't think she could handle this. Instead, she grabbed her keys and went out to her car to drive up to Richmond to find out if Mark actually was sleeping with somebody else.

When I turned over, the cop was just staring down at me with his mouth hanging open. He was about my age, and I think he recognized his mistake pretty quickly, because he just turned and trotted off towards the Campanile. There were a few people walking past me, and I think they must have seen what had happened, but none of them stopped to help me, or to give me their names as witnesses, so I just lay there for a minute trying to bring my thoughts into something resembling coherence. The first fully formed idea to cross my mind, strangely enough, was that it probably wouldn't be worth the hassle of pressing charges. And then I rubbed the back of my head. It was a little sore, a lump, but there was no blood, at least.

So I wasn't really hurt, at least in a physical sense. But the whole experience had kind of disrupted the pure focus of will that had sent me rushing out to find Karen and to kiss her, and as I lay there, I felt that I didn't have the will to do much else anymore either. It seemed too much of an effort even to stand up, although I didn't feel that there was anything physically hindering me from doing so. I just turned my head towards the Campanile and vaguely wondered if Judas and Karen were still there. And that was the first time I saw Viv, with the big bell tower behind him, half a thousand paper airplanes flying from its peak, each with its own unique message of hope and peace, like an ironic reversal and deflation of 9/11. And if the idea had sounded idiotic and juvenile in the meeting earlier that night, it seemed glorious to me then.*

He was kind of huffing as he ran up to me, out of shape. Not someone you'd have expected to become the sort of larger-than-life figure that he is today: half Chinese, on the shorter side, with remnants of what had once been a major acne problem. Not exactly the picture of the charismatic leader. But even then he was charming, and he only honed that charm in the next few years.

"Holy fuck." Those were the first two words he ever spoke to me, and in a way they describe him better than any others. "I saw what happened. Are you okay?"

"No. I don't think I am."

"Let me get your information. I'm going to write an article about this for the *Daily Cal*." It's strange to recall that he had such mundane beginnings. In any case, he offered a hand, helped me from the ground, and I gave him my "information":

* While some commentators have pointed to the World Trade Center attacks as possible inspiration for the Towers of Ideological Apocalypse, I would argue that they were inspired much more directly by the Campanile this night.

name, abbreviated background, email address, and phone number. And that was how he got in touch with me a week later, after I was already starting to get involved with Bendix and his teachings. Which, incidentally, makes me a pretty major footnote in the history of how SOFA was founded.*

Anyway, so then I headed home. I don't know why I went from determination to despair so quickly, without any concrete, objective correlative for that despair; in those days I guess I was just sort of an emotional windsock. I went home, and I brooded, and Judas didn't get back himself until about three in the morning. I was awake. I recall thinking that at least he hadn't spent the night with her. A song was just ending when he tapped twice on my door.

"Come on in."

"Hey, how's it going?"

I reached over and turned on the reading lamp that sat on my bedside table. His cheeks were flush from the cold.

"I'm doing okay."

He walked into the room and took a seat sideways in the chair by my desk, and I sat up in bed and put some pillows against the wall behind me.

"Sorry we didn't call," he said, and I inwardly winced at the word "we." "I guess you probably saw how crazy things were out there. We couldn't find a phone."

---

* I think it fair to say that SOFA wouldn't have employed the methods that it does if I hadn't introduced Viv to Bendix. SOFA's model of "ideological activism" was basically indistinguishable from Bendix's conception of magic: half placebo, half propaganda.

"Yeah, no big deal. I was in a weird mood anyway. What wound up happening?"

He shrugged. "Not much, really. I mean, there were cops everywhere. I guess blocking the freeway was the big event, but I didn't really see any of that. There was supposedly some halfhearted attempt to start a looting riot on Telegraph, but I think it was like two guys, and they got arrested pretty quickly. We were just at the Campanile, though, and that was pretty tame. Protesters shouting at the cops and the cops just standing around, a few reporters interviewing that chairman guy. I don't know what it is exactly that makes modern times different from the sixties, but all in all this felt like a pretty cheap imitation."*

"I saw you guys on the news."

"Really? Wow, that's cool, I guess."

"Just in the background."

And then we were both silent for a moment, and I could feel a constriction in my chest as he bit his lips in thought.

"So, I kind of have some good news," he said.

"Oh?"

---

* Viv was disillusioned, too, though the difference between him and Judas was this: while Judas took the events of the night to indicate that protest in general was a dumb and passé concept, Viv took it as a challenge, prompting him to study the history of social movements in search of what had been lost, what could be salvaged, how old structures might be refurbished to fit a modern context, etc. He looked at Algeria, Tibet, Guyana, May '68, the SLA, the Weather Underground, the Zapatistas, the Seattle WTO protests, the Basque, even al-Qaeda. More important, he looked at the tactics employed by agents of the other side, like COINTELPRO. But he eventually found everything he was looking for in the teachings of Bendix.

"Yeah. I guess it's confirmed that Karen likes you."

This hadn't been what I was expecting to hear, and I wasn't sure how to respond. "What do you mean? How is it confirmed?"

He shrugged again. "She told me as much. I mean, I asked her."

I was sitting up straight now, no longer leaning back against the pillows. "You just randomly asked her? How did it come up?"

"Um, well, it's kind of a long story, I guess."

But I just turned a palm upwards in solicitude, and so he proceeded to tell it to me.

"You are useless to me right now," Selah said to Mark about thirty seconds after he let her in. "I don't need you high; I need you here to support me."

Mark smiled. "This is my friend: the one I was telling you about. I call him O. Carmen, but you can call him O." There was someone sitting on the couch whom she had never seen before, but she vaguely recalled Mark mentioning the name. Looking at him—bald, black, a few years older, and obviously built at one point, though he'd now gone to pot—she recalled that he was an ex-marine.

"What does the 'O' stand for?"

"Nothing, it's just my nickname for him. O. Carmen, Mike Harmon."

"Like my nickname for him is Markie Cunt."

"I don't get it."

"He thinks he's funny," Mark said. "Likes to give people offensive nicknames."

"I still don't get it."

"My last name, you know. Mark Seaward."

"Oh," Selah said.

"That's me," O. Carmen said.

It occurred to her only then that she had never thought to ask Mark's last name before, and this didn't improve her disposition towards him. He and the guy he called O. Carmen were playing some video game, projected on the wall, that involved running around and shooting each other. And in addition to a bong, the coffee table held a small mirror spread with cut lines of coke and a rolled-up two-dollar bill.

"God, seriously, what the fuck?" she said. "This is what you do with your spare time? Get high and play video games?"

"We were making revolutionary plans," Mark said. "Like saviors of America, you know? And then we got to talking about soldiering for real, and drugs as a tool of social change, and all that shit, and so we thought we'd practice a little."

Selah huffed. "And to think that I called you my boyfriend. You don't even answer the phone when I call."

Mark just smiled again. "You're like Jesus."

"What?"

"You know, when he was like, 'Hey, I'm the only one here without sin, so let me cast the first stone.'"

O. Carmen laughed.

"Fuck you. I'm going through some desperate shit here. I might lose my job, and you can't even be bothered to act like you care."

"I thought you told me that you don't even need that job."

"That's not the point." Selah felt as if she was about to cry. To stop herself, she said, "I'm going to try some of that coke."

Mark nodded. "All right, but it'll cost you twenty bucks."

"What?"

"You need to learn that I don't get this stuff for free. I mean, I ignore your klepto shit for the most part, like when it's just a bowl of weed you're grabbing, but I don't want you to start getting any bigger ideas."

Selah gaped, then said, "All right, if you want to be an asshole like all the other assholes in my life, then fine." She picked her backpack up from off of the chair where she'd set it and pulled out her wallet. When she opened it, however, she found that she had no cash. "God, fuck you," she said, and she threw the wallet at Mark's head. It missed and landed on the couch behind him.

"You gotta control your woman," O. Carmen said.

"Fine," Mark said. "Snort a line or two if you really want. But are you sure that's what you really want? I mean, have you ever done coke before? Do you even know what you're in for?"

"I can handle it."

Selah picked up the two-dollar bill and held it to her nose before leaning down to inhale one of the lines off of the mirror, closing her eyes so as not to catch sight of herself.

"Fuck," she said in response to the numb sting in her nostril. And then almost immediately she felt a sense of elation, combined with the desire to do more coke.

"So how does this game work?" she asked, flopping down on the couch.

The details aren't important. There's no need to go into every word that Judas said to me that night, or the warm horror that expanded in my bowels as he spoke, or how this feeling was mingled in my midbrain with a dull anger and an anticipatory desire for revenge that rendered me incapable of uttering more than a few syllables in response to him.* A brief summary will do.

Karen liked me, he said. She had revealed as much when he confronted her directly about it on the walk home from the Campanile. He had walked her home. They were closer to her side of campus than mine, so they'd decided to go to her place to use the phone. But they hadn't called me right away, because she was so confused about what he had told her, and she wanted to talk about it first. She had a bottle of Irish whiskey in her room, and they opened it. Why hadn't I made a move, if I liked her too? The way that Judas told it, he had been my fiercest advocate, and he had basically done everything short of lighting the candles in her bedroom for me. He'd

---

* Nicholas Bendix explained to me a few weeks later about how he had once used magic to achieve revenge:

> "Jan Moldinowski was the name of my enemy," he said. "And I destroyed him through magic."
>
> "What sort of spell did you use?" I asked.
>
> "Rumor and propaganda, Thomas. While careful to avoid libel, I tainted his name across the academic world. I accused him of intellectual dishonesty. I implied plagiarism. I cast vague aspersions on his virility. He eventually committed suicide."

Which is sort of how I got the inspiration to write a book about Judas.

done all he could for me, and all he'd done had been for me, with one small exception.*

He had kissed her. He had explained to her that she and I would live happily ever after, and she seemed to look forward to the prospect, but then he went on to say that the only problem was that he liked her too, and so he wondered if, just once —before that happy future came to be—he could kiss her himself. And she'd said yes. He claimed that was all that happened, and that he'd come home immediately after, and that his last words had been to promise her that he would tell me everything and have me call her to set up a date or something the next day, and he tried to reassure me that the kiss really didn't mean anything in comparison to what I had in store for me, but I already knew at this point that it was hopeless. However well-intentioned, he had worked his emotional judo, redirecting the force of her infatuation from me to him, and nothing I could do would be able to turn it back.

* I sincerely believe that Judas's intentions were good. But intentions are beside the point. It always seemed to me that he was the Fool of the Tarot inverted. He tripped through life with hardly a pause for self-examination—hardly a thought for the world. It can be tempting to see such a carefree attitude as an admirable quality in a person, but in Judas, it was not; his Fool-ish nature explains his perpetual state of *infatuation*. In this moment now, looking back at the text that I have composed, I am trying to be sincere: to reveal myself clearly through the filter of these notes. I hate so much. But this is my attempt to overcome that hatred. This is supposed to be therapeutic. I am trying not to hate Judas. I am trying to understand him.

Mark was pontificating. It was much later in the night, and more lines of coke had been snorted, and many shots of tequila had been downed as well. O. Carmen had just left to go chase after a girl who had texted him.

"A crush is like cocaine," Mark said. "Each little interaction with the person is a lightning flash that momentarily illuminates everything, but afterwards all you're left with is the desire for more. Abusive relationships are like heroin. Low-level unpleasantness punctuated by thrilling highs and harrowing lows. Not a lot of fun overall, but hard to break the hold, regardless. Good relationships are like weed. They make simple things seem profound. They feel *good.* Warm. Happy. Occasional paranoia, sure—if your partner is on an airplane without you or something, or if you think he's cheating—but the body high makes up for a lot. One-night stands are like nitrous oxide. That's self-explanatory. Now with us, at first I thought I was just booze to you, something you used to numb yourself, right, but also to loosen yourself up: so you could have some fun, uninhibited, even if it's going to leave a bad hangover. A fling. But I'm starting to worry that you're treating me more like ketamine. Burrowing down into a k-hole that you don't want to crawl out of."

Selah waited a moment, and then she leaned down to snort another line of coke. "Fuck you," she said. "I'm going dancing in the City." And then, without further discussion or thought, she picked up her backpack and left. Though she did at least choose to walk to the BART rather than trying to drive.

I called Karen the next afternoon, but she just told me that she was confused about everything and that she thought it best that she not see me outside of work for the immediate future—and that she definitely didn't want to see Judas either. It was all just too weird. I said I understood.

Anyway, I could probably write out some genuinely disturbing shit about what went through my mind, and how violently I wanted to reject what I knew was happening with the two of them, but I don't think there'd be much point. Suffice it to say that I was feeling pretty negative and not completely balanced. I mean, for a moment after I hung up the phone, it seemed to me that 9/11 might have been an elaborate cock-block on the part of Osama bin Laden: that his masterminding of the plan to crash the planes into iconic buildings had been to give America a reason to invade Afghanistan, specifically in order to inspire the antiwar protesters in Berkeley, which would give Karen something to study for her anthropology class, but which would also give the police a reason to be out on the streets and to hit me over the head before I could get to her and kiss her, giving Judas the time to kiss her first. But then I realized that this was a slightly solipsistic way of looking at the situation.*

The two of them didn't immediately acknowledge their

* It's only now that I realize how petty I've been about all of this: that if Bendix was my Ancient One, then I was his Mordo, not his Dr. Strange, and that the latter would have to be Viv, who actually used Bendix's teachings to change the world rather than simply to exact some minor, personal revenge; it hurts to admit that while I was the facilitator of greatness, I wasn't ready to embrace it for myself: I let my acquaintance with Bendix fall off after a month or so, while Viv cultivated it for years.

romance, but Karen and Judas did, of course, wind up together. He invited her out to try to explain why he'd acted so weirdly that night, and to apologize, but that just wound up turning into a long walk and an intimate conversation, at the end of which they made out again. And things progressed from there: explicit dates, Judas spending the night at her place, Karen halfway moving in with us—I mean, imagine, having to watch her close-up, every day, falling more and more in love with him; having to see the joy that almost could have been mine; and having to listen through the walls as they made that love—until one day she told him that she was thinking of going off to grad school in Chicago, and he said that he didn't think a long-distance relationship would work, and that he didn't see himself ever wanting to leave California, and so he casually discarded her, and that's when I kind of started to hate him. It wasn't that I felt bad for her exactly; I knew that she could handle herself. And it wasn't that I was angry that he had screwed me over, moving in on the girl whom he knew I had a thing for; I know I should have acted sooner. It was the fact that he never even considered these things, didn't think at all about the pain he might be causing to those around him. Even after he started working for the county and got his own place, I'd still see him on occasion, and it was always the same. I saw it happen again and again, to girl after girl, all the way through Hannah, and I would get angry about it each time: how they seemed not to even exist to him. Until eventually I realized that what was making me angry was that I didn't exist to him any more than they did. The last time I saw him before he left, he actually said to me, "You know, you should have dated that Karen chick. I think the two of you would have made a better couple than she and I did." And that's why I don't know if I can ever forgive him.

The next morning, Selah lay sick and aching in her bed for an hour, unable to sleep, before she decided to give up the effort and write in her journal.

Dear Adam,

I feel like shit. I feel like dog shit that someone has stepped in and accidentally tracked across an American flag, which then had to be burned. I have drifted in and out of semi-consciousness, but I have not rested for a long while.

Last night, I tried to go dancing on my own. This seemed like a good idea: trying to have fun in an independent activity without relying on someone else to give me meaning. But, logistically, it didn't quite work out that way. I got a late start, which wasn't bad in and of itself, since I was wide-awake from all of the cocaine that I had done, and dancing is an activity better suited for the darkest hours anyway. But the problem with the lateness, in practice, was that BART service stops at 12:30, and I wasn't thinking about how I would get home. Or I didn't really care, I guess, because I thought I was going to dance until at least four in the morning, which is when service starts back up again. But then that was the other problem of the night: when I got to the Café (a gay bar, because I didn't want my dancing to be about anything other than movement), the bouncer asked to see my ID. Which would have been fine—flattering, even—except that I had left my wallet at Mark's apartment. And no matter how much I begged and tried to explain, even when I was on the verge of tears, the bouncer wouldn't let me in.

I headed back to the BART then, and that's when the lateness came into effect. Because I hadn't realized that it would be closed. I'd walked from 16th Street, and it took a while to get back I guess, and by the time I got there it was 1:00, and it was dark, and there was no one around except for crackheads and people smoking outside of bars that wouldn't let me in. And it occurred to me that I might feel scared. But really, instead, I just felt profoundly alone. I don't know if this will make you happy, but I thought of you.

I sat down on someone's front step a block or two from the BART stop, and I wrapped my hands around their opposing biceps, and I just generally tried to feel less trapped inside of myself. But I was coming down off the cocaine, and the alcohol was still pretty strong, and it was hard not to feel a little melancholy. But then, even though chemically I had no cause, I had this weird little wing-flutter of hope: a car slowed down on the street in front of me, and I somehow knew who it would be driving the car. It would be an old man named Stu, whom I had met at the bakery right before I met Mark for the first time. Our conversation had been short but had seemed meaningful to me, even though I wasn't sure how, and I felt as if this, finally, was what the meaning had been all about. But then the car sped back up and moved on, so I guess it wasn't Stu after all.

But in that moment in which I thought it might be—though it only lasted a moment—I'd had this incredibly elaborate fantasy, in which he would recognize me, and I would cry, and he would offer to take me home and ask me where I lived, and I would tell him, "Richmond. Richmond is my home." Which is weird, right? Because Richmond is not my home. Don't worry, I know that. I guess I'm still trying to figure out where home is. And I realize that one of the things making that difficult is that you were my last home, and I didn't exactly take my leave in the most formal or final of ways. If you want to leave a place, it helps to be there. Maybe I'll come for a visit.

But anyway, I don't suppose any of this necessarily means that the feeling of meaningful connection I had with Stu was wrong, exactly. I mean, sometimes when we feel that a person is meaningful in our lives, it might come down to some fact that we can never know—like he's secretly the proprietor of a company that makes all of the spray paint that your boyfriend uses to vandalize things. We all drift blindly by, but we touch one another with invisible tendrils. Or maybe the sense of meaning was only chemical.

So, whatever, it wasn't Stu, and I just walked up to Market, and I found a bus full of other drunk people who were heading back to the East Bay. And we were together in our separateness, I guess, as I was saying. But mostly I still just felt alone. I didn't go to Richmond; I took the bus to Berkeley. And I crept into my room as quietly as I could, and I writhed in my sheets all night —or all morning, I should say—until I couldn't take the frustration anymore, and that's when I decided to grab my journal to write to you. Which is where I am now.

I think I may head to Richmond later today, though. I have to get my car, at least. And Mark left a worried message on my phone. It's good to know that he cares, at least a little bit. In any case, I may not know exactly what I'm doing right now, but I do know that I need a break. I think.

Love after all (though still only of a sort),
Selah

PART FOUR

BAKERSFIELD

Ah, what image was there of his love which had no image? It was not rose or bird or star, for all would not suffice though he should encompass all . . .

—Marguerite Young, *Miss MacIntosh, My Darling*

All of this ends here, the Central Valley's southern tip: shit-hung horizon where the mountains rise up to catch the poison air. Bakersfield, California, which on a quartered postcard depicting its essential qualities could be fairly represented by an oil derrick, a potato, a cowboy hat, and a field of dirt. For Judas this was a bit of a homecoming; he'd been born in Southern California but had moved progressively northward with his mother after his parents' split, and Bakersfield had been the first way station on that journey. It was where he'd spent sixth grade, and he recalled it still as the worst year of his life, as much for the locale as for the pain of the divorce.

Driving down into it now in a cheap white two-door rental, he found the city much as he recalled: a pointless sprawl, larger than most imagined (if they'd ever even heard of it), though not as flat; the wide-laned roads and highways were sometimes hilly as they traversed this expanse of nothing. But, as opposed to the sprawl of cities farther south, in Bakersfield the nothing in the middle connected only to other nothings at either end.

Judas had flown into LAX the previous afternoon and spent

the night at his father's place in San Fernando. They hadn't seen each other for a few years—not since Judas's grandmother's funeral—and though they never had much to say to each other, it seemed wrong to pass so close without at least stopping by to say hello. Malcolm Hodge had once been six foot four, but Judas found him now reduced—not only in height, but in other ways as well: his white beard was wispy over sunken cheeks, and a nail hole had been added to his belt to cinch it tight enough to hold up his jeans.

"Are you all right?" Judas asked when Malcolm opened the front door of his little two-bedroom ranch house.

Without immediate verbal answer, Malcolm just smiled and hugged his son—his arms were strong at least, if bony, and Judas felt a child again within them—though "ulcer" was the eventual explanation Malcolm offered to explain his appearance: the single word—his voice a deep, tobacco-colored croak—and that was all that he had to say on the subject.

The two of them chatted for a while in Malcolm's darkened living room, where an old Frederic Remington print depicting men with guns on horses hung above a television that was blaring NASCAR; Judas remembered this well. Half shouting to be heard above the race announcers, he told his father about all that he'd been up to lately: the move to New York, etc. Malcolm listened mostly, interrupting occasionally to opine that New York was the one place that Judas could have found to live that was worse than Berkeley. Malcolm had been a National Guardsman in the sixties, involved in the Battle of People's Park, and so had taken it as an almost personal insult that Judas had attended that hippie school; the fact that those SOFA yahoos had started there only deepened this conviction. And though he hadn't ever been to New York—or, indeed, outside of California at any point in his adult life—he said he could imagine.

When Judas ran out of innocuous things to say, Malcolm talked for a bit about his garden: how he'd sculpted the earth and clover to resemble his idea of the Scottish highlands, and how he'd been looking into their ancestry, and how he thought that he'd figured out what their family tartan looked like—all of which made Judas laugh, silently, since the only other time Malcolm had expressed any awareness of his Scottish heritage had been over the phone once when Judas was in high school, his sixteenth birthday, and Malcolm had asked him if there were any particular girls he liked, and Judas had said, "Kind of," and Malcolm had asked her name, and when Judas revealed that her last name was Campbell, Malcolm had forbidden him from dating her—on the grounds that the Campbells were traitors; though this had been an unnecessary injunction, as she wouldn't have dated Judas anyway. After exhausting the subject of the family tree and the garden—without offering to take Judas outside to see it—Malcolm asked briefly after Judas's mother, and then he ordered a pizza for dinner and sat quietly while Judas ate, not touching it himself. "When you don't eat much, you don't get hungry," he explained. Overall, he said, he was happy. After dinner, they watched an old Sam Peckinpah western, and then Malcolm told Judas that he wanted to get to bed early, and he showed Judas into the guest room.

"I mostly use this as my office, for business and things. But the couch is good for naps, and I expect it'll last you through till morning. I found a box of your old stuff in the garage if you want to check it out. It's in the closet. Otherwise I'm probably gonna toss it. And you can use the computer if you want. The password is 'buttermilk.' It's the same for Netflix, too, if you want to watch a movie online or anything."

"Thanks, Dad. See you in the morning."

Judas threw his backpack in the corner of the room and immediately turned on the computer. He had to wait a few minutes for it to boot up, and then, when the desktop finally appeared, he was slightly saddened to see a folder labeled "Porn" sitting right there, three down from the top left, following the "My Computer" and "Internet Explorer" icons. Somehow it seemed worse to find his old man's dirty pictures in this digital way rather than under a mattress or in the back of a sock drawer. He didn't click to open the folder but got right online to check his Facebook and his email.

After he'd read all of his new messages—which didn't consist of anything more exciting than a cute cat picture from his mom—he just sat there in his dad's old, wooden swivel chair, Gmail tab open, staring at the screen without typing, clicking, or reading. He had his Gchat status set to "Available," and he was hoping that Caissa was out there somewhere, also online, but that for some reason she just had her status set to "Invisible." He was hoping that she would see him and type something. He thought vaguely of writing her an email, but then he recalled that he had promised to send her a postcard or a letter, and he didn't want an email to serve as a reminder that it had been almost a week and that he hadn't yet kept his promise, though perhaps such a show of indifference would make him more alluring. But then, after a few minutes of just sitting there and staring, he started to feel as if he were acting desperate—like a hooker with her breasts hanging out—and he closed the tab.

He didn't know exactly what it was that had set him off, but ever since leaving New York he'd been thinking way too much, pearling over thoughts that should have had no more substance than grains of sand. And it wasn't just a case of second-guessing his instincts with Caissa; he was questioning everything: wondering why he had moved to Brooklyn in the first place, what he was doing now trying to track down some obscure Tibetan novelist in what was basically a California desert town—and also what else, more productive, he might be doing with his life instead.

To distract himself from the trap of self-consciousness, he shut down the computer and opened up the closet to pull out the box that his dad had found for him. It wasn't big, maybe eight cubic feet, mostly filled with books that he had left behind when he'd stayed in San Fernando the summer between his junior and senior year of high school. Still, he was curious to see what he'd been reading back then, out of the general fondness he had for his own past. Or, actually, fondness was a gentle way of putting it, as he occasionally even felt that such nostalgia fettered him in his present dealings: the box before him made him recall that back in Brooklyn he had another box, about an eighth as large as the one before him, and that within it he kept a Magic-Markered oath of brotherhood to his best friend from kindergarten, and the drunken deed to a college roommate's soul; he had a letter written to him by his fourth-grade teacher telling him what a special student he was, and rereading this never failed to lift his spirits; he had intricately folded notes of friendship that had been passed to him by girls in high school with whom nothing romantic had ever happened, and these were dearer to him even than the memory of his first kiss.

It was sometimes hard for him to find half as much meaning in events that were actually taking place in the present moment. He knew this was a problem, but he did have hope that he might come across some similar treasure here in this box of forgotten books.

The only thing that came close was an old paperback copy of *The Sorrows of Young Werther.* For a bookmark, he'd apparently been using a photo of a girl that he'd had a crush on back then: ACA, as she'd signed her name on the back of it—April Christine Amberson—a yearbook photo of her in her tennis uniform, and she'd written a lengthy note along with her signature. It ended with an exhortation, which—if he'd ever understood it—he had now entirely forgotten the meaning of: "Don't be such a Nightingale, but don't become a Student, either." Possibly something to do with the fact that they were both going off to college?

In any case, he had enjoyed the Goethe book, but he recalled now that what had stuck with him most about it was a small choice of the translation. A central scene involved a fragment from James Macpherson's Ossian cycle—in itself a forgery—which Goethe had translated into German for his purposes. Yet in Judas's edition, this fragment hadn't been presented in Macpherson's original wording, but had rather been retranslated from the German into a brand-new English version. A note explained that the choice had been made in order to capture Goethe's idiosyncrasies of expression, which the translator deemed more important in this context than the idiosyncrasies of the original poem. He supported his assertion with a quote from Goethe himself, which read, "There are two ways of going about the business of translation. You can either try to give your audience something slavishly faithful to the original text and its context, or you can just use that text as a rough guide for your own creation, which is something that your audience might be better able to relate to." This was a minor and esoteric point, but for some reason it had provoked young Judas into fierce imaginings, and rather than moving on to, say, *Faust*, he had decided instead to read everything he could find by the same translator.

That had been the point at which he had realized what he wanted to do with his life: he wanted to be the next Charles Moncrieff, or William Weaver, or even Peter Rosetti. In those days, he'd thought of everything according to its largest scope. He didn't just want to be a translator who made a living; he wanted to be a translator who made a difference. And he didn't think of this goal in terms of the individual books that he would bring into English, but rather in terms of how he would filter an entire culture through the body of work that he would amass over the course of his career. These days, though, he couldn't see much further than the desire to find Jigme Drolma, possibly to translate the new book, and maybe to keep working on his own pet swordplay translation.

Looking back at the photo of April, he found that his ambitions had diminished in other areas, as well. Where he'd once dreamt of finding his one great love, now his thoughts on that subject didn't reach far beyond getting back to Brooklyn and having sex with Caissa again—or for Caissa to love him, and tell him that she loved him, even if they didn't end up together forever. And beyond all of this, he wasn't sure what any of his next goals would be—what he would have in his life immediately worth living for.

This is the moment at which things might have turned: his mind flickered briefly towards the romantic possibility of Jasmine Green, who along with Jigme Drolma provided one of two points in a triangle that was completed by SOFA, and compounded with the revelation that he had nothing immediately worth living for, Judas might at this point have decided to join the movement: to surrender himself to something larger so that he needn't worry about goals of his own, and—not incidentally—to make himself into someone more attractive to a girl who could distract him from his own emptiness. Luckily for all of us, Judas was too much his own fanatic for this; the possibility crossed his mind, but he decided that he would much rather *be* Viv than serve him. He might not know what he was doing with his life, but—strangely—he felt that he was okay with this.

Thinking too much about the future had never made him any happier, he realized; the narrowness of the present instant and the breadth of the continually unfolding process of existence—both of these extremes seemed to be more likely places at which he might locate a sense of meaning in his life. The moment, now, and the building, continuous: the incremental process of trying to bring something into existence—whether a friendship, or a political change, or a self, etc.—rather than trying to achieve happiness through some specific, individual achievement. And so, for the present moment, he decided to forget the future, forget the past, and to just turn his dad's computer back on, log in to Netflix, and focus on watching a movie unfold before him, frame by frame.

• • •

That night Judas dreamt of his high school crush, April Amberson. Among his friends he had always referred to her as "the Magnificent," and tonight's dream was a dream that he'd had before, rooted in an actual memory: senior year, their high school prom, and all he could ever remember about it was their one dance, sleepy and dreamish—in fact, set to a song that he was sure had the word "dream" in the title—as rain began to trickle slowly down the side of the sky, and he rested his dazed sweaty head, the outer rim of his ear, right on the tiny lump in her long white neck (which seemed strange in retrospect, because he was a little taller than she, but he clearly remembered it being this way, and that's how it happened in the dream), exactly halfway between the subtle indentation in her upper lip—which shimmered with the slightest blonde of down—and the vertex of the V-shaped neck of her dress: a wedge of negative space carving out the interior curves of her cleavage; in his dream, he could see this all from a third-person perspective, and it was a cold crystalline moment in his memory.

The next morning, after a mostly silent breakfast with Malcolm, while he was driving over the Grapevine with nothing worth listening to on the radio, Judas started having imaginary conversations with April: out loud, asking advice and then pausing, listening, trying to hear what she would hypothetically say in response. He hadn't seen her in years—he didn't even know her anymore, had maybe heard some vague update about her once every three or four years; she apparently had a steady girlfriend according to the last report—so none of this had anything at all to do with the actual her. Instead, he just had this living idea of her in his head based almost entirely on what he knew of her from high school, and it was this idea that he was having imaginary conversations with. But since the picture he'd found had been part of the basis for this idea, he felt that the message on the back was sort of like a message from her—from the ideal April—and it was a message that meant something to him. So he felt justified in responding to it aloud.

"You always seemed so aloof," he said as he drove down into the edge of the city. "Even when we were close, and you would tell me about your woes—your parents making you go to cotillion, or that boy, Jeremy, in your after-school driver's-training class who harassed you every night—I felt that you were somehow above it all, laughing despite your complaints. I felt that, as happy as you were to have an audience, it didn't matter that the audience was me. And I guess that probably partially had to do with the fact that you weren't interested in boys in general, but—realistically—it must have also had to do with the fact that you weren't interested in me in particular. I mean, I understand that I was sort of an oaf. And my idea of what constituted a romantic gesture was pretty embarrassing. But at the time I suppose I sort of hoped that you'd find all of that endearing. I was naïve."

She didn't immediately answer.

"There were times when I tried to fool myself into thinking that we were dating. Like when we went to the movies once on our own."

This prompted her to overcome her reticence. "I remember that. But I don't recall what the movie was."

He shook his head. "It doesn't really matter. But anyway, there was a moment that night, before the movie, when you inspired a sort of revelation in me. It's something that's stuck with me over the years. We'd stopped at a little grocery store to buy some sodas, and we had some time to kill, so we sat out on the sidewalk to drink them. I remember I wrapped my lips all the way around the mouth of the bottle as I took my first gulp, and you said I was 'nigger-nursing' it."

"I did not say that."

"You did. You had that whole streak of pseudo-racist humor that year . . . What was that about, anyway? I always hoped it was some kind of subtle mockery of the actual racists, all around us in the Central Valley."

"Well, that's generous of you. But if I really said shit like that, I think it probably just comes down to the fact that I had a really immature sense of humor."

"Huh. Well, whatever. But so we were sitting there drinking our sodas, and the lights were burnt out above us, and at some point you noticed the moon hanging over the parking lot: a ridiculous orange as it shone through the smog. And while you were looking at the moon, I was looking at you: your little inhale, your forward lean, hand to your mouth, the awestruck expression on your face. The fact that you were the sort of girl who could lean into the mystery of life and hold your hand to your mouth in wonder: I felt like it was half of something incredibly profound."

She laughed. "What was the other half?"

He shook his head and tapped on the steering wheel. "Well, I still haven't figured that part out."

"Hmm." He pictured her turning towards him and smiling. "All right, I'll give you a little help here. The boy thing aside, I would have been a lot more interested in you if you had been leaning into the mystery of anything other than me."

"You would have liked me more if I wasn't into you? That doesn't help me much."

"You're not listening. I didn't say that. I said that I would have liked you more if you were interested in something, you know, in addition to me. Like I could appreciate your passion more if I could see it directed towards something else."

"Oh." He wasn't sure what else to say.

He felt that, if she'd had a head, she would have shaken it. "You go about loving all wrong. What you see as 'appreciation' of a girl is all taking and no giving. You just admire and you try to reflect what you see. Like, that girl Caissa is into Guyana, so you learn everything you can about Guyana, because you want to understand her better. And you come to have a genuine interest in the place and its politics and its culture, including but also going beyond an understanding of what makes it meaningful to her. But what does she get out of that? She already had Guyana before you came along, and I already had the moon."

He beat a finger roll on the steering wheel. "Wow. I wish you'd told me some of this stuff back in high school. It could have saved me a lot of trouble."

She laughed again, throaty. "You weren't ready to hear it. Besides, I don't really think you were into me nearly as much as you thought you were. You were into torturing yourself, getting high on the frustration. Making an aesthetic object out of the purity of your burning desire. Your courtly love shit was safer than actually risking your emotions on anything real."

He nodded. "Well, that much I knew, I guess. At least on some level. But it still doesn't make it any easier."

He tried the radio again but turned it off as soon as he heard the voice of Buck Owens singing "I've Got a Tiger by the Tail."

The Tibetan girl whom Judas had contacted and who claimed to have slept with Drolma hadn't known his exact address. She had just come up to Bakersfield from L.A. for a party, and she said that Drolma had sort of crashed it.

"It wasn't even a book party or anything," she'd explained over the phone. "One of my girlfriends who was born in Bakersfield wanted to go back there for her birthday to see this boy she'd always had a crush on, and they decided to have a karaoke party, so we got a room, and then like half an hour later, while we were all singing and everything, this random guy just walked in and sat down without even talking to anyone. I guess everyone must have thought that someone else knew him or something, 'cause no one asked what he was doing there, even though he was like a hundred years older than everyone else. I mean, I guess it helped that he brought a bottle of whiskey with him. And he even cut a few lines of coke for everybody, and did a bunch himself. Which I don't do, you know, but some of my friends were into it, so whatever. But so he hung out and sang a few songs and stuff—like old Prince songs that I'd never heard before—and then he sat down next to me and asked me if I was Tibetan. And I was like, 'Yeah,' because no one ever guesses that. And then he told me his name, and I was like, 'Oh my God.' I mean, more because his son is totally hot, you know, because I'm not into old guys, but still. It was like one degree of separation or whatever. So anyway, I let him take me home and stuff, but I didn't ask for his address or anything, and I don't really know Bakersfield geography. But yeah, he had a nice setup and stuff. So unless he has like a billion houses, I think he's probably still there."

"Thanks," Judas had said.

He had tried Google, of course, to narrow the search, but that hadn't turned up anything useful, and so his best hope at this point was a guy he'd been in the dorms with freshman year of college—Byron Stoat—who'd grown up here. He and Judas had never really been close, but they'd played chess a few times when they were drunk and had a few fond memories in common. And they were friends on Facebook, so Judas had the easy means of communication. He hadn't really followed Byron's life closely in the years since he'd seen him, even through status updates, but he knew enough to suspect that he might be a valuable resource when it came to finding out about people in Bakersfield.

Byron hadn't ever actually wanted to go to college in the first place; he'd wanted to go to the police academy, but his father had insisted that he try Berkeley first, since he had done well enough in school to get in. So he'd shown up there freshman year, though it was obvious from the beginning that he was just going through the motions to please his dad, and maybe to indulge a bit in illicit activities before pursuing a course of life that would make such things more difficult; his favorite pursuits included getting high and harassing people with his Maglite, while going to class was something like a distant fifteenth down the list. He had managed to stay enrolled for only a year, but Judas understood that he now worked for the Bakersfield Police Department in some capacity and hoped that Byron might thus have access to city records or whatever: something that might provide a clue about how to track down Drolma. He hadn't mentioned any of these specifics in the Facebook message that he'd sent, but they had arranged to meet for a late lunch today, and Byron had responded enthusiastically, so it seemed as if there was at least a slight chance that he'd be willing to offer whatever help he could.

Judas felt that he should have been excited at this point in his adventure—that all of his effort might finally pay off—but he was actually still pretty ambivalent about it all. He had found another Chinese-language novella of Drolma's in a used-book store before he'd left Bloomington, and he'd read it on the plane. It was fairly recent—must have been the last published before this new one—and just as with the novel that Caissa had given him, it reminded him of another book that he'd already read; this time a German novel called *Die Unbefreundung von Laura Müller.* He didn't recall the details of the plot of that one, but Drolma's book was about a Chinese girl who makes some ill-considered comments on a YouTube video and eventually kills herself after all of her Facebook friends become her Facebook foes—and that had at least been the basic framework of the German one, with the obvious exceptions of nationality and technology. Judas wasn't exactly a fan of either—both were a little stark for his tastes—and this, again, made him question how wise it was to have signed on to work on a book that he probably wouldn't have much passion for.

Further, if Drolma did turn out to be a plagiarist, it cast the whole translation enterprise into doubt. Did Judas really want to be attached to a project that promised such literary embarrassment? The possibility was almost enough to make him reconsider the validity of translation in general, despite all the value that he had invested in it to this point in his life; after all,

Drolma's fraudulence, if proven, would consist of little more than translation without attribution. Judas had ethics, yes, but he and Drolma were still both just faithless Qabbalists working through permutations of someone else's master text. And Drolma's works were, at least in some sense, original: adapting the basic concepts of a piece rather than sticking slavishly to the words, while Judas had always regarded that sort of freedom as a temptation that must be resisted. Drolma was, at worst, the Qelippah to Judas's Sephirah.

He asked the Idea of April after an hour's silence. "But what's the alternative? Give up on all of this? Find something else to do with my life? A forty-hour job that lets me get by. Head back to Berkeley and try to patch things up with Hannah?"

"That's a bad idea and you know it.* Not even an option. Your reasons for getting involved with that whole thing were wrong in the first place. Why not try to make a new start in Brooklyn? A real start this time. Get a day job to pay the bills. Find something you're passionate about and pursue it. Something besides Caissa. In addition to Caissa. Build a life for yourself rather than hoping for some single thing to come along and make you happy. And, in the meantime, work on the swordplay novel, since that's something you're actually at least semipassionate about. Focus on contentment rather than joy."

"Hmm. Right. But for now, at least, I should just focus on the task in front of me, right?"

---

* This is granting Judas, perhaps, an unrealistic amount of self-knowledge. But I find that I am not quite as discerning when it comes to his nature, or as in control of his narrative, as I presumed myself to be when I wrote this.

"If you say so."

"I'll take that as a yes."

He had finally arrived in Bakersfield proper, and his first task was to find his hotel and check in. He still had about an hour before his lunch with Byron.

Byron had suggested that they meet at a little Mexican restaurant in the East Hills: cracked vinyl covering the seats in the booths, poorly wiped tables, and a view out the windows of dirty streets. The only detail in its décor that set it apart from an average diner was a mural along one wall showing a winged man rising up beneath the skirt of the Virgen de Guadalupe; a blue flower opening like a Buddhist lotus blossom farther below her; a soldier with an AK-47; a wide-mouthed bass; green and red peppers; stalks of corn; a black-skinned goddess that looked more Hindu than Aztec or Mayan or whatever to Judas's untrained eye; an eagle eating a snake as if it were the intestine of Prometheus; and lovers wearing wide-brimmed, tasseled hats. The place was half full, though, with young couples and families, so Judas hoped that the food might possibly belie the look of the place. Byron was already there when Judas walked in, sitting in a corner booth and tapping his fork tines on the table, a big grin beneath his mustache as he waited. When he saw Judas, he swaggered over to give him a rough hug.

"Judas! Shit, man, good to see you. You're looking good. Kept the weight off." Byron slapped his own paunch where it shoved against the buttons of his uniform. "I mean, I saw a couple of the other guys in Vegas a few years back, and I think you're the only one who's actually gotten better looking. Hah! Of course, you were a pretty ugly motherfucker back then, so it would have been hard not to improve at least a little, right? I'm just kidding. Have a seat, though."

"Thanks for meeting with me, Byron."

"Hell, you come all the way to my town, the least I can do is take you out for a meal. I'm just sorry I couldn't offer you a place to stay. But I wouldn't want to force you to put up with my wife and kid, know what I mean? I'm just kidding."

"Yeah, no problem; my hotel's not so bad."

"Yep, yep, not so bad. It's a nice little city when you get to know it. Where are you living, though? Still up in Berkeley?"

"Brooklyn, actually."

Byron squinted and reared back his head. "Brooklyn? As in New York Shitty? What the hell brings you all the way out here, then?"

"Well, it's a long story."

Byron nodded. "Yep, yep. Oh, I hear you. My life is one long story, let me tell you. Very busy time for me, actually—work is pretty crazy of late—but, you know, I'm happy to squeeze you into my schedule."

"You're living the dream, I hear. Doing what you always wanted to do."

"Yeah . . . Still, sometimes . . . Sometimes. I mean, this case I'm on right now, this white-trash high school girl got herself shot a couple nights ago out on Cottonwood Road. And, ironically, everyone is acting like it's the end of the world. Hard on the nerves and shit."*

---

* His saying "the end of the world" is only ironic, of course, in that he couldn't have imagined the sort of catalyst that her death was to become.

"You're a homicide detective?"

"Me? Nah. But I am in the Crimes Against Persons detail. Detectives get all the glory, but, you know, it's really a group effort. This girl, though, it's a tough one. If she'd been black or Mexican, it wouldn't be half as bad. I mean, there'd have been one story on the news, and then we could just work the case, without everyone looking over our shoulders and shit. But they're acting like this is the story of the century and shit, which only makes our jobs all the harder to do."

"Wow, sounds like you have a lot on your plate then."

"Yeah, well"—Byron grinned and rubbed his belly—"I'm about to have a lot on my plate. They serve pretty good portions here." Just then, the waitress happened to walk up to the table and asked what they wanted.

"What do you recommend?" Judas asked Byron.

"Hmm, I'm gonna have the *chili colorado* myself," Byron said, looking to the waitress. Then, looking back to Judas: "But you don't really strike me as a *chili colorado* kind of guy. Unfortunately, I don't think they have a tofu platter. Hah! I'm just kidding. The corn smut is pretty good."

"The what?"

"They call it *huitlacoche* on the menu, or some Mexican shit. I call it corn smut. Should be right up your alley, though."

Judas read the description and nodded. "All right, corn smut it is."

The waitress waddled away.

"Shit, man, what happened to your finger?" Judas had stopped wearing the splint, but his finger was still pretty bent and swollen.

"Nothing. I fell. No big deal."

"Huh. Well, anyway, this little Okie girl, three in the morning, I figure she was probably just down there buying drugs or whatnot, doesn't realize how dangerous it is—or maybe she's even excited by the danger, gets her all wet and shit—but then we're the ones who have to clean up the mess. Not to blame the victim, you know."

"Of course not."

Byron adjusted himself in his seat and put on a sober face. "I mean, I try to take each case seriously—and personally. It can get to be a bit much if you don't. You know, thinking about a hundred murders and two hundred rapes every year could get a bit overwhelming, so I like to keep it focused on the individual. Just do what I can about one thing at a time. I'm married now, you know, and I have a daughter of my own. And if my daughter got shot up by some crackhead, I know I'd sure want the police to treat her like an individual person rather than just 'murder number one hundred sixty-eight' of their career or whatever. Like, this white-trash girl's name is Sarah Nightingale, and I keep that in mind. Keep it so she's a real person in my mind. Never forget." His face had assumed an ever more serious expression as he spoke, ending in wrinkled brow with corners of mouth curled down.

"Right. I think I understand where you're coming from."

"You know the funniest part, though?" Now Byron smiled. "I talked with her brother, and he went on record as saying that he'd always advised her to go to boarding school, and that a girl as hot as her in a town like this could look forward to a long future of multiple rapes. Sounds like a real caring individual there, don't he?"

"Yeah, I don't even know how to respond to that."

"Hah! That reminds me. How do you know if a girl in Bakersfield is a virgin?"

"I don't know, how?"

"If she can run faster than her dad and brothers!" He slapped the table as he laughed, but then he tried to put on a straight face again. "We'll see, though. Like I said, drugs is the most likely explanation. She had a joint in her purse. Though I guess if she already had a joint, you have to wonder why she was looking to buy more drugs. But I don't get paid for idle speculation; that's what detectives are for, when they aren't sticking their thumbs up their asses. Mine but to do and die. I'm just kidding." He narrowed his eyes and smiled again. "But there's maybe another angle, too. She had a letter in her purse. Nice stationery, neatly folded in an envelope. Not like your average high school girl notebook origami."

"Should you be telling me all this?"

"Hell, why not? You're not gonna write a story about it in the *Bakersfield Californian*, are you? But anyway, get this, it was from her guidance counselor. She went to school right over here: Highland High."

"So you make him for the perp?"

"Hah! Listen to you. 'Make him for the perp.' Nah, most likely not. I mean, I can imagine a scenario—like, she threatens to blackmail him with the letter, he panics and shoots her to keep her quiet—but too much about it doesn't make sense. Why would he leave the letter on her? Why take her down to Cottonwood Road? Why would a high school guidance counselor be carrying a gun? The drug angle seems more likely. But, like I say, mine not to reason why. All I've done is interview people in the neighborhood, as if they'd tell us something even if they witnessed it. Lots of fun, right?"

"So what else is new with you? Sounds like work is going well. Or at least keeping you busy. And I didn't realize you had a kid. Congratulations."

"Yeah, thanks. She's the light of my life and all that. You should have seen this letter from the guidance counselor, though. It was all"—Byron affected an effeminate voice—"'I think I need to stop seeing you. Getting to know you over the past few years, listening to your problems, I think I've fallen a little in love with you. I don't mean this to be sleazy and shit 'cause I know I'm your fucking guidance counselor. But I feel all like I could happily spend the rest of my life in your company, and that's a problem, since I'm married and I'm also your fucking guidance counselor.' Or some pansy shit like that. Anyway, I mostly just thought it was funny, but I guess it's something to follow up on. He's apparently one of these SOFA wackos, and I figure maybe he got her all mixed up in it too, which might have precipitated whatever situation led to her being out on Cottonwood Road that night. Just a theory, mind. Still, no one ever asked me for my opinion, so I just do what I'm told. It's not as if I need the glory. Just the way my noodle flops. Yep, yep, just doing my job."

"There are SOFA people in Bakersfield?"

"Shit, where aren't there SOFA people? Don't you watch the news?"

The waitress arrived with their food, then, and Judas used the break to segue into the favor that he had come to ask. Byron nodded and chewed chunks of his *chili colorado* as he listened.

"Shit, I haven't thought about that Gabe Stilzkin asshole since my last colonoscopy," he said once Judas had finished. "I'm just kidding. He was a weird motherfucker, though. Never really liked him. But he's doing all right?"

"Yeah, he seems to be making a decent little life for himself out on the East Coast."

"Well, that's good to hear. But so this dude you're looking for is an author, huh? You know, I got a buddy at work—this guy Horatio Sponge, a records clerk—and he's trying to write a book too. I think it's about working for the police department and shit. Not that he's shown me any of it yet. Been working on it almost a year, now, you'd think he'd show me one page. He's a smart motherfucker though. You ever read any Joseph Wambaugh?"

"Name doesn't ring a bell."

"He was another cop who wrote books. Pretty good, too. Though, knowing Horatio, I just hope he's not trying to be all clever and boring or whatever. Like making it about a records clerk instead of a real cop, you know? I mean, I got plenty of good stories I tell him all the time; all the shit I've been through, you'd think I was an anal squeegee. Hah! At least enough to fill a book, though."

"Yeah, I don't know. But what do you think about looking into this other thing for me?"

"The Tibetan dude? Yeah, shit, man, I don't see why there'd be a problem with that. You just want me to help you figure out how you can contact this guy and he's gonna get a book deal out of it? That sounds like I'm doing him a favor rather than violating his civil liberties or whatever. But sure, I'll see if I can find some time to look into it this afternoon. Send me a text or something to remind me if you don't hear from me by tomorrow."

"Thanks, man. I really appreciate it. Let me get the check."

"Well, that's mighty white of you, but I got this one. You're my guest here, compadre. And maybe I'll give you a call later if we go out for drinks after work or something. You can meet my buddy Horatio. The one writing the book."

Around this time, across town, Horatio himself was pulling up in front of the house of his friend Espiri Santos, who was working on his car. Horatio wasn't mechanically minded, and he couldn't have explained what Espiri was doing with any degree of certainty—he took his own car in to be serviced every three months or three thousand miles, very regular about it, and it never gave him any trouble—but Espiri seemed always to be tinkering with something under the hood. *The Mustang is his novel*, Horatio thought.

"What's going on, *maricón?*" Horatio said by way of announcing his presence.

"Hey." Espiri took his eyes only reluctantly from the engine. "I was just thinking about you. I think I came up with a perfect title for your book; you can call it *I, Cabrón*. Like *I, Claudius*, you know?"

"Hah. That's good. Maybe I'll use it. But, you know, if you were a classics professor, you wouldn't be Robert Graves; you'd be Robert *Fag*les."

"Yeah, and if you were a real writer you'd be *Gay* Talese. So, what's going on, man?"

"Not much. Day off. Wasted the morning. You probably heard about Viv's niece, right?"

"Shit, yeah, I think everybody's heard about it. They got you working on that?"

"Nah, all day yesterday I was on that church thing."

"What church thing?"

"You didn't hear? Somebody painted pentagrams in pig blood on the doors of five churches. And if you draw connections between the churches on a map, you can sort of make another pentagram. Which we only know because we got a letter from the perpetrators telling us that this was the case."

"You don't think it's for-real Satanists, do you?"

"Nah. I mean, it was probably just some of our folks, trying to get these hard-core Christian extremists riled up against Satanists to distract them from shit where they can do real harm; all the churches they targeted were pretty vocal opponents of marriage rights. But of course the police have to take it seriously. Kind of funny, though, anyway: there are a couple loons from the churches walking around downtown carrying crosses on their backs, trying to exorcise the devil. I don't know if that's supposed to be some kind of protest or what, but I guess people are pretty invested in the sanctity of their churches or whatever. Or maybe they're SOFA, too, playing both sides. It's getting hard to tell, but I guess that's kind of the point, right?"*

"People just got too much time on their hands is what it is, *joto.*" Espiri wiped engine grease from his hands onto his blue jeans. "You want to come in and have a beer or something?"

---

* I have to assume that these two were involved with SOFA in some minor way, or my whole conspiracy theory collapses; which is also to say that, if Viv didn't exist, I would have had to invent him.

"You got any iced tea? I had a little too much to drink last night."

Espiri lived with his older sister Letty, but she was at work, so he and Horatio had the place to themselves. The two of them had been friends since high school: in honors together, and they had somehow felt even then that they had more in common with each other than with any of the others in those classes. Physically, there was a fairly sharp contrast between them; Espiri was a good two feet shorter than Horatio and half as wide, though he tended to take more the alpha role in the friendship. Temperamentally, though, they were, if not the same, at least complements.

Espiri poured Horatio a glass of iced tea from a pitcher in the fridge, popped open a bottle of cola for himself, dropped in a handful of peanuts, and took a long pull. The two of them then made their way down the hall to the den, taking their seats in leather-covered armchairs in the unlit room as Espiri turned the TV on to provide some background noise; it was a show about the plight of the red panda.

"So, how you doing, man?"

Horatio exhaled. "I'm okay, I guess. I'm thinking I should maybe try medication, though. Therapy hasn't been much help on its own."

"Fuck medication, *ese. Your* mind's not the problem; it's your wife's mind that's bothering you. Get her to go in to this therapist with you or something."

Horatio shook his head. "She says she doesn't want to hear about my issues with everything; she's dealing with it in her own way—with the Blog—and that talking about it directly to a therapist or whatever would only make her feel worse."

"Uh-huh. The Blog is the real problem, right there. What Maya *would be* doing? Shit. Anyway, how's your sex life lately?"

"*Ay, no mames.*"

"I'm just saying."

Horatio sipped his tea. "I mean, yeah, it's been better. But what are you gonna do? Not exactly the first thing on my mind these days."

"Bullshit. I could tell just looking at you. Not getting laid, man, that's nine-tenths of your problem right there. It's just the way guys are wired; you may not even realize it yourself, but your brain is devoting almost all of its energy right now to the problem of how you're going to get back to being fucked on a regular basis. And how are you supposed to think clearly about anything else under those conditions?"

Horatio looked down at the pea-green shag of carpet and eventually started to nod.

"It's all tied together and shit," Espiri explained. "Like one problem is a symptom of another. And with you, I don't think the fundamental problem is what happened with Maya; it's how Lekha is dealing with what happened with Maya."

"What am I supposed to do, though?"

"Well, when you can't see any way to get the outcome you want, maybe what you need is to readjust your goals."

"What are you talking about?"

"Just, maybe Lekha isn't what you need. Maybe she's the big distraction holding you back from achieving your true potential."

"Shut the fuck up."

"When you got nothing, you got nothing to lose."

"Did you just quote Dylan at me?"

"I'm just saying, man, maybe the cause would make you happier than this woman of yours."

"You're just saying that because you don't like women."

"Yeah, but look how happy I am."

"What about your car?"

"I'd give it up in a second if the revolution can liberate us from petroleum dependency."

Horatio took another sip of tea, and then the two of them were silent for a while as they watched the red panda move across the screen.

Lekha and Horatio had been married for nearly ten years. Their first date had been at a bar that Horatio had only gone to once before, and though it'd seemed normal enough on that previous occasion, on the night that he showed up to meet Lekha, the other patrons were almost all dressed up in some manner of garb that seemed to blend flapper style with goth, and they were dancing to songs that all sounded rainy and British. Rather than suggest a change of venue, though, Horatio sat at the bar with Lekha and sipped his beer; then, after they'd had a few more laughs, he began to gulp, until he was feeling loose enough to suggest that they dance, even though neither was dressed appropriately and neither had a real appreciation for the music.

As he recalled it now, his thoughts on the dance floor that night had been primarily anthropological: observing this weirdly specific subculture, and noting how he and Lekha were themselves being observed, in turn, as outsiders. But also, he was watching Lekha in this same distant way: knowing that she and he had established some sort of connection, and feeling the contour of this connection as she would come in close for a moment, lock eyes with him, and then retreat, teasing him, balancing her enticing movements with movements of denial. At least half due to the fact that she was Indian, the whole thing reminded him of a Bollywood movie. But then at some point —he wasn't quite sure how it happened—he found that they were making out on the dance floor. It had felt nice in a way that transcended mere tumescence. They held hands in the cab that took her back to her apartment, and they made out again at her front door. He'd expected to be sent home from there, but then suddenly they were fucking in the swivel chair of her bedroom desk.

It seemed to Horatio, at that moment, that sex was a mode of expression limited in its range only by the meager scope of most people's emotional imaginations: an artistic medium in which lust and romantic love were but the two most common genres, like police procedurals and reality shows on TV. But the form itself was capable of so much more. Sympathy, appreciation, friendship. Anger, guilt, revenge. Blends of various proportion. And in the relationship that had developed, all of this had been on the palette. There was sex as comfort from grief. There was sex to end an argument. It seemed that there was sex to solve, or at least ameliorate, all of their problems. But then Lekha had actually gotten pregnant, and she'd started the Blog, and—he wasn't sure that there was a direct correlation—after that she'd spent pretty much every night devoted single-mindedly to that, and sex started to fall by the wayside. And after the birth, it had stopped pretty much completely. It didn't help that she wouldn't talk about what had happened, either, revealing more of herself to the internet than she did to him in private.

One night after work, in the first few days, before Lekha

got home from the hospital, he found himself just driving, east along the 178—out to where he couldn't see anything except for what was directly in front of his headlights, radio off, occasionally cursing or sounding inarticulate phonemes not often associated with the English language—then up to Hart Park, and finally looping back into town on the Alfred Harrell Highway. He was still too keyed up to even think about sleep, so he decided to head out for a drink instead, and within half an hour he found himself back at the bar where he and Lekha had had their first date. On this, his third visit, the place had transformed again back into a normal bar, with men who wore cowboy boots and large belt buckles dancing to modern country with women who had been known to wear the same, the flapper-goth phenomenon apparently some sort of Brigadoon. Others hovered around a pool table in the back, beneath the brightness of a bare bulb housed within a green conical shade, which seemed most sharply to illuminate the nicotine cravings on their faces. Horatio stepped to the bar and ordered a gin martini with olives, started a tab, took the drink in one long draft, ordered an IPA to chase it, then slid the three olives off the little plastic sword with his incisors and proceeded to chew.

"Piss," he said as he swallowed the olive bits. He didn't know how to think about the problem in front of him. Or not problem, but pain, from a wound that he knew was there but which he was not yet sensate enough to feel the shape and depth of—as if he'd woken on an operating table and found his anesthetized leg wrapped in bloody gauze. He drank the beer down and ordered another round of the same.

"Thirsty, eh?" the bartender asked as he poured.

Horatio felt the urge to smash the bartender in the face with his empty pint glass. It was a far-off sort of feeling, barely perceptible in the firelight of his awareness, but still it surprised him. Despite his size and musculature, he wasn't a violent man. Besides, if he got in a fight with this guy, it would mark the end of the night's booze flow. "Parched," he said.

The bartender nodded and set a full glass in front of him.

As he continued to drink, though, the violent urge kept venturing in closer, a wild dog growing ever more bold as its hunger grew. He watched it with a sort of fascination, wondering if this was the thing that had gnawed his leg. Wait, no, those were completely separate metaphors. Or were they? Even in his growing drunkenness, he was fairly certain that the two of them were related, the beast born perhaps through some abiogenesis from the wounded tissue. He would just have to observe it in action and see what its behavior could tell him about its nature and its origins.

"I am only a passenger," he said aloud as he rose from his stool and walked back towards the pool table. "I'm much too drunk to drive."

Horatio stood by the table as one of the players lined up his shot, and then he tapped the guy on the shoulder right in the middle of the stroke, resulting in a miscue.

"Hey, who has next game?" he said.

The guy turned, angry, but some of the anger visibly abated as he took in Horatio's size.

"What the fuck, man?" he said, his voice pitched high, beginning the sentence with eye contact but ending focused on a dust bunny beside Horatio's shoe. "You couldn't see I was in the middle of something?"

"Oh, you mean like the way your face is going to be in the middle of my fist in a minute?"

The guy shook his head. "Look, man, I don't want a fight here, just: I would have appreciated it if you'd have waited till I was done with my shot before you tapped me on the shoulder."

"Oh, I'm sorry. What about when I tap you on the face? With my fist? Go on, you take the first punch."

The guy nodded, set his cue on the table, and walked away. Horatio realized that he'd have to find a guy who was trying to impress a girl if he really wanted to start a fight: someone who would be ashamed to walk away. He turned to scan the other patrons and realized that a good number of them were already looking at him with varying degrees of boldness. And yet, despite how generous Horatio was feeling about such matters, none was quite bold enough to be interpreted as a challenge.

"Hey, compadre, what's going on?"

The voice came from in front of him, no more than forty-five degrees off to the side, but he still had to turn his head before he could see who it was that spoke.

"Everything okay?"

Byron Stoat. From work. Horatio paused to consider whether maybe he should try to start a fight with him. It usually didn't take much time with Byron for Horatio to reach his saturation point, as the guy was kind of casually racist. So the provocation might be there. But otherwise he wasn't actually that bad a person. Anyway, he was hardly in good enough shape, physically, to put up much resistance, and Horatio was still lucid enough to realize that the fact that they worked together meant that fighting him would probably cause more trouble than the satisfaction of the pummeling was worth.

"I've been better, Byron," he said.

"I can see that. Why don't you come take a seat with me? I'll buy you a beer."

"I'm not sure I need another, but thanks."

"Don't need another? What the shit kind of talk is that? Of course you need another. You can drink it slowly if you want, but you have got to come sit with me and have a beer."

Horatio didn't think this was a good idea, but he felt powerless to resist. And strangely, sitting and periodically sipping from a pint poured from Byron's pitcher, he actually felt his drunkenness begin to diffuse. Not dissipate, but spread out through him, becoming too blunt to pose any further danger. For a long time, he didn't speak, just sat and allowed Byron's plentiful babble to spread over him.

"Yep, yep, just figured I owed myself a drunk after the shit I went through today at work: a little something so I can go home and face the wife and daughter, know what I'm saying? I'm just kidding. But shit, I tell you, my girl Megan may still just be a toddler, but I swear, females of any age, they team up on a motherfucker. You can't fight 'em, though; all you can do is leave 'em to their own devices and hope eventually they turn on each other. But that's what love's all about, I guess."

Am I bothered that he is talking about his child when I have none? Horatio thought. *I would have expected to be, but I don't think I am. I think I am not very in touch with my feelings.*

Byron continued to chatter on for an hour before Horatio spoke to say that he thought he should probably head home.

"Yep, I hear you. Getting to be that time. Let me give you a ride, though; I don't quite trust those eyelids of yours to stay open much longer than this bar. I think I'm legal enough. Especially with this badge!"

Horatio had little memory of it, but on the ride home he knew that he'd finally blathered a bit about the baby: about Maya, his girl that he didn't have. He didn't recall what Byron had said, and they never really talked about it again directly, but they'd started bullshitting with each other a bit more at work after that, and they occasionally went out for drinks together. It helped just to share a beer every now and then. But they never talked about it. Byron had invited him out for drinks, actually, on the day when Horatio went to visit Espiri, and it probably would have been nice to go, but Byron had wanted him to meet an old buddy from college or something, and Horatio hadn't been in the mood for new people. Instead he drank a few beers in his room as he worked on his novel, Lekha out on the couch updating the Blog, trying to live life as if it were the way she wanted it to be or whatever.

A lot of the hard-copy records for older cases, such as unsolved homicides, were kept in a privately owned file-storage facility downtown. Same-day delivery of files stored was among the services offered by the place, but on the rare occasions that he needed access to something, Horatio liked to actually head over himself and check it out on premises—mostly just for a change of scene, but also because it was located fewer than two blocks from his favorite sandwich shop. So though he didn't exactly *need* anything, looking into some old cases of church vandalism the next day seemed like a good excuse to grab himself a decent lunch.

The storage facility was a small operation, staff of maybe five including the owner, usually no more than two or three people working on a given day, but Horatio was still a little surprised when he walked in and found that there wasn't anyone behind the front counter, and even more surprised that no one responded within two minutes of him pressing the little white button that sounded an electronic bell in multiple speakers throughout the building. He pressed the button again, and then he wandered back around the counter and tried the door on the other side; it opened onto a small break room—table, microwave, fridge, and coffeemaker—from which another door, already open, led out to the main space of the warehouse: two steps leading down to a concrete floor that spread off to the three far walls that bound the place, though two were invisible behind rows of metal bays built six tiers high. It reminded him of the storage area of IKEA. The room was lit with fluorescents hung from a thirty-foot ceiling, dim at that distance, though the rolling door of the loading dock was pulled all the way up, letting some sunlight in. About twenty feet in front of Horatio, Lester Brightman—a worker whom he recognized, though he'd never spoken to him—sat on a pallet of boxes between two blue scissor lifts.

Lester was tall, maybe six-four, Sioux, with the shy suggestion of a mustache and his hair tied into a shoulder-blade-length ponytail. He wore a beige jumpsuit and leather tool belt, and he was rocking back and forth while he cursed to himself atop the boxes. He looked up when Horatio came through the door but hardly seemed to notice him.

"Fuck, man, what the fuck?" he muttered, shaking his head and looking back down at the concrete in front of him. "Just trying to get rid of me, but I didn't do shit. Just scratched an itch. I didn't do shit, I didn't do shit. I know how this works."

"Is everything okay?" Horatio asked.

Lester's shaking head modulated into a nod. "Oh yeah, everything's okay, sure, you expect me to run out to the counter when you ring, when they're just going to fire me, right, like I should even do my job, like it's my job, like they'll probably use that as an excuse to fire me, that I didn't answer the fucking bell, right? I know how this works. If someone asks for his box, I give him his box, that's how this works. If they give me the numbers, I go to the row, and I go to the stack, and I go to the bin, and I get the box. Why is that such a problem? Why is that so hard to understand?"

Horatio took a deep breath and released it. "Is there someone else here I can talk to, maybe?" he asked.

"Oh yeah, see, and they act like they don't need me. No one else here to get anything done. I don't see anybody else here, do I. Just Lester, holding down the fort." He made eye contact with Horatio for the first time. "Yeah, what? A customer? What do you need? You need something? You want me to help you? Yeah?"

"Well . . . if you could. I was hoping to retrieve a few files. I'm with the Bakersfield Police Department, and—"

"Fuck you, man, fuck you." He spoke in normal tones without raising his voice. "He deserved my spit. It should have gone in his eye instead of his nose. Arrest me again for the same thing, sure, I got civil rights. I got rights. I don't have the right to drink a beer on my own front lawn, is that what you're telling me? I'm not getting you a box. I'm not retrieving you a file. You go tell your friend that. You come over here and I'll spit on your face, too. I put skewers in my pecs, man. I pulled myself free. You do that. You do that, and then you come over here. And I'll still spit on you."

Horatio chewed his tongue for a moment and nodded. "You know what, I have no idea what is going on here. You may have hacked your coworkers to pieces for all I know. But I'm going to be a nice guy and just leave you alone."

"Hacked up my coworkers, hah, that's funny. What? You think I have a fucking tomahawk? You racist fuck, racist just like the rest of them, you fuck."

"Okay." Horatio backed through the door and pulled it shut. Out in his car, he considered what he was supposed to do about this, if anything. The guy seemed like he could be a threat to someone. Hell, he had in fact threatened Horatio, if only with spit. Though Horatio might technically have been trespassing once he went out into the warehouse itself; he wasn't sure if that affected anything. He pulled out his smartphone to give Byron a call and ask his advice, but the screen notified him that he had an email from Lekha, and he clicked to read that first, and by the time he finished reading, he had put the matter of the mentally unbalanced guy in the warehouse completely out of his mind.

Lester had started the previous day balanced enough, relatively speaking. He was never a calm person by disposition, and he always talked at least as much to himself as he did to any other person, but he hadn't actively been angry with anyone when he arrived at work. He'd even made a few attempts at bantering with his coworker Dontay Weems. Dontay's brother Milton, who usually drove the van, had called in sick this morning, so today it was just Lester and Dontay, and they were taking turns with the deliveries. Dontay had just got back from a run when Lester found him smoking out on the loading dock around ten in the morning.

"Smoke 'em if you got 'em," Lester had said.

Dontay had just pulled his head back and squinted at Lester. "What the fuck you talking 'bout, you retarded motherfucker? You telling me you want a cigarette or something?"

"Nope." Lester smiled. "But smoke 'em if you got 'em." Then he went off to reshelve some boxes.

Lester recalled the last time that Milton had called in sick, and how he'd come in the next day complaining about Jägermeister and swearing that he would never drink it again. So at lunchtime, Lester started smiling as he paid for his tacos from the roach coach, and his smile grew as he made his way to the break room and sat down at the table across from Dontay. "Jäger," he said as Dontay bit into a white bread and bologna sandwich. "Jäger bomb. Hey, Dontay, where's Milton? Jäger bomb. Jäger bomb."

Dontay slammed his sandwich down on the little Formica table. "Lester, don't take this the wrong way, but would you just shut the fuck up, please? Can I have one meal without listening to your crazy-ass shit? I'm saying this for your own good, motherfucker. You think Kevin gonna be happy if he walks in here with you talking about Jäger bombs? Who he gonna think's been hitting the bottle then, huh? Especially after you getting yourself locked up last week for being drunk in public. And you know you're lucky that was the only charge. You lucky to still have a job, motherfucker. So don't you be going and trying to get my brother in trouble."

Lester made a little moan. "Shit, Dontay, you know I'm joking. You can't take a joke. You think you're such a joker, why can't you take a joke?"

Dontay picked his sandwich up again and looked down at it as he spoke. "Lester, I'm just looking out for you, okay? I don't want you getting fired. You do all the heavy lifting round here; you think I wanna do that? No. But after last week, and after that shit with Kevin's daughter a month ago, you know he's just looking for a reason to fire you."

Lester moaned again and shook his head. "I didn't do nothing, man. I didn't do nothing. I just had to scratch myself. What, like I can't scratch an itch? Just because there's a lady present? A lady. A lay-uh-dee. Who's the lucky lady? What if I had a tick or something making me itch? What if the lady gave me Lyme disease? What then? Then I'd sue the shit out of Kevin, that's what. He should be happy I scratched myself, 'cause then I'd be a millionaire and he'd be lifting boxes for me. Maybe I'll sue him anyway. Maybe a box will fall on me. You never know. You never know. It's a warehouse. Accidents happen. Warehouses are exactly where accidents happen."

"Lester!" Dontay spoke in a bark. "Get ahold of yourself! This is exactly the sort of shit that Kevin is gonna use against you. I know he's a punk, and you know he's a punk, but you can't give him shit to use against you like this. Just eat your lunch, man. And do your job. Then he won't have nothing on you."

Lester breathed in through his nose and hugged his hands around his shoulders and nodded. "Yeah, you're right. Thanks, Dontay. I know how it works. I don't want to lose my job. I hope Milton's okay. He's not too sick, is he?"

Dontay shook his head. "Nah, man. Don't worry. Milton's okay. He'll be back tomorrow."

From the office came the sound of the telephone, and Dontay got up to answer it. Lester picked up one of his tacos and took a bite. He couldn't decide if he was angry or grateful.

"Hey," Dontay said as he came back into the break room less than a minute later. "We got a delivery. Three boxes. You go load up the van and I'll drive."

"It's my turn to drive."

"I know, man, but this one's right off Cottonwood, and I want to stop by and see Milton. Besides, I need to pick some shit up while I'm out. I'll owe you one, okay? Anyway, you need to cool off and shit." He slid a piece of paper with the box numbers and locations across the table to Lester.

"Yeah, yeah, okay. You do what you want, I guess. Nobody asks Lester what he wants." He shoved the second taco into his mouth whole, chewed a bit, then added the remainder of the first and went out to find the boxes and put them into the van. He spoke as he left the break room, but the shape of the words was mangled by the mixture of meat and tortilla in his mouth.

Fifteen minutes after Dontay left, while Lester was busy driving up and down the aisles of the warehouse on one of the scissor lifts, raised to maximum height, the bell rang to indicate that someone was at the counter. He halted and lowered the lift and then walked at a leisurely pace to the front room.

The man on the other side of the counter just looked like any old white guy, dirt-brown coat, dome-blue shirt, dark red tie, glasses, and a stupid French hat. Probably in his seventies, though Lester just thought, *Old as balls.*

"Hello," the man said. "I haven't been here in a few years,

but I would like to collect a few items I filed away back then. I hope they're still on the premises."

Lester nodded. "Should still be here. We don't just get rid of stuff for no good reason. Let me look in the computer, though." Lester took the guy's information, found the location of the single box, and then said, "Yeah, okay, let me go get it for you. Just a second."

He found the box easily enough. It wasn't very heavy, nor was it as dusty as he would have expected it to be after sitting untouched for years, but he just brought it out to the guy, who then explained that he wanted to close his account.

"Hokey-dokey," Lester said, smiling.

In five minutes the guy was gone, and in six Dontay had returned.

"You get anything done while I was out, or did you just sit there grinning?"

Lester didn't deign to answer. The rest of the day passed without incident, and he left work in a good mood, relatively speaking. He bought a twelve-pack on the way home, and over the course of the night he worked his way through it with his dad, and the two of them wound up pulling out an emergency bottle of whiskey as well, but he didn't get so drunk that he couldn't wake up in the morning and make it in to work. Or he was a little late, but not even an hour, and Kevin wasn't supposed to come in anyway. Though in his rush out the door he hadn't had time for more than a Mexican shower—two quick *fwooshes* of spray to the underarms—and he was worried that he would smell like booze; what if Kevin decided to stop by today after all? When Lester arrived, though, he found that his problems were of an entirely different kind.

Milton was back, and he was upset, flaring his nostrils and nodding his head over and over as Dontay shrugged and threw his hands in the air.

"Those fiery redheads," Lester said aloud as he walked out onto the warehouse floor.

"What'd you say, motherfucker?" Milton asked. "You're late."

"Hey, Milton, how's it hanging? Like a hangover? I may be late, but you didn't even come in to work yesterday."

"Well, Lester, let me tell you something: it's not hanging the way I would like it to be hanging at all. And I have reason to believe that this is partially your fault."

"Whatever, Milton. I didn't do nothing."

"No, but nothing is precisely what you should have done. You did something, and that's the problem."

"Leave him alone, Milt. How was he supposed to know? Besides, we know where the shit is, so let's just go get it back. Yelling at Lester ain't gonna do shit for us."

"You're lucky my brother is here, motherfucker. Because I am in no mood for this sort of shit after what I already been through the past few days. I don't know why they didn't fire your ass before they even hired you—would have made my life a whole lot easier."

"You wanna fight, Milton? Huh? I'll fight you. You think you can just yell at me, but why don't you put your fist where your mouth is? Or I'll put my fist where your mouth is, huh? That's even better."

"If I had the five seconds to spare, motherfucker—"

"Both of you cut this shit out. Don't pay attention to Milton, Lester. He's just had a hard couple days. Let's go, Milt."

"Get your hands off me, D. But yeah, fine. Let's go."

The two brothers headed out the loading dock door, got into Dontay's lime-green El Camino, and drove off, and it was only after he was alone that Lester began to think that he might have actually done something wrong, and that he might be fired for it, so he sat down on the pallet of boxes, between the two scissor lifts, and he began to bemoan his fate.

"Motherfucker" succinctly summarized Milton's feelings on the subject of all that had happened in the past few days of his life, including the business with his halfway serious girlfriend, Sarah, being too stupid to keep her mouth shut and how he still didn't know how to feel about the whole thing—he wasn't going to cry like a pussy, but rage, no matter how intense, didn't quite seem to release what he was feeling, and he wasn't sure what the other alternatives were—not to mention the entirely serious issue of a boxful of drugs being handed over to a random motherfucker when he came in to collect a box that hadn't been touched in five years. Which had seemed as if it would be the perfect stash: a place to store the stuff until all the shit coming down in their neighborhood, the business about Sarah, had lost its stink. Five years. He and Dontay had thought the guy was probably dead, or at least that there was no way he'd randomly come in after five years, at the exact wrong time. Like lightning struck itself. But seriously, shit. The worst part though was the embarrassment. They'd looked like punks in front of this guy Mark, who'd come all the way down from Berkeley to buy from them, and then there they were up on a scissor lift, moving boxes around even though they could see right away that the shit wasn't there, having to apologize to the motherfucker, saying, "Oh, I have no idea where it could have gone, but don't worry, we'll find it and get back to you later today." Like a bunch of pussies.

Mark hadn't actually come down from Berkeley just to do business with Dontay and Milton—he was a professional, and Viv was counting on him, so he had appointments lined up all day—and he wasn't too concerned about whether or not they'd actually get back to him later; he had gone into this trip fully expecting that he'd have to deal with at least one or two sets of amateurs, and there were still a few other places where he might find the particular drug he was after. He was looking at this all mostly as a vacation, anyway. Yesterday he'd taken Selah around to some of his favorite places from his youth: out along the bluffs, down to the train yard where he'd tagged a freight car in broad daylight, then lunch at this Basque place that he liked. Then at night she'd been excited by the hotel, the Rosedale: a bar with a mechanical bull, sadly not running, though they'd played a game where they'd spun a wheel to determine which shots they would take, and after a brief sit in the hot tub they'd run back to their room, slammed the sliding glass door, and fucked while she let him keep his eyes on her. The people next door had audibly expressed their displeasure at the banging headboard, but that hadn't stopped them.

This morning, though, Mark had left her to fend for herself. Today was devoted to business. They'd argued about that, and it was one of the first times that they'd seriously fought.

"So you have me drive you down here and then you expect me just to sit around in this crappy hotel room?"

"I don't expect you to do anything. I mean, you can do whatever you want, as long as you do it on your own. I just don't want you getting hurt, okay? Some of these guys I'm dealing with can be a little dangerous."

"So it's because I'm a woman, then, and I need a big strong man like you to protect me? I can handle it."

"Shit, are you even listening to me? This has nothing to do with the fact that you're a girl. It has to do with the fact that these guys will be carrying guns, and they might get suspicious and/or angry if I bring along someone they've never met before when I told them beforehand that it's just going to be me. But you know what? I don't care if you understand the point I'm making or not. Because I don't have time for this. So you do what you like, and I will see you tonight, okay? We'll celebrate."

Selah said nothing as he walked through the door. She had moved well past the stage of wondering what she was doing here, or why she was with Mark in general, and she realized now that these weren't so much questions with rational answers as they were koans: standing there in the hotel room, in his absence, she slapped herself on the forehead, and in that moment she was enlightened. She would have to ride out the rest of this trip, and she would have to make some changes once she got back to Berkeley, but that was no reason not to make the most of the present. About half an hour after Mark headed out to meet Dontay and Milton down at the warehouse, Selah showered, and then she headed out to see if this city had anything more to it than the meager showings that Mark had presented her with yesterday. She figured that she'd begin with the Bakersfield Museum of Art and see what the place had to offer by way of high culture.

The weather here was slightly warmer than in Berkeley, though by no means as sweltering as Mark had made it out in the tales he'd told her on the car ride down. She supposed it was well enough into autumn now that she couldn't actually expect it to be any warmer than it was, but somehow she had come to associate Bakersfield with heat. She turned on the AC in her car on general principle, though she kept the fan on low.

The museum was nicer than she expected. It had four different exhibits going, mostly composed of regional artists. There was a woman who made photorealist watercolors, a man who painted abstract horses, an exhibit focusing on works that incorporated cotton into their design, and—Selah's favorite—a collection of quilts from the 1970s. It was while she was looking at the lattermost that she noticed a dapperly clad elderly gentleman—tweeds and horn-rimmed glasses, atilt beret, reddish leather briefcase that matched his shoes—who seemed to be looking her way with unusual intensity. As soon as she made eye contact, he jerked his head to beckon her over; without thinking, she responded.

"You're not from here, are you?" he said.

"No. Berkeley. Or Santa Barbara, originally."

He nodded, as if he understood some hidden profundity in this statement. "Berkeley. I'm headed there myself, later today as a matter of fact. But Santa Barbara interests me more. Less than a degree of latitude away from here, and yet all the world. But what brings you here, then?"

"Bakersfield?"

"This museum."

"Looking for culture, I guess."

"And why try to find culture in Bakersfield?"

For some reason she blushed. "I guess I want to believe that every place has something good about it."

"And so it does. But I think perhaps you need to broaden your definition of 'something good.'"

Her blush deepened. "Well, what are you doing here then?"

"Killing time. I have a train to catch later. And a friend of mine made a few of these quilts." He gestured vaguely. "But now that I've seen them, let's head elsewhere."

"You'll show me the good to be found in Bakersfield?"

"Hmm." He smiled, revealing a mouth full of small white teeth, and a whole new set of wrinkles spread through the softness of his face. "Well, you've already met me. But we'll see what else we can come up with, shall we?"

She bit her lip. "All right. I guess I'm curious."

And so he took her by the hand and they headed toward the exit.

Out in the parking lot, the day felt brighter than it had before. Not clear and blue, but strewn with a smoggy whiteness that seemed to prevent light from escaping its dome. Selah led the man to her car.

"The Basque," he said as he walked around to the passenger-side door. "The Basque are something good about this place. Or at least here, away from their native mountains, they seem to have overcome their genetic predisposition towards blowing up trains. Which is not to devalue their penchant for revolution as much as their means. Though I can't say that I care much for their cuisine. Pickled tongue has never been quite to my palate."

She paused before opening her door and looked hard at

him. He wasn't unattractive, despite his age. White hair and beard, pale blue eyes, but with something vaguely exotic in his features and his voice. And he carried himself with a sense of style. Attractive, in fact. Though this judgment was perhaps colored by her general affinity for the aged.

"What else?" She sat down behind the wheel and reached across to unlock the door on his side. He opened it and settled slowly down into the seat beside her. "Besides the Basque, I mean?"

"Well, the air quality is poor, and the summers are intolerably hot. The people tend to be narrow-mindedly conservative, and the great number of migrant workers intensifies the already prevalent class-based racial tension. But subtract these aspects, and you're left with the good. It's the town that electrified country music."

"Uh-huh. Wow. You're really not selling this." She started the car. "So where do we go from here? You're going to have to give me directions."

"Hmm. We could go to my place. Though I have to be at the station by five."

She laughed. "Not so fast. Show me something else worthwhile, first, and then maybe I'll consider it." She wouldn't really consider it, she told herself, though she enjoyed verbally toying with the idea. Did this make her a tease? She'd never thought of herself as one before.

"All right. Take a left out of the parking lot."

And so the two of them were off, with him giving her directions as she went, though he refused to name the destination in advance.

"God, seriously?" she said when they arrived. It was the same ice-cream parlor that Mark had taken her to the day before. It was pretty full—end of the lunch hour—but they went in and managed to grab a table by the window. "This really can't be the best you have to offer."

He tilted his head. "Not the best, but something good. I have a sweet tooth. Besides, we should embrace the basics of life. Eating and fucking, that is, with sleep a distant third. These are things that most people are unaccountably shy about. Ashamed of being seen naked, or chewing, or drooling on a pillow. Most people go to great lengths to hide the fact that they are human."

"Or maybe you're just not a very creative date."

"Nonsense. I simply have a preference for living honestly. It's why I include so many scenes of meals in my novels, as I find that so much of actual life takes place during them."

"Is that supposed to be a smooth way of telling me you're a novelist."

"You're very antagonistic, aren't you? But no, it's just a statement of fact."

"So what sort of books do you write?"

He shook his head. "Nothing is more boring than talk of books that one has never read. You forget that I hope to charm you."

"Well, what's your name? Maybe I've read one."

"Doubtful, but yes, how rude of me not to have introduced myself earlier. Jigme Drolma."

"Shut up."

"Excuse me?"

"Seriously? You're seriously Jigme Drolma, the novelist?"

"If there is only one of us, then I suppose I'm he."

A moment of stupefaction. "I know you. Or at least of you."

"I gathered as much. And you are?"

"Oh God, sorry. Selah Park. I'm a grad student, focusing on Uralic and Altaic studies. Kind of impossible for me not to have heard of you, you know."

"Fascinating. An unusual name, Selah. Your parents were religious, I take it?"

"Um, yeah."

"My mother was as well, though that has little to do with my name."

"Right."

He beamed, close-mouthed, as he waited for her to speak.

"But, hey. You don't exactly look the way I would have pictured you. I mean, what are you doing in Bakersfield?"

He smiled, again displaying his teeth. "Yes, most people expect me to be somewhat darker. I usually prefer not to broadcast my somewhat shameful heritage. My father was a Nazi, you see."

She laughed. "Of course." Laughed again. "Schäfer expedition, no doubt?" And then she laughed a third time. A throaty "hah."

Drolma squinted at her and bit his thumb. "Yes, as a matter of fact. And this is funny to you?"

"Well, 'ridiculous' might be a better word. Your father's expedition is probably going to get its own chapter in my dissertation, if I ever get around to it. This is too much."

He rocked back and forth in his chair. "Yes, a remarkable coincidence. But let us not dwell on it, as we are faced with more immediate necessities. What are you planning to order? I suggest anything with caramel. Lynn's Favorite, for example."

"Wait, no, seriously, you don't think it's meaningful that you just randomly ran into, like, the one person in America who would possibly know who you are?"

"Now, I don't consider myself an egoist, but, in fairness, you must admit that I am a bit more well known than that. But in any case, no, I'm sorry, I just don't place much stock in coincidence. It's unfair to reduce others to the roles they play in our lives. It's necessary to realize that other people are real, that they have their own lives, even when those lives fail to intersect meaningfully with our own. Or when they do intersect with our own lives in ways that we find unpleasant."

"That's not what I'm saying, though. It's not reducing someone if you're just noticing how you're each meaningful to the other. Like, back in Berkeley, I was working in this bakery, and one day I met this old guy named Stu, and—"

He upraised a hand to halt her and sighed before he spoke. "An illusion. We can't help but underestimate how hard it is to be anyone but ourselves. My mother used to make up stories about people to explain their bad behavior. If someone was rude to her, she'd say, 'Well, his family must have just been brutally slaughtered, so you can't really blame him.' Perhaps that's where my own impulse to make up stories derives from."

"Sure, maybe that's why you make them up, but it's not why you publish them. That's all about meaningful intersection with the life of another."

"You seem to know a lot about me. But we should order our ice cream."

"You know I'm right, though. That's what gives the whole

thing urgency, isn't it? I mean, if you make mittens and don't let people wear them, then they're no better than tangled yarn. You can keep yourself warm, maybe, but a story out in the world is a mitten that you share with a cold-handed child. And even if you're writing for yourself, it's still nice to think that somebody might be made warmer by your mittens. Envisioning blue child-fingers turning pink again can keep your own fingers warm as they work the cold knitting needles."

"A pretty if meaningless metaphor."

"Bullshit. No. You don't get to do that. You know the flaw in your reasoning? Meaning isn't something that exists outside of us; it's something we create for ourselves. So you can't tell me it's meaningless that I met you here, or what I just said about mittens. Because it means something to me. And even if you don't realize it, you're still giving out mittens to kids in need."

He nodded. "But what is the real warmth in your metaphor? The great myth is that novels increase our capacity for empathy as we pause and reflect on the distance between our own lives and the lives of those we read about. And this is supposed to help us to imagine the inner lives of the actual others around us, and thus to think of the universe less solipsistically. But no, the truth is that literature—all of the hours that we spend reading or writing alone—isolates us. It's a distraction from the most fundamental truth of existence: that we are alone within our own minds, incapable of ever actually touching another human consciousness, and we must make do with these empty simulations, words on a page, or platitudes from my mother's mouth. The only real alternative is to placate ourselves by touching another human *body*, which is at least more direct. And that is precisely why we should be fucking instead of talking about literature."

"Right. That again."

A shrug. "It is what it is. Whenever given the choice between writing and fucking, I have always chosen fucking. The great tragedy of my life is that I've written so many novels."

Selah nodded. "Let's have that ice cream now."

If the two of them had skipped the ice cream and left at that moment to head back to Drolma's home, they would have arrived there roughly at the same time as Judas, who had been given the address the previous night when he'd gone out for a few beers with Byron Stoat. A wide driveway led alongside a lawn that was overgrown—yellow, but wet nevertheless from automatic sprinklers—up to a dirty white garage door attached to a house that was itself a sickly beige and roofed with rounded tiles of red. A small cement path led from the front of the garage, past some dead bushes, to a front door that Judas found half open.

He knocked and peered inside and called out hello, but there was no answer, so he took a step inside. At which point two young men, Milton and Dontay Weems, emerged from the hallway, coming at him quickly, with a purpose to their movements not unrelated to the sense of meaning that seems to imbue every action in a dream.

"What?" Judas managed to say, but Milton was already speaking.

"Where the fuck is it, motherfucker?"

And before Judas could answer, Dontay had grabbed a marble-based bowling trophy from the mantel, and—grasping it by the miniature plastic bowler coated in his metallic veneer—he'd swung the trophy at Judas's head; Judas managed to trip backwards, avoiding the swing, but in his attempt to regain balance he brought his face forward into Milton's fist. He was dazed by the pain, but aware enough to be distantly impressed at his own ability to stay upright and even stumble back through the door.

"Do I need to repeat myself?" Milton said, following him out onto the cement walkway. "Where is our fucking shit, motherfucker?"

Judas straightened up and tried to throw a punch, but then he crumpled again in pain as his broken finger made the barest contact with Milton's chest.

"Look, we can make this simple," Milton said, puffing himself up over Judas. "You tell us where you stashed our shit, and we leave your ass alone."

"Hey!" came a voice from the street. "Hey, what are—I know you!"

At this sounding of recognition, Dontay moved instinctively, swung the trophy yet again, connecting this time with a mouth that had just opened for further inquiry—marble against teeth—cracking both Judas's upper lip and his upper incisors, spinning him around and knocking him face-first into the wet grass. But between the fall and the smash into the fallow blades, there was time enough for a small flash of thought, forced to the surface of consciousness by the sharp sensation; intense pain can heighten our awareness. The collapse was brief, yes, and the white light of pain even briefer—but in the way that entire lives can spool out in a moment when one is faced with the prospect of death, so did Judas experience a protracted spark of self-reflection in this moment of only slightly lesser fear.

He realized, first, that he knew nothing about why he was being attacked by these two young men. He knew nothing of the trauma that they had experienced over the past few days, which had brought them to this point in their lives. He knew nothing of how the discovery of a letter from an emotionally troubled high school guidance counselor had led to what could, at the most generous, be described as Milton's unintentional manslaughter of a loved one. Judas knew nothing of any missing drugs, or of the trouble that the disappearance of these drugs would cause for Dontay and Milton, or of the connection between these drugs and the man for whom he long had searched.

Further, Judas knew nothing of the voice that had called up from the street. He didn't realize that it was the voice of a man whose name he had heard but one day earlier: Horatio Sponge. He knew nothing of the slough of despond in which Horatio and Lekha had been mired in the wake of a child who had died within days of birth, or of how their mutual methods of coping had subtly deepened the rift between them. Judas knew nothing of the email from Lekha that had sent Horatio flying home from the file-storage facility, to find his own house empty and to discover that his wife had, indeed, left him for another, just as she had written, or of how all of the little absences in the house, things she had taken with her, had crowded around Horatio like ghosts with Lekha as their undead queen. He knew nothing of how this absence that Horatio had discovered had prompted him to spiral out through the neighborhood, looking—ostensibly—not for his wife, but rather simply for a picture frame that she had grabbed from the mantel when she left: a picture frame that Horatio had chosen and which held an image of the two of them beneath a wedding arch in Santa Barbara.

Judas knew none of this, and in recognizing the extent of his ignorance, he achieved a point of connection with the outside world that he had heretofore been lacking: an instinctive awareness that these people of whom he had previously known nothing may actually have something to do with him—beyond, even, the tangible something that they had to do with the moment in which he found himself. And the awareness extended beyond, even, these people. As the first grass-blade grazed his nose, he recalled Adam flattened in a Bloomington driveway by a kid from Spain. He thought of Martin Pope, back in Brooklyn, whom he himself had once wanted to punch. He didn't quite extend so far as to think of Viv or of how the world around him was on the cusp of a change that had nothing directly to do with his own personal experience, but it was the beginning of a broadening of perception that might eventually lead to such a wider awareness.

Of course this is all, admittedly, a fairly simple revelation that he had here—and yet, in fairness to Judas, it must also be admitted that it is one that, in the tumult of daily life, might be easy for anyone to overlook. The experience nudged him slightly out of his habitual solipsism, and the sense of existing within a larger context left him strangely elated, even in his pain, rendering whatever momentary worries he had slight in contrast. It was a sort of satori whose blossom folded back in upon itself as soon as the moment had passed, but it left him with a distinct afterimage in his mind's eye: a remembrance of what it would mean to be more fully self-conscious.

Now, "self-consciousness" is a funny term, since it implies not just the literal consciousness of one's self but more specifically the consciousness of one's self as perceived by others, along with the attendant anxiety. But awareness of others—of one's self as part of a complex of mutual others—is perhaps the highest form of self-awareness. And prior to this trophy-to-the-teeth incident, Judas had just rarely been afforded the opportunity for the sort of self-reflection that might come more naturally, say, to someone who had bad teeth. As the moment of revelation passed, he turned himself over and looked up to see both brothers standing there in nervous jitter, staring down at him; he wanted to say something to them, but—broken-toothed—he couldn't have spoken even if he'd known what to say.*

"I know you," Horatio repeated, calling up from the street, and this time the word "know" was invested with an anger that suggested something much deeper than mere recognition. He was up the slight grade of the lawn in seconds.

As he ran up to Milton, he knew that he should identify himself as police, but he decided just to take a swing. Unfortunately, he pretty obviously telegraphed it, and Milton had reached up to grab his shoulder for leverage as he kneed him in the balls before the swing was even halfway finished. Horatio dropped to the lawn beside Judas.

---

* I once felt that Judas deserved the trophy to the teeth; now I feel that what he deserved was the attendant illumination.

"Shit, man, let's go," Dontay said.

A guy across the street had walked out onto his porch and was observing the scene as he dialed his phone.

Milton nodded. "Yeah. Motherfucker anyway." And he kicked Horatio in the stomach before loping down the lawn to the El Camino, followed closely by Dontay, who leapt behind the wheel and peeled off down the block.

"Shit," Horatio said, struggling to regain his breath. "I know who those guys are." He looked at Judas, bloody mouthed beside him and struggling up onto his elbows. "Are you okay?"

Judas sat up fully and put his hand to his mouth. "No," he tried to say, but all that came out was the vowel and a piece of tooth.

"All right. Well, let's get you to a hospital then. I mean, fuck it. I guess she can keep the frame."

Selah's midday dessert with Drolma turned into a full meal, and it went long. She wound up telling him all about her life: about Adam, about Mark, but also, and more important, about things that had nothing to do with men. She told him more about her idea for a dissertation, for instance, and—though he kept injecting sex into the conversation—as she spoke she began to recall what had first excited her about the project.

"I will make a deal with you," he told her once he'd paid for the meal. "Go home today. To Berkeley. Leave this Mark fellow behind. He is your way of distracting yourself from what is actually important in your life. And if you do this, I will give you an interview for your dissertation. I'll talk about my father, my writing, Tibet in general. Even my son, if you like."

"You have a son?"

"I was married. But she's long gone, and nothing to prevent you and me from enjoying ourselves."

"And why exactly would I want to talk about your son? Does that turn you on or something?"

"Oh, I just assumed you would know about Viv, since you know so much else about me."

"Viv? As in LaRevolution? Not Viv LaRevolution."

"Well, that's what he's calling himself these days. Tibetan tradition has it that you can choose your own last name."

"Well. This is, to say the least, a fascinating proposal."

"I wouldn't make it to just anyone. But I feel that you and I are kindred souls. And I will, of course, allow you to print anything you like. You're in a rut, and you need something, some moment, to jar you out of it, and I will try to provide you this, out of sympathy. Your life revolves around secrets: a secret drug habit, a secret boyfriend, even a secret diary in the form of letters to your secret ex-boyfriend. Letters so secret that the recipient never even gets to read them. So I will tell you my secrets as a demonstration. And then after we get to Berkeley, we shall have sex, and you will tell everyone."

"Hah! So I get the interview in exchange for sex? Wouldn't that be considered prostitution?"

He shook his head. "No. The sex will be purely consensual and separate from our transaction."

"You think about your dick a lot, don't you?"

He shrugged. "A man worries about his penis in the same way that a woman worries about her face. Besides, as I have mentioned, I have reasons of my own to travel to Berkeley. Viv is there, and he's set up a meeting for me tomorrow with that Hal Auerbach fellow, whom I may allow to translate my latest book. A gift to my son. But it would be more restful to travel in a passenger seat near someone whose company I enjoy than in a slow-moving train surrounded by . . . other people."

"That would be hell, right?"

"Yes. Though it's equally true that I is another. But what do you say?"

For once, Selah decided to pause and reflect before acting. She had no real intention of having sex with this man, despite his odd aura of celebrity. And she realized that he was offering no lasting alternative to the general malaise that had beset her life of late; even if she did something drastic like leaving Mark behind, it wouldn't in itself be an act that set her on any better course. But being with Mark was basically stupid, she knew, and he had pissed her off this morning, and she didn't want her actions to be defined by the parameters that he set for her. And the sooner she got back on the track of figuring out what she needed to do for herself, the better. Which would probably involve getting back to Berkeley, with or without this guy. And maybe then she really would head back to Bloomington, to the Tibetan Cultural Center, and finally put in the work that she needed to do in order to finally get started on the writing—not to mention settling things with Adam in a more concrete way. The lack of having done so, as she had considered in the past, possibly being what was ultimately stopping her from moving forward. But why not travel with this guy in the meantime, if that would make things a little more interesting?

"All right," she said. "Let me just give him a call. Mark, I mean."

"Please do."

She opened up her purse and slowly withdrew the phone.

"What's going on?" was how Mark answered. "I'm kind of in the middle of something here."

"I need to head back to Berkeley," Selah said, making it true as she spoke it. "Can you get back on your own?"

"Are you fucking kidding me? Seriously? No, you don't have to answer. I don't have time for this shit. Do what the fuck you want. I have to go."

"See you when you get back maybe?"

"Not fucking likely." He paused for a moment without hanging up. "Good luck, though," he said. "You can do better than this."

"Not better. But maybe more right for me."

She imagined him nodding on the other end of the line. "Yeah, fuck you, too," he said. And then he hung up.

"All settled, then?"

"Yes, I think so." She nodded. "I'm telling you now that you're either on the couch tonight or in a hotel. Just so we're clear."

"We'll see. I was planning to stay with Viv, but I hope I won't need to."

"Okay, so do we need to stop by your place and get anything?"

"All that I require for the trip is in this briefcase. I plan ahead, you see. And I believe in traveling light."

"I see." Selah stuck her fingers into her cup and fished the final ice cube out from the bottom, crunched down on it, and then, as she did so, she felt a dead molar with an old mercury filling start to crack. "Fuck!"

"Excuse me? Are you all right?"

"No, I'm not fucking all right," she mouthed around the ice cube, trying not to swallow. And though she heard him and also heard herself, her thoughts were far away.

"Is there anything I can do to help? Is it your tooth?" He lowered his voice. "In my briefcase I happen to have—"

She spit into her cup. "Just shut up for a minute, will you?" She looked him in the eyes, the pale blue; she saw his small-toothed smile of concern. "You know what?" she said. "I think you're gonna have to take the train after all."

Drolma didn't speak for a moment. "Are you quite certain? That is, are you still heading back up yourself? You shouldn't, if you—"

She winced. "I'll drop you at the station, okay? You don't need to worry about me." She thought then for a moment about what she had said. "I mean, I think I'm gonna be okay."

While he was recovering the next day in his hospital room, Judas finally wrote a postcard to Caissa. He sketched out, quickly, the details of what had happened to him, but he also said that he missed her, and then for some reason he just started to write down everything he knew about her. Or at least a few representative facts: that the linden was her favorite tree and the lily of the Nile her favorite flower, that her manner of shrugging could make him grin, and that her right eye was stronger than her left. Not that these things were important in and of themselves, but he was pleased to find that they seemed important to him now, and he was eager to get back and find out if he still had a chance to explore what they might mean. As he was running out of room, he wrote in tiny letters that he would maybe try again to contact Drolma once he got out of the hospital, but that what was more important to him in the moment was getting back to Brooklyn. He said that he was looking forward to seeing her again. He wrote that what he liked most of all about her was that she was Caissa-esque.

This was all probably too much. He hoped that the fact of his pain would elicit enough sympathy to mitigate the harm he was doing, but even as he wrote it he knew he was doing harm, and that such a direct display of affection would more likely scare her away at this point than draw her close to him. But it seemed important to be direct just now, and he was willing to accept whatever consequences may come. In an ideal world, she would find his directness refreshing. But he knew this wasn't an ideal world, so he did his best to imagine the actual.* He would head back to Brooklyn with less purpose than ever before. He would take Gabe up on the offer to help him find a fact-checking job. He would continue to see Caissa socially and hope that

---

* He couldn't imagine the aftermath of the impending SOFA events, of course, and how these would affect his plans: how attending the Brooklyn event hosted by Caissa's sister, together with Caissa herself, would both affect their relationship but also help encourage Judas's enlarging sense of the world. But then Viv himself couldn't imagine how Judas's subsequent exposure of Jigme Drolma's plagiarism would contribute to his own downfall as figurehead of the movement, at the same time allowing it to grow beyond the limits of his own petty concerns and develop into something truly populist in spite of him. Nor could Viv imagine how Selah's interactions with his father, once she had reconnected (non-romantically) with her ex-boyfriend Adam in Bloomington, would further contribute to this downfall, in the form of a ridiculously overblown article that Adam would contribute to issue six of *E* ("Eugenics") on the subject of Viv's Nazi heritage. But, then, the future must always seem to each of us like a failure of imagination.

there was still the possibility that they could make each other happy. The Drolma translation, needless to say, would not be his. Though even as he thought this, he realized that he no longer cared; he still felt a bit of dental immediacy—a sense that meaning was to be found in the present moment rather than in this fictive emblem of future greatness that he had been hoping to harness to himself. Instead, he would work on his swordplay translation in his spare time.

Caissa wrote an email in response three days later; it wasn't overly affectionate, but it expressed concern for his well-being and also mentioned that she too was looking forward to his return. She asked about the new magazine that he was supposedly putting together, and whether it was really true that he was hoping to scoop Drolma for himself and screw over the editors of *E*. She told him a bit about what she'd been up to in the brief time since he'd been gone, mostly about how she was finally making progress on the book, and she was putting together a pitch for an article based on the first chapter, but that even if she didn't sell it, at least she was writing; in fact, she'd started a blog, too: about Guyana, and her father, and just her life in general. She wrote that she was rediscovering childhood methods of eating tropical fruit.

Judas was reading this email in the morning, in an internet café, where he'd gone to check the status of his flight before heading down to LAX, and that last part about the fruit made him smile, revealing the temporary caps that had been placed on his incisors until it became clearer whether they would live or die. Remembrance is a funny thing; he was smiling because he was thinking of his mother's company picnic, held every year when he was little, in different parks in different cities. He had all these lushly vivid memories, each one like precious, tiny, brightly colored pieces of celluloid in his head, though thinking back on them now, they were all sort of retrospectively melted and merged into this one big plastic Picnic of Memory, with only a few little tendrils rising individually from the mass.

He remembered his first kiss, at age five, behind a half-fallen tree; the shiny black hair of a girl named Stella something, water-ballooned, soaked in her Superman T-shirt; dripping summer day and wood-planked tables; translucent neon squirt guns and Frisbees; go-karts that he never got to drive; the promise of cans of Hawaiian Punch in deep metal tubs, reaching to the bottom, ice and water up to his elbow, searching fruitlessly amid all the Coke and Tabs; melon-eating contests with red sugar-water dribbling down his chin; submerging his whole head in a mad bob for apples . . . All in this humongous park that had been cobbled together from all the parks in all the different cities that his mother had dragged him to. None of it quite came together, none of it quite made sense, and as he looked back now upon these happy images of his childhood and tried to reconstruct them into something real and meaningful and true, he felt much as Bizarro must have felt, trying to rebuild Krypton from the rubble of the Metropolis that he was destroying in the process. Metropolis in this instance, he supposed, standing in for the actualities of his present life.

But in any case, clearest of all—the one memory that had brought all of this back—he recalled once swimming the length of an enormous pool without taking a breath, watching the sunlight somehow manage to bounce up off of the water's undulating surface rather than sink below when he came up at the other end, and then—after, lying flat on the burning concrete to dry himself off—he'd marveled further as the light continued to dance in the leaves of the trees above. And he could recall the very end of the day, as well, when it was almost time to go home, pattering across the hot coals of cement to grab his towel from the back of a folding chair, and there was suddenly just this man standing next to him: an Asian man, miles high, with a small cart of fruit. Judas remembered just squinting up at him, trying to recognize him and not; the sun was right behind the man's head, eclipsed by his head, which was become a corona-ed silhouette. Or almost a silhouette, though Judas could clearly recall the man's protrusively crooked upper incisors: *a bucktoothed Chinaman*, he'd thought at the time—a phrase he'd heard his father use. But this man said something to Judas, something Judas couldn't quite make sense of, and he seemed to tower above Judas although he wasn't actually very tall, and he handed Judas a large multicolored fruit unlike any Judas had seen before: a fruit that Judas would later try to bite into only to find that his teeth were not strong enough to penetrate the peel. And the man told Judas that this fruit was a gift, and he started to lean forward as if to speak to Judas more intimately, though Judas had no idea what words could have followed. Because as this strange man squatted, the dusking sun hit Judas directly in the eyes, whiting out everything in the world, burning him right to the retina. He was blinded, but it was the blindness of seeing too much rather than the blindness of seeing nothing, and he could recall feeling a bit giddy as a warmth filled his body, and for a long bright moment he had wondered if he would ever see anything again.

HEREBY ACKNOWLEDGED

This book wouldn't exist if it weren't for the talents of Ed Park and the entire Little A team. Thanks also to cover designer Rex Bonomelli.

The idea of the men in masks in the précis of the fictional novella *Tourneé du Chat Orange* was sparked in part by Jeff VanderMeer's story "The Transformation of Martin Lake."

The character of Nicholas Bendix was very loosely modeled on the character of Dr. Crucifer from Alexander Theroux's *Darconville's Cat,* though Bendix is much toned down from his Mephistophelean original.

The device of a character who remains central to while not always being the focus of the novel's individual parts was inspired by Tyrone Slothrop in Thomas Pynchon's *Gravity's Rainbow.*

Innumerable bits and pieces were stolen from conversation and correspondence with Sarah Raymont.

The distinction between "complex" and "complicated" was taught to me by Katherine Sharpe.

Matthew Laird and Dan Peretti lived in Bloomington, as did several other people.

Some character names, situations, and even occasional pieces of prose were pulled from a novel that I wrote in my undergraduate days.

The idea of acknowledging specific examples of literary theft is lifted from a few novels by Alasdair Gray.